I0785056

Published by Kinematic Studios and Entertainment

ISBN 979-8-9860467-0-9

eBook ISBN 979-8-9860467-1-6

Printed in the United States of America

1 2 3 4 5 6 7 8 9 10

First Edition Printing

Book Design by Martellia

The
Circle of Ten

"Seeds of Omo"

By R.G. Rios

Table of Contents

For my children, without you all, none of this would have been possible. Remember to always dream and dream big because anything can happen!

Prologue

There comes a time in everyone's life when they must accept their fate. All of us came together as one to stop an evil force that was going to destroy mankind as we know it. But, not like this, just 2 years ago I was a single free-spirited girl in high school planning my future. Who would have known that my future consisted of so many trials and tribulations only to end like this? We have come a long way and I refuse to believe that this is the end. And like I said we must accept our fate, but this is the one time that fate will have to change. They need me, and with all my powers and abilities I will make sure that my family is protected from now until my dying breath.

It took nearly two years for all of us to find each other, and it was something that drew us all together to Fairfield Park one gloomy Saturday. We talked and that next weekend we all brought scrapbooks full of stories of impossible acts in the newspapers. We wanted to explore and evaluate what would be best for all of us. The questions lingered in all our minds on whether this was the solution or if we should all just let things go and move on with our lives. But the kinship was too strong for us to let go and to think we did not even know our true bloodline. The stories fluctuated from happiness to sorrow. From wealth to poverty, we all knew there was something special in all of us. It was amazing what all of us could do and none of us knew why, but we were all going to find out. And never in a million years did we ever believe our gifts were going to change the world forever. We wondered if we should keep our abilities a secret, but they were too strong to hide or hold onto. We were always careful at least that is what we all thought. However good things sometimes come to an end and people become confused and want to know more or do not understand.

So instead of unleashing and presenting our powers to the world, we all agreed that it was best to find out how we all came to be. Our heritage and history determine if this was something brought down from generation to generation. Were there more like us, or were we alone? One thing was common among all of us and that was the name Cryogen. An infertility facility would pay willing mothers to test infertility medication, but that was not the only thing they were testing. It was a secret military experiment that not only brought into this world who we would come to know as our father, but allowed him to manipulate the tests and give us life, or was it life? We never asked for these abilities, but as time would tell, we needed them, and we needed each other.

Chapter I

"Senior Year is the Best Year"

The blaring sound of the alarm made me cringe as I knew the summer had ended and the first day of school had come too soon, but what a summer it was knowing this year would be my final year at Cambridge High School in Groton, CT. Your senior year should be the best part of anyone's life knowing that in no time at all I was going to be an adult. My job, my own place, my own......ugh the alarm. Looking at it, it cut off almost immediately, oh what a wonderful senior year this is going to be. Slowly getting out of my bed the cold of the floor made my heart skip knowing there was nothing more I would have wanted than lying back down, but this was going to be my year, the year I got noticed, the year of unbelievable accomplishments. Gazing at my shelf and all the trophies I have already won for physics, theory, and relativity, made me realize the fact that there was one thing that I still need to accomplish everything I wanted. Homecoming Queen! Quickly looking back into my closet, my slippers guided to me allowing me to jump into them and rush my way downstairs to greet my family. Realizing that I still did not have full control of my powers I went forward...my shoes...did not. Bracing myself for the worst, all I hear by the door is "Gotcha!"

"Well, well, well what do we have here?" my loud, obnoxious sister says.

"Looks like you owe me big time, and I don't mean doing my chores either," Adrienne says.

Looking around I realize she had stopped time to keep me from falling, and yes, this time I did owe her, there was no way I was going to show up to school with a busted lip, especially not on my first day.

"Ok, ok we'll figure something out, but in the meantime can you please allow me to get up?" I asked. "Sure, no problem," she says. Starting time in motion, I thud against the floor ever so slightly knowing it could have been a lot worse. "Thanks," I said sarcastically.

"Anytime," she mutters.

After getting up I looked outside my bedroom window, watching the leaves fall from the trees I could only imagine what this year would have in store for me. Thinking to myself, I already knew that Sam was going to be on the top of my list of things to try to keep away from. Seems like every year he is trying to get closer and closer to me, but why? Was it my beautiful looks, my long brown hair, or was he really, truly in love with me? Either way, I cannot let him get too close to me, or my heart. All these changes would be too much for me to deal with let alone someone trying to be in my life.

"Hey, mom's calling us breakfast is ready," Adrienne says.

"Ok, I will be right down" I responded.

Looking out the window, a final thought passed through my mind, why keep pushing him away, knowing that I did have feelings for him, but was too afraid of what could happen if he ever found out about my powers. Only time will tell as my sister always says.

Walking down the stairs towards the kitchen I could hear my mom and dad talking about me and my future.

"So, what are we going to do about tuition and money," Lilly says. My mother was a strong woman having been at her nursing job for more than 15 years she made sure we always had what we needed and then some. But this time their conversation was odd since they were talking about money, something they had never worried about, well at least until now.

"I don't know, maybe we can take out another mortgage on the house, I will come up with something," Roger says. My dad was another story. He was always different for some reason with me and my sister, but we always knew he would do anything for us and was always there for us.

"So, what are you guys talking about?"

"Nothing honey, your father lost his job yesterday and we are trying to figure out how to pay for your tuition when you start college next fall," she says.

"Honey, I will find another job very soon, please don't worry about this, we will make sure you have everything you need," he says.

"Guys, I am not worried, you all have always provided for me, and Adrienne and we are not worried at all," I say.

Seeing them just standing there as if frozen I knew exactly what happened.

"Adrienne, seriously what is the issue?"

"Look this isn't the only issue that we have," she says. "Did they even tell you why Dad got fired?"

"No" I responded.

"Well, it seems that he was going through old files and brought up something called Project Nimuel. It had to do with some type of kinetic energy and the alternate reality that the government was working on. They ran tests on people and tried to create a serum that would give people abilities. Unfortunately, they saw his access ID on the system and stopped him from reading anymore" she says.

"What are you talking about, like the ones we have?" I ask.

"Yes, just like us and the others" she exclaims. "Supposedly Cryogen was set up as an infertility clinic and they were trying to create soldiers that could do almost anything. Imagine all our abilities put together, we would be unstoppable. Wouldn't that be exciting; we would be like soldiers going into battle to stop anything that was trying to destroy us."

"No Adrienne, that would not be exciting, that would be dangerous, and what happens if we can't control these powers, then what? I ask. "We could destroy this entire city, let alone possibly the entire world, and we wouldn't have anyone to blame but ourselves."

"Aren't you even a bit curious about what's in those files, maybe there are more like us in the world" she says. "All I am saying is this, I will use my powers we go in see what the files are, and leave. Or are you too scared to even try, we might even find a way to get dad his job back, who knows."

"I am not afraid, dad got me the internship there to help boost my career, not possibly hinder my future, and what if we get caught?" I ask.

"We are not going to get caught, you get me into the facility, I will do my thing and we are in, piece of cake," Adrienne says.

"I don't know, this all seems too easy, but I guess taking a look isn't going to hurt anyone, I mean dad already lost his job, what's the worst that can happen?" I ask concerned.

"Exactly, now let's go before we are late for school" Adrienne boasts. "Oh, wait I'll start time up again as soon as we get there, wouldn't want to ruin my perfect attendance," she says laughing.

"Uh, what about mom and dad they were just talking to us don't you think it's gonna be weird us here one second and then gone the next?" I ask.

"Besides, I need to know what's gonna happen not only with my tuition but your tuition also for next year," I say.

"Look stop worrying all you do is worry about everything, but you know how things work now, we got family outside of our own, and I am sure we can all come up with something if things get rough," Adrienne says.

"Fine but let me put mom's cup down and dad's coffee on the counter so that they don't burn themselves when things are started again," I say.

"Cool, oh, and don't forget to grab my school bag and lunch, seeing as you owe me a favor, we will start with this first, and work our way up," Adrienne says sarcastically.

"Fine, but don't get too pushy, it's not gonna last forever," I say.

"Funny if I want it to, it actually could," she says walking out the door.

Using my untrained powers, I feel a force push from my body knocking her out the door.

"Don't try me fool, you may be able to stop and start time, but I know I will be a lot stronger than you one day and learn how to stop you from messing around" I say.

"Seriously!" she exclaims. Jumping to her feet she runs at me with all her might to try and knock me down, closing my eyes I feel the energy rush through me again. Slowly opening them all I see is my sister's fist right in front of my face.

"If you don't let me go, I am going to stop time just long enough to make sure you barely make it to your senior prom!" she yells.

"Ok, ok, you don't have to get all emotional," I say. "But as I said sooner or later you are going to realize that every minute, I am getting stronger and stronger. You may have your powers in check, but we can always learn a little bit more to better not only ourselves but this world."

Getting into my vehicle I clip our seatbelts together and start my car not even realizing my keys are still in my hand.

"Pretty cool sis," Adrienne says, surprisingly.

"Yeah, it seems like the things I am doing are becoming more frequent, it kind of scares me sometimes, but I am letting things take their course and see what happens," I say.

"Well, it's about time, now if we can just remove that stick up your butt all of us can live a better life," she says.

Smirking a little bit, I realize that things needed to be different somehow. We have always had a good relationship and I would dread it if anything happened to her. But me worrying all the time about how reckless she is, is the only thing that keeps me sane. How do I let go? Where do I start? Oh yeah school, I cannot wait to see how this year is gonna be. Leaving the driveway, I hear a loud honk!

"Why don't you look where you are going moron" Mike shouts. Mike is the jock Varsity football player who believes he is God's gift to women. Talented yes, smart, no chance, but I can see that John is with him as well. John, the varsity quarterback who every girl at school loves, but he could care less unless they were wearing short skirts is another story.

"Sorry guys," my sister says sarcastically.

"Whatever just watch where you are going, I wouldn't want my dad's 64 Mustang to get totaled" he yells.

Burning their tires all, I can see is smoke filling the air, and just like that, they remind me of the part of school I hate the most. The bullying and teasing they do have tormented so many kids, maybe just maybe this year I can put a stop to all of that. Driving off to school gave me a sense of excitement and fear, but I know this year is going to be my year.

Driving into the school parking lot I slam on my brakes almost hitting Vincent. All dressed in black with a hooded sweater and jeans that were so worn out, his piercing green eyes were the only thing that I saw peering out from under his hood. Slowly walking away, I could feel my heart racing a bit as if something were wrong.

"Take your time jerk" my sister yells.

"Would you behave, geez it seems like every year your attitude is getting worse and worse" I say.

"Well, we are running late, and I am tired of having to use my powers to get here on time" she states.

"Well excuse me miss I can do what I want whenever I want," I say.

"Let's please just go, I have to get to practice, and I am not going to be yelled at again by the team captains," she says.

"Ok sorry, I'll make sure we leave earlier next time, but with the whole mom and dad thing, I couldn't help it," I say.

"It's ok, oh, and don't forget about this evening, I want to get this over with and see what exactly is going on with this facility dad worked at," she says.

"Fine, and please don't tell anyone about this, I am not gonna lose my job there and then hate you for the rest of my life," I say.

"Rest of my life, man with the way I am going I sometimes hope to see the next day," she says jokingly.

"That's not funny, now hurry up before the Blondes decide to make you run laps instead of practicing," I say.

"Seriously this time next year it will be just me, they need me," she says.

"They need to stop dyeing their hair and picking on people," I say.

"Fine gotta go love ya."

"Love you too fool," I say.

Slowly getting out of my car I get startled by a grabbing of my waist.

"Hey, beautiful how are things. Finally, our last year of this place then on to bigger, better things" Sam says.

Sam, the kid that grew into a man too quickly, always following me around telling me how beautiful I am, but not getting the hint that I am not ready for anything serious. His piercing blue eyes and dimples could make any girl fall in love with him. Why me? What was it about me that he cared for and loved so much? Maybe I have feelings for him but knowing what I know now and these powers that I am learning about the last thing I would want to do is hurt him or even worse get him hurt.

"So, can I walk you to class," he says.

"Uh, actually I am good Sam, but thanks" I utter nervously.

"Look, what is it about me. Every year it seems like you become more and more distant, and I don't know what to do anymore?" he questions. "I have been trying for years to try and talk to you and show you how much I really, really like you and nothing," he says.

"Sam, it's not you, I just don't think I am ready for anything serious," I say.

"Ever since you moved on my block since we were seven you have done so, so much for me, but I don't think right now is a good time" I state. The ringing of the bell reminds me of how late I am for class.

"I get it, there's someone else, well I hope he makes you happy and treats you as I would," he says. "Have a great senior year, I won't bother you anymore" he mutters. Grabbing onto his arm I delay him from leaving.

"Sam please don't take this the wrong way, there are a lot of things that you don't know about me. Things that if you only knew half of them would make you run away and never look at me the same way" I say.

"Well then let me be the judge of that, you have always kept me in the dark and hid your feelings for me, why not just give me a chance," he says.

"In time Sam, I have to find myself first before I can allow myself to ever care for someone as much as you care for me" I state gently. "Please just give me time."

"I understand, but will you do me the honor and go to the senior prom with me," he asks?

"Uh, it's the first day of school, don't you think it a little too soon to ask anyone," I ask?

"Just know that I asked you first, and if someone comes along and sweeps you off your feet then fine, I know your answer. But if not then give me the honor of taking you to prom" he says.

"Fine, I seriously doubt that's gonna happen, but I will keep that in mind," I say.

Watching him walk away for some reason is hard because I can feel his love, his kind heart that seems to break every time we part ways. But I do know I was not wrong, I must find myself first, and then I can begin to see where our future will take us. Right now, is not the best time for me to even think about a boyfriend or falling in love. Oh no class, I forgot through all this emotional downward spiral that I am going through, that I am now 10 minutes late. I wish I had my sister's powers, but I know that in the end, I am way better off.

Walking into the classroom I could feel the glaring eyes of the two idiots that almost hit me this morning. Mike and John Montgomery are not the smartest of our senior class, but their athletic skills have set them apart from every other kid that has hopes and dreams of playing on our football team. Seeing them also reminded me that Christian has tryouts today. Christian was a quiet kid, but man can he manipulate things like no other. I am sure he will do fine if these two idiots do not mess up things for him.

"How's it going sweet thing," John says. "Looks like someone grew up over the summer."

"Keep your comments to yourself and leave me alone," I say abruptly.

"Awe, is the little princess still upset about this morning," he asks?

"I could care less about this morning you just need to leave me alone," I say.

"I can't wait until this year is over and I never have to deal with you or your dumb brother ever again."

"What are you gonna do about it if we don't," John says angrily. "You gonna get your boyfriend to stop us."

"First off Sam isn't my boyfriend, second I don't need anyone to protect me I can take care of myself," I say. "So, don't try me, not this year."

Grabbing onto my arm as I turn and jerking me closer to him, John has this glare in his eye that becomes very disturbing. I begin to feel this growing heat within my body, and then it happens.

"STOP!!!" I yell loudly. Feeling a hard vibration my vision becomes very blurred, but the hardest part was not seeing John flying backward into the cabinets knocking him to the ground.

"What the hell you freak," Mike says concerned. My vision clears.

Running out of the classroom I could only imagine what the rest of the people were saying, or even thinking. Vincent, sitting in the corner of the classroom watching, under his dark hood glaring and wondering himself what he just saw. I run past everyone into the back hallway realizing what I have just done, and it felt as if I was losing my mind. What a feeling, a feeling of freedom and insanity at the same time. But the reality is setting in a little quicker than I expected, and I needed to control this power somehow. There must be some type of safety protocol that I have to create so that this does not happen again. But what do I do? Sitting against the lockers I look up and see a hand raised out in front of me. It's Christian.

"Come on, it's gonna be ok," Christian says. "We all need to stick together before we all lose control." Slowing rising he hugs me gently.

"I feel lost right now and I know this is a big deal for all of us, but what are we supposed to do?" "We know nothing about why we are going through this, and I don't know if I can keep feeling this way," I say.

"Everything will work out in the end, ok?" "All we have to do is take one day at a time and we will all get through this," he says.

Hugging me again, I slowly glance to the end of the hall where I see Sam standing there in confusion.

"Sam wait!" I yell. But, to no avail, I can see the pain in his confused eyes as he slowly turns and disappears around the corner.

"Who was that?" Christian asks.

"My downfall" I exclaim. "Thanks, Christian I needed that."

"Don't worry about Mike and John I'll take care of those two, next period" he says.

"Please don't do anything dumb, you have too much to look forward to these next two years and I would hate to see you blow it for nothing," I say.

"Don't worry I think I got an idea of how to keep them from bothering any of us ever again" he says confidently.

"Please be careful and we'll talk about this later. As a matter a fact why don't you meet me and my sister around 10 pm this evening at the Stop-N-Mart, I want to show you something and we can sure use your help if you can" I ask.

"Sure, see you then."

Watching Christian walk away I can only imagine what Sam was feeling. I do not want to hurt him, but I am sure he thinks the worst without knowing the truth. I wonder sometimes if I am ever going to tell him what is going on in my mind and my heart, but for now this must be kept between me and the others. One day, I promise.

Walking through the hallways it seems like things are going in slow motion. Everyone is looking at me, some scared others laughing as if I was a freak. Is this who I am, is this what my life was going to be like? I cannot allow my emotions to get to me anymore I have to control them so that I do not hurt anyone, especially my family. Gym is my next class, and I cannot stand it because of the 3 airheads that I have to deal with every day. I cannot do this if I do, I will lose control.

Chapter II

"Christian's Rise"

Walking out to the football field I skip gym class to watch Christian during his tryout for the starting Varsity football team. Watching him walk out on the field made my heart skip for a bit knowing that John and Mike are going to do their best to keep him off the team. But I am sure he can hold his own. Sitting on the bleachers I kept thinking about Sam and how he looked. I could not get his face out of my mind knowing he must think the worst of me.

"Hey," Sam says, slowly walking up the bleachers and taking a seat right next to me. He looks like he had been crying and I felt so bad.

"How are things going," I ask.

"They are good just wanted to talk to you about earlier today," he says. "I am going to stop bothering you about us, and everything in between."

"Sam don't do this you don't understand what's going on with me and it's hard to explain," I say.

"I know already, you're going through a lot of changes and becoming a woman, but I never expected you to do this to me and not tell me," Sam says.

"Sam, you are right, it isn't fair to you, but becoming a woman has nothing to do with this or us," I say. "This is a bigger issue than you think, and I don't want to get you involved with anything that I am going through right now," I say.

"Just trust me right now isn't a good time for me to get involved with anyone."

"Like Christian, who I saw hugging you and making me feel like I am not good enough," he says worriedly.

"Sam he is a friend, there is nothing else going on between us, please understand that," I say.

"Ok, I am sorry, I just feel like we are slipping apart ever since we got to high school and I feel like I am losing not only our friendship but a chance," he says.

"You're not losing me, Sam, ever," I say.

Hearing the whistle blow loud I turn my attention to the field and notice that Christian is standing in front of both Mike and John. That warm feeling in my body begins to swell up again, but I breathe deeply to control it.

"Well, I'll let you get back to what you're doing," Sam says.

"Thanks so much for understanding but believe me we will have a much-needed talk soon so that you can understand the truth, and understand everything, but when the time is right, not now" I reply.

Watching him walk away down the bleachers was a lot harder than I imagined. But it was for the best. Walking down the bleachers I took a seat by the athletic trainer to watch Christian's tryout and hope that everything works out for him.

"Hey, new kid think fast" John utters. Throwing the ball at his head the thudding sound of the football was the only thing that can be heard from a distance.

"Good one, next time throw it harder I barely felt that," Christian says.

"Oh, I'll throw it harder next time," John says.

Hearing the whistle blow from the head coach got everyone lined up and ready for a tryout that I will never forget. They began by running sprints and hurdles, then having them line up face to face to put hits on each other and ending on offense versus defense. This is where it got out of hand.

"Alright, lineup, defense, offense, new kid go play wide receiver for now I want to see what you got," Coach Johnson says.

"Got it, coach," Christian says.

Knowing that John is the quarterback, and Mike played safety I knew this was not going to be good watching them talking to one another from the sideline.

"Blue 18, blue 18, set, hut, hut" John yells.

Christian takes a direct route to the sideline, and as I see the ball released in the air, I knew it was going to be bad. He let go of it too high leaving it hanging in midair for Christian to wait for it to come back down and then it happened. SLAM!!! He is hit in the chest so hard there was no way he could have hung onto the ball let alone even see Mike running straight at him.

"Whoa, their new boy how did that feel" Mike boasts.

"That was not bad, maybe next time you can hit a little harder, that kind of tickled. Watching Mike and John high fiving each other I knew it was going to happen again, but Christian did not.

"Ok ladies line up again; this time John make sure you get it to our wide receiver quicker so that no one gets hurt" Coach Johnson yells.

"Blue 18, blue 18, set, hut, hut," John says.

Here we go again, watching Christian come near the sideline the ball is thrown high enough to cause the same impact that happened earlier. But for some reason this play was different, Christian grabbed the ball out of the air with confidence and upon coming down to the ground Mike seems to hesitate and allows Christian to go right by him.

"What in the hell was that Mike, what are you doing letting him just run on by you," Coach Johnson says.

"Coach didn't you see that," Mike says confusingly.

"See what Mike, what was it."

"I saw my mom standing in the end zone waving at me," he says. "But she's been dead for 5 years now."

"Dude, getting thrown into the cabinets must have messed you up," John says.

"Whatever, I saw her," Mike says.

"Well, whatever you saw get your head back in the game and get focused" Coach Johnson says. "Now switch sides, new kid, play strong safety, Mike move to wide receiver, and wake up.

Lining up I could tell Mike was still shaking his head confused, but nowhere as confused as I was.

"Blue 20, blue 20, set, hut, hut" John yells.

Mike takes a sharp right then left and comes charging down the sideline with Christian watching his every move. The ball is thrown very hard and as Mike was about to catch it, he lets up looking into the stands. SLAM!!! The hit was so hard Mike's helmet came flying off at least 10 feet away from him. Christian got his revenge, or did he?

"Bet it doesn't feel the same when you're on the other end does it" Christian boasts.

Grabbing onto his facemask Coach Johnson begins yelling, as he always does letting him know the consequences and repercussions of his activity.

"We are practicing here it's not the damn Super Bowl if you want to show off, go show off somewhere else," the coach says. "But, with the looks of how Mike is, you're taking his spot next Friday so get your game together and be ready" Coach Johnson says.

"What are you talking about coach, he is just some kid that hasn't even proved anything," John says angrily.

"If he can take out the leading all-state free safety as he did, I think he will do just fine," Coach Johnson says.

"This isn't over, you hear me this is only the beginning," John says to Christian.

As practice ends Christian runs over to me to gloat just a little.

"So, what did you think, are you happy now," he says.

"Uh, I never asked you to do anything like that, plus you could have killed him," I say.

"Nothing would have happened; I just gave them a little taste of their own medicine," he says.

"Don't do me any favors, if I need to take care of them, I can do it on my own" I say.

"Ok, ok I am sorry but other than that how did I do?"

"You did good, but why was Mike just standing there and looking all confused," I ask?

"Well, one thing I learned over the summer when we were all together is, that I can manipulate reality. I can make people see things and make things that aren't real seem like they are real" he says. "I made him think his mom was around the end zone and in the stands, I overheard them talking in the locker room before practice on how they wished their mom was around to see their final year of high school, so I used that."

"That wasn't nice, but I guess it worked," I say. "Good job getting on the team, I guess now we will have to see what happens Friday. But be careful John didn't look very happy and I am sure Mike is going to want to get revenge."

"I'll be ok, you worry about you, and I'll deal with my situation, see you tonight," he says running past me to the locker rooms.

As I begin to walk away, I notice Braelyn in the distance working out with the varsity cheerleaders. Waving to her I get the ugly death stare from Cassandra, the head fake cheerleader who believes is better than any girl that goes to our school.

"Do not look or even converse with that piece of garbage" Cassandra says.

"We are above everyone one else that comes to our school, and we will always be the best varsity cheerleading team in the nation. Isn't that right girls?"

"Yes, we are" both Heather and Michelle agree. They are the varsity co-heads or airheads as we like to call them.

"And we sure as hell are way above that pale-looking thing right there," Cassandra says angrily.

Ariel puts her camera down slowly as she realizes they are talking about her. She is different, light-skinned, and dark all around. Her black clothing, fishnet stockings, and combat boots do not help her either, as she is always picked on by the cheerleaders for the last four years. She has a strong heart and loves to take pictures for our journalism class. Meeting her this summer gave me a whole new sense of taking flight. She has this little knack for levitating things and flying around making her one of a kind. All in all, she is a good person, but no one understands her and one day I am sure she will do all she sets out for.

"Hey, freak, why don't you take pictures of me so that you can put value to that camera and make yourself useful for once," Cassandra says.

"Why don't you go jump off a bridge and leave me alone," Ariel says.

"Excuse me honey what did you say? Because I sure as hell know you are not talking to me that way" Cassandra says sarcastically.

"I think she is trying to be a little smart ass," Michelle says.

"Look, I don't want any trouble, I am just sick and tired of you always picking on me and it's getting annoying" Ariel states.

"Annoying, picking on you, you're sick and tired of us," Cassandra asks? "If it were not for us sweetie, you would not even exist in this school. But then again who do you belong to? Didn't your mom take a little ride down the highway and crash her car off a bridge? And your dad where is he, oh that's right he was in the car too wasn't he?"

"Please stop it," Ariel says sadly.

"Awe are you going to cry," Cassandra says.

"Cassandra, please leave her alone," Braelyn says. "If you were in her situation, you wouldn't want people talking about you and your family, so just stop."

"Little one, you have no right to speak at all, so just butt out of this ok" Cassandra states.

"I can say whatever I want, Ariel is a friend of mine, and I am not going to let you talk to her like that" Braelyn states.

"Well, then I guess we are just going to have to teach you a lesson in proper manners aren't we," Cassandra says.

Slowly raising her hand Braelyn stood confidently taking the strike from

Cassandra not even budging a millimeter.

"Owwww" Cassandra screams! "Your face is like a rock, what are you taking, steroids," she asks?

"Nope, I just think your bark is louder than your bite," Braelyn says smiling.

"Let's go Ariel I got better things to do than listen to these three."

Walking away Michelle and Heather console Cassandra who is holding her hand and crying to no avail. Watching this transpire I am starting to believe that there is hope for us all. We are working together as a team, and that is how it should be. But one thing that still lingers in the back of my mind is how many of us are out there. What powers are still unknown to us and how are we all going to be able to use them to our advantage, not as a hindrance. I wonder how Dean, David, Megan, and Cheyenne are doing. Megan and Cheyenne go to Maple Grove High School about 20 miles from here and Dean and David are homeschooled considering they cannot be out in the sun for too long unless they wear sunscreen. Their skin is so sensitive to light that even being exposed to direct sunlight for longer than 10 minutes will begin to irritate them and develop boils. Megan on the other hand is studying to become a doctor, with her healing abilities it is no wonder she volunteers at Maple Grove Memorial Hospital as much as she can. And Dean and David their abilities to manipulate water and fire makes them double trouble for anyone. As for Cheyenne, she is a little different than the others as she is what we call our necrokinetic or deadflayer. She can manipulate the dead and all of us were amazed at the things she can do.

"Are you coming with or?" I ask Adrienne.

"No, I am getting a ride with Braelyn" she responds.

Wow, I almost forgot about tonight. I hope we can find enough information to get Dad his job back, or at least see what is going on there. Walking to my car I see Sam walking into the field leading to the back of our subdivision.

"Hey, you want a ride?" I ask.

"No, I am good thanks anyway though" he responds.

"Come on get in I'll give you a ride it's not a big deal, my sister got a lift from one of our friends."

"Alright I guess," he says.

Getting in I can feel his frustration, but I leave it at that, I do not want to start a conversation knowing that he is hurt. I allow him to sit there on our way off campus feeling awful, but at least he knows where we are at for now. I am desperately trying to hold back my tears knowing that I can feel his love and that it is a love I have never felt before and know that it would be forever.

Chapter III

"Who Wants to do a B and E?"

Sitting in my bedroom I could only imagine what we would find, especially knowing that it could hold a key to not only our father's future but could contain information about us. Not two months ago, I heard the main secretary talking to another lady in the restroom about how the DOD (Department of Defense) found information against the CEO and CDO that had to be investigated further. I thought it was just a lot of hot air, but now I am starting to think my internship and my career could be in jeopardy. I needed to find out what exactly was going on and my sister running back and forth in her all-black hoodie and jeans did not help my nerves.

"So are you ready to do this or are you gonna chicken out," she said. "We need to see what's going on in there and clear all of this up once and for all."

"I know, I just want to go in and go out and look for what we need to as soon as possible, but I don't want to get caught either," I say.

"Don't worry I got a little surprise for you just in case anything goes bad" Adrienne says.

"I don't want anyone hurt plus we can get in trouble for breaking and entering, but if anyone gets hurt it's gonna be our heads," I reiterate.

"Don't worry leave it all to me, I got this," she says.

Getting into the car we take the five-mile journey to Cryogen. It seems like a great place to work, but over the last 3 months that I have been there, it seems like people are getting more and more stressed out and cannot seem to control their nervousness about each other. Something must be going on there that has rattled their sense of security, and tonight I am going to find out why.

"Ok we are here, and remember Adrienne we go in and out regardless of what we find, and no one gets hurt, do you understand?"

"Don't worry so much, in and out, no one hurt, got it" she says.

I parked about two blocks from the entrance, I know Joe the old security guard is on duty tonight and he cannot hear anything to save his life. Before opening the door, I hear a loud knocking on the window.

"Hey there guys are we too late," Dean says.

"Yeah, are we too late" David repeats.

"Are you serious, Jesus, you almost gave me a heart attack!" I yell.

"Told you I had a surprise," Adrienne says.

"Ok look now that we four are here we have to get one thing straight, in and out, no one gets hurt and we don't get caught, those are the rules," I say.

"Sounds good to me," David says. "Me too" Dean replies.

"Ok now let's go around the corner behind the bushes and..."

Before I can finish my sentence Christian walks up from around the corner to my sister's surprise and gets frozen in his tracks.

"Adrienne, it's Christian geez what's the deal," I say.

"Well, hello, how was I supposed to know you invited him," she says.

"Just like you told me about Dean and David, right?"

"Ok, sorry," she says. Waving her hand Christian begins to move again and does not seem very happy.

"Seriously, it's a good thing that we know each other because if not I am sure, I could have made your day very, very bad," he says.

"My fault, sorry, it's been a long day and you sneaking up behind us didn't help" she apologizes.

"It's cool it kind of tickled," he says. "Anyway, what are we doing here?"

"I have an internship here, and this morning our dad got fired, and we want to know why," I say.

"Ah, I see well and these two are?" he asks.

"Christian this is Dean and David, I met them last summer at our day camp my sister and I went to. They were the last two I found that were kind of like us" I say.

"Kind of like you all" Dean says. "More like identical, not like me and my brother, but you know what I mean."

"No, what exactly do you mean" Christian says.

Standing next to each other, their blue eyes become like light and their bodies begin to glow blue and red just like the aura of their fire and water powers. Dean begins first by making a metal mailbox begin to melt, David while extending his hand begins to make it steam as he extinguishes the heat to nothing. Watching Dean light up even stronger I remind them of why we are here, not to get caught.

"Guys I think you have proven your point; can we please get focused and get this over with" I exclaim.

"Sorry Alyssa, my fault," Dean says. "Nope, all mine" David utters.

"Ok guys, nice job, I won't ever get on your bad side," Christian says.

Looking at the mailbox to our disbelief it is there as if nothing ever happened to it. Now was Christian playing with our heads or did the twins not do anything to it? Anyway, it was time for us to find answers.

Walking up to the south side of the gate I forgot about the barbwire that was surrounding the top of it. How were we supposed to get inside, we cannot climb over the fence, maybe I can attempt to control my energy and float or fly or do something? Reaching for the fence, Dean reacts with a surprising solution.

"I got this," he says. Holding onto the fence it begins to turn red and melt with ease. "I knew I would come in handy for something."

Creating a hole, we begin to slide one by one heading towards the back of Building E, the only building I have the access code to. Running behind the security guard shack I can see Joe sitting there half asleep not realizing that anyone could have gotten in even walking right by him. Running into the shadows we move in single file from building to building bypassing all the security cameras that I know are working this late. Slowly arriving at building E and walking up the back steps my security card is not allowing us in. Over and over the light stays red making me worry that my dad's firing could have ended my career here, but I keep trying.

"What's going on, why isn't it letting you in," Adrienne asks?

"I don't know, I don't know if when dad got fired, they took my access also, I can't get it to work," I say.

Thinking of the cold chill in the air I breathe heavily on the back of it hoping the cold is what is making it not work. Swiping it one last time and praying, the light turns green.

"Ok, let's go and make this quick I don't want any of us getting caught," I say.

"Don't worry about anything, I think we have everyone here that can make a difference, we will be ok," Christian says.

Running through the corridors I go into my father's office hoping I can find the files that he was looking up. But it is going to be tricky, I do not know if they erased the files from my dad's computer when they caught him, or if they erased them permanently, thank God for all my computer classes last year.

"Hey, we are gonna go, uh, walk around a little while you are doing this ok" Dean says.

"Yeah, just walk around" David repeats.

"Seriously, do not touch anything and don't get caught in 20 minutes Joe is gonna do his walkarounds, so please just stay out of everything and don't be seen," I say.

"We will be fine don't worry; we won't touch anything," they both say in unison.

"Ok, the files are still on his hard drive, but they are encrypted. I have to get around this encryption, if not we are not going to get anything" I say worried.

"Get to it then, you are the one wanting to get in and out remember," Adrienne says sarcastically.

Password, password, what would my dad have used for the password? Adrienne, Alyssa, date of birth, case sensitive? Thinking more and more I remember the tattoo my dad had on his arm of my parent's anniversary. 01/01/2004? Got it!

"Alright, I am in," I say excitedly. "Let's see files, files don't seem like they erased anything."

"Well, that's good, I am going to go check on Dean and David, I'll be back," Adrienne says.

"Please be careful and don't do anything that's gonna draw attention, Joe is about to do his rounds soon," I say.

"I promise I won't do anything that is out of the ordinary" she responds sarcastically.

Going through the files I see the file "Project Nemuel", clicking on the account more and more files open to reveal something dark and yet overwhelming familiar, something that has been plaguing my mind for several months now, who we were. Reading more and more of the files I connected my USB drive so that I can research more later but, the final file was encrypted and needed a little more work and I knew exactly who to ask. Removing the USB drive, I did not even notice the lights coming on in the building knowing that we needed to get out of there as soon as possible. With everyone running back to the office I could see the panic in everyone's eyes.

"We got to get out of here now," Christian says breathing heavily. "Guards are surrounding the building and helicopters everywhere."

"Ok, everyone sticks together, we need to think this out and do this the right way, ok, no one gets hurt," I say. "I don't care how bad it gets we can't reveal ourselves to anyone."

Feeling all of them looking behind me I slowly turn around and realize Joe is standing there with his gun pointed right at me.

"Oh, okay now guys, don't move," Joe says shaking. "I don't want any trouble, but Alyssa you are the last person I thought I would see here, and breaking in?"

"You don't understand Joe, there are a lot of things going on here that you wouldn't understand, so just put the gun down and let us walk out of here, this doesn't need to involve you," I say.

"I c-c-can't do that Alyssa; you know I need my job and can't r-r-risk losing it," he says sadly.

"I know Joe, but please just put the gun down and let us walk out of here, this can only get worse, and I don't want to see you get hurt, please," I say.

"I-I-I guess I should have taken early retirement as they asked me to," he says jokingly.

Slowly lowering his weapon, the doors burst open from the side creating such a blast that Joe accidentally fires his gun.

"NOOOOOO!" Adrienne shouts.

Raising her hands, I can see the bullet slowing down and coming right at my chest. Slowly gathering my energy, I create enough of it to disintegrate the bullet before it could cause any harm to myself or anyone else. I could see Adrienne moving at normal speed and pushing us through the corridor as if we were pieces of paper. The hardest part for me was realizing as time was slowing the blast that came through the building was slowly engulfing Joe, he was not going to make it, and this is all my fault. Reaching out my hand towards him I saw the fire consume his body and watch him turn to ash as if he never mattered in this world. Slowly placing us in a corner Adrienne allowed time to catch up with us.

"Are you ok, are you'll ok, is anyone hurt" Adrienne worriedly asks.

"We are good, I think, guys you, ok?" Christian responds.

"Yeah, we are good" the twins respond together.

"I need to think, I need to think, how are we going to get out of here," I say to myself.

"Let me take care of it, I got an idea, pretty crazy but, it might be our only way" Christian says.

Slowly closing his eyes, I can see our clothes change and materialize into

Army uniforms, the brothers and my sister look just like military soldiers but, it is not us, we look just like them with machine guns and faces that are unrecognizable.

"Ok, we have to stick together but, don't make it too obvious we need to make our way through the south side of the building, that's the fastest exit to the main gate," I say.

Walking through the side of the corridor we begin to mesh in with the soldiers that are standing near the south exit.

"Hey, where did you'll come from," one of the soldiers asks.

"Oh, we thought we saw some shadows going through the back end of the building, so we went to check it out," someone says. I can't even tell who-is-who with our faces being different.

Slowly glancing over my shoulder, I could see a man in a white coat, it was Dr. Peterson, the medical director here at Cryogen that has been developing so many vaccines and helping women with infertility issues for the past 30 years.

"Look at this place General, all I asked was to blast open the door so that we can get inside and see who was going through our system, not use napalm to destroy everything in here," he says disturbed.

"Well, we are inside, and looks like we got the culprit, turned completely into ash" General Collins says.

"That was Joe, our security guard, he was harmless but, things happen, maybe now I bet he regrets not taking that early retirement," he says jokingly.

"Well, the security systems are down due to the blast, no thanks to you, and our backup system was melted thanks to the napalm, so you pretty much gave our intruders an easy way out."

"Listen Doc, I don't have time for antics, or to listen to some crazy scientist who thinks he can change the world. You were supposed to have our serum ready two months ago, and nothing. Remember what happened 18 years ago, we don't need that happening again, Project Nemuel has been given the green light again, but this time we need to prepare ourselves. We have a fresh batch of women that are willing to use the medication knowing they are at full risk" General Collins says. "We can't risk a security breach again, this time I have come prepared."

Eighteen years ago, what was he talking about, security breach, what happened back then, was it on the file that I downloaded that was encrypted, why are they doing this, to protect what? I had to go find Amorette the local geek who knows anything and everything about encryption. We also needed to get out of here, but who is who, I could not tell the difference, and everyone was scattered around. Slowly backing up I felt a push to my back.

"Hey sis, you ready everyone is waiting for you," Adrienne says.

"Yeah, let's go we have to find Amorette, she is the only one that can bypass this encryption there is no way I can do it," I say.

"Ok, it will be hard to find her, you know how she goes from location to location hiding, she is wanted by so many people for breaking into systems, I hope we can track her down," Adrienne says.

"I think I know of a way let's go but we can't take my car it's too close and I don't want to be followed," I say.

Walking out of the south exit and walking past the guard shack I see Joe's cup of coffee and donut that he left there. The sadness started to become overwhelming, but I could not let down my guard, walking into the parking area, our disguises began to fade leaving me to realize that Joe would still be alive if I just thought this through and planned it out a little better.

"Alyssa, this isn't your fault," Christians says. "They were monitoring us somehow; I am sure they had the computer system tapped and as soon as anyone accessed it, they would ambush us as they did. Joe was collateral damage, he was in the wrong place wrong time, but this has nothing to do with you" he repeats.

"I don't care, this is my fault, but next time this will not happen, I will make sure we plan this out before even attempting anything like this again" I state. "Understand?"

Feeling the tears build up in my eyes my anger takes over and holding my face within my hands never realized or saw the destruction I was leaving behind me as we walked into the forest back to our home.

Walking into the house very slowly, so that my parents would not wake up, I could hear sobbing coming from the living area. My greatest fears were realized.

"Mom, are you ok," I ask?

"Alyssa where have you all been, I have been sitting here for an hour worrying, calling around, and couldn't find either one of you, where were you?"

"We were at the park hanging out with our friends and talking," I say.

"At midnight," she asks?

"Ok, well we lost track of time and I didn't have my phone to call you, what happened?" I ask.

"Mom, what is wrong" Adrienne states?

"Your father was taken from the house by some military men and didn't say anything on why they were here and where they were taking him," she says.

"They dragged him out of the bed while we were sleeping and I couldn't find you all and, and....
Seeing her just sitting there motionless I look at my sister.

"What's going on," I ask.

"This isn't good at all Lys; I don't like where this is going" she states. "We logged into his computer and used his password, I am sure they thought it was him doing it, but you also have to figure with you working there too they may be suspecting you as well."

"I have been thinking about that the whole way back and it's starting to freak me out, but we need to keep calm and just go with the flow, if not mom will know something is up," I say.

"Ok" Adrienne agrees.

"And I thought they took you too" mom finishes.

"Mom we are fine, and we are sorry we didn't call, did dad say anything?" I ask.

"He just kept saying sunshine, sunshine, I have no clue what that means, but it scared the hell out of me," she says.

The sound of thunder and rain begin to make me feel even more somber than I was.

Sitting there in disbelief why would my dad say something like that, it makes no sense in his last act of desperation he would say the word sunshine? Think Alyssa, think was the only thing I could keep telling myself, why would he say that? Then it hits me, it was a song that my dad used to sing to me when I was little "You are my Sunshine, my only sunshine, you make me happy when skies are grey, you'll never know dear, how much I love you, please don't take my sunshine away." It is just a song, but my dad always said right afterward not to forget him and if anything, ever happened to him, to take care of my mom and my sister because he knew how special me and my sister were. What did he know though, was there something he was hiding or even my mom? He worked at that place for so long and seems like there were so many secrets that are starting to come out. What exactly was on this USB drive, what is it that they are hiding. This is when I knew I had to find Amorette. She was in my computer class my freshman year but got in trouble changing grades and putting a virus in six school districts that still has not been solved. Now I hear she has been tapping into the government systems and now is a top ten most wanted fugitive. Where do I even begin to look for her, no one has seen her for three years. Then there was a sudden knocking at the door.

"Oh God, they are back" my mom exclaims.

"Mom, relax nothing is going to happen" I state. "Adrienne, get behind me and be ready."

"Got you sis, I am ready" she replies.

Opening the door there she was, Amorette, standing in the rain with a black hoodie on and no umbrella. Slowly raising her head, I could see her mascara smeared down her eyes as if she had been crying for years.

"Hey guys, I know this may sound weird but, Joe was my grandfather, and after finding out what happened tonight, I went through the security system and saw the video, I think we need to talk, and I think I may be able to help you" she states. "I want to give a little payback to those bastards that did this to him."

"Sure, sure please come in," I say. "Mom, this is Amorette she was, is in my computer class at school, she is going to help me with an assignment I have is that ok," I ask?

"Honey it's after midnight and too much has gone on, I don't think that right now is the right time," she says.

Holding onto her arm I can see my mother's expression change.

"Alright, and if she needs to stay over, she can use the third bedroom," she says.

"Thanks, mom I appreciate it," I say.

Walking upstairs I could feel the anger and frustration that Amorette was containing inside. It was as if a furnace were about to explode but kept in very well. She sits on my bed as Adrienne brings her hot coffee to soothe the cold, but nothing could ever soothe her need for revenge.

"Ok Amorette, now that we are here alone, what all did you see," I ask?

"Well, I see you'll standing there in front of my grandfather one second, then an explosion, my grandfather turned to ash, and you are all untouched" she exclaims. "Now how does this happen, I asked myself how is it that you're standing there one minute and then gone the next?"

"Well, the reason why is because..." but before I could finish, she stops me in mid-sentence.

"Look it doesn't matter, I ran through their system and realized that there was a file downloaded through their encrypted database, and knowing you from computer class, I am sure you can't decode it, so if there is anything on there that I can use to get them back or help my grandfather's death not go in vain then I will help you," she says.

"I am very sorry for your loss, I loved Joe like a grandfather of my own he was a good man," I say.

"Is a good man!" Amorette exclaims.

"Sorry, I hope whatever is on this drive is going to not only help me but help you do what you need to do" I state.

"Me too, but we can't do it here, I have a place we can go to," she says. "I must put a decoding device on it so they can't track where I am opening it from, from there we will get the information you need. But right now, I am going to rest, we are going to have a long day tomorrow, so you'd better get your rest, you are going to need it."

"Sounds good," I say. "Adrienne, please go get the third room ready so she can..." Not evening noticing she was already asleep in my bed; I use my extra blanket to cover her body.

"Well, looks like you're sleeping in the third room tonight," Adrienne says jokingly.

"That's fine, I hope she can help us with this drive tomorrow, I am sure there are a lot of things we are going to discover that is either going to help us or hinder our future," I say. "Either way we need to know the truth."

"Very true, well good night, I am going to sleep in my comfortable bed, good luck sleeping on the rock in there," Adrienne says.

"Good night jerk" I exclaim.

Walking into the third bedroom I can hear my mom crying silently in her room. Walking in she wipes her eyes as if to hide the fact that she is losing it little by little.

"Mom, are you ok," I ask?

"Yes, baby I am ok how is your friend" she replies.

"She's good, sleeping, something you should be doing don't you think?"

"Yes, but without your father here it's going to be a long night for me," she says sadly.

"I know mom, but I will find out what happened and get dad back" I reply.

"Don't go do anything foolish, I am sure your dad is ok, I just worry about, well, I just worry" she says.

"Mom is there something you're not telling me?"

"No dear, don't worry, things will work themselves out, in the end, they always do. I am going to rest for a little bit, don't worry about me" she states.

"I will always worry about you, you all are my parents, and I will always be there for you, ok?"

"Ok honey get some rest you will need it also," she says.

"Ok, good night mom" I reply.

Closing the door, I could hear her begin to weep again, but I could not do anything about it, I had to allow her to grieve the only way she knows how to. But I can be sure now that there is something my mother is hiding, and I hope I get all the answers I need tomorrow. Now I need to sleep and hope whatever lies ahead will give us the peace that we need. Looking into my sister's bathroom, I can see her in the mirror wiping away blood from her nose.

"Are you ok?" I ask.

"Oh, hey yeah, of course, just a little nosebleed, nothing to be worried about"
she says nervously.

"I have never seen you have a nosebleed, all these years and now you start to have them," I ask?

"Ok, look I don't want you to worry, but over the last couple of months, I have been experimenting with my powers. And have been traveling back in forth in time. Yes, I can travel in time, isn't that amazing!" she exclaims.

"Are you serious?" I ask. "What are you thinking, do you realize what could happen if you're seen, or even worse change things that can affect the future?"

"I can only go back and forth a month or two but imagine if I can control it enough to go back years or decades at a time, I can go back and see what happened

18 years ago and find out what was going on at that facility" she states.

"The only problem I have now is that a part of me is in multiple timelines, and grown to realize that if anything changes, I get really bad nose bleeds," she says concerned. "And over the last 2 weeks they have been getting worse, so I have been meditating to increase my power and feel like I am ready to attempt years," she says.

"Seriously, don't even think about it," I say angrily. "Even a slight change can affect not only the past but the future, and we have no idea what that will cause."

"Look I know you want to be the big sister, but I can handle this and don't need for you to try and control everything around here, ok? I just need to know what's going on and when it's going on and I will stop once I know I can control it" she says.

"Fine, please just talk to me and we can do this together ok?" I ask.

"Sounds good big sis, now let's get rest, I am beat and have no clue what Amorette has in store for us."

"Ok, love you creep, see you in the morning," I say.

Walking into the third bedroom, I think about her time leaping back and forth and wonder what damage she may have caused, or why her nose bleeds were getting worse. What is happening and when?

Chapter IV

"Amorette's Battle"

Slowly opening my eyes, the next morning, I hear conversations happening in the kitchen downstairs.

"Well, well, look who decided to join our morning festivities," Adrienne says.

"Good morning sunshine, how did you sleep?" Christian asks.

"Uh, what are you doing here?" I ask.

"Well, this morning I went back to get your car seeing as I had these," he says.

Jingling my keys in my face I started thinking, how the hell did he get my keys?

"Alright, I guess, what time is it?" I ask.

"Eight-thirty," Adrienne says.

"Feels like I slept for ages" I respond.

"Well with all the talking and shouting you were doing in that room; I didn't want to wake you up too early. Do you even remember what you were dreaming about" Adrienne asks?

"No, but my body feels like I worked out for eight days straight," I say.

"Well, we need to hurry up and go, the place we are going to is pretty far from here, and going there at night isn't a good thing," Amorette says.

"Ok let me get dressed and we will leave," I say.

"Am I going to be able to go with you all or am I not invited anymore?" Christian says.

"Last night was enough for a lot of people, thank you for my car, but I will call you tonight, and then we will talk about all of this," I say.

"Sounds good, ladies, have a great morning, Amorette, good to see you it's been a while," he says.

Walking out the door, he glances behind again at her. Watching her smile makes me think something was going on between them, but that is another story. Walking up the stairs I began to think about my father and why this is happening, but today all of that will change.

"Hey honey, are you leaving?" Mom asks.

"Yeah, we have to take care of some things, and I don't want for us to be out too late" I respond.

"Please be careful and take care of your sister please," she says sadly.

"Of course, mom, don't worry everything is going to be ok," I say.

"I know, you are just so grown now, and you remind me of your father," she says suddenly.

"What do you mean?" I ask.

"Um, just what I said you're just like your father," she says.

Walking away, again my heart and mind are starting to believe that she is keeping something from us, and it is becoming very hard to believe anything she is telling me. Grabbing my keys and heading outside Adrienne and Amorette are waving me to the car as if something were wrong.

"We need to go now," Amorette says.

"What's wrong?" I ask? But before I could even finish the panic in Adrienne's eyes told me exactly what is happening. Standing in the distance near the woods is a very large dark figure, with gold flames surrounding him, making it appear as if the entire forest was engulfed. With his hand slowly rising I could feel the heat sensation beginning to boil inside of me.

"Hurry, hurry start the car let's go, I have tried everything and it's not working!" Adrienne says.

"What do you mean it's not working?" I ask.

"No, it's not working, and I am freaking out, go, go please start the car!" Adrienne yells.

Turning the key, the car is winding and grinding but I am not getting anything, closing my eyes, I start the car.

"Uh, is there something going on that I should know about guys, you'll are freaking me out big time?" Amorette asks.

Driving off I can no longer see anything in the rear-view mirror, except the fact that Adrienne's nose has begun to bleed again. Using her jacket, she looks at me in panic, making me think that she did something that she is regretting.

"What did you do Adrienne, is this your fault?" I ask.
From behind her jacket, all I got was a muffled "I'm sorry."

"We will talk about this later, but until then Amorette where are we going?" I ask.

"Go towards, the old factory that's behind Cryogen," she says.

"Seriously, that's where we are going. Why didn't you say this last night? You said that this place was far away."

"Well, the only way I could get you to even go by there again was not to tell you," Amorette says.

"Ok, look things are happening that you wouldn't even understand, so please just keep things simple and we will all get through this," I say.

"Ok, I am sorry, take a right up here we will go in through the back entrance near the woods, so we aren't seen," she says.

Driving into the back of the factory, I can still see military personnel around the building, Joe lingers on my mind again, but I must keep my head straight. The factory has been abandoned for 18 years now and has graffiti across the ceiling, making it look like an artist's paradise.

"Behind there, on the left, go into that little area we can hide the car there," Amorette says.

Driving into the narrow corridor, I stop abruptly noticing that the car is swaying a little from side to side.

"You ready for this" Amorette says excitedly.

Slowing taking a control out of her pocket the car begins to lower assumingly to another level. The chains can be heard straining along the elevator shaft as if it had not been used for years, lowering ever so slowly as we hit the bottom of the shaft.

"Home sweet home, here we are guys what do you think?" Amorette asks.

Getting out of the car there was paperwork everywhere, papers on the wall, codes, mathematical equations, a small bed in the corner with just a pillow and blankets that look like they had not been washed in months. On the corner table was a picture of Joe and Amorette, the feeling was unbearable as I picked it up to take a closer look.

"Amorette, I just wanted to say that I am sorry about Joe, and I didn't mean for anything to happen to him," I say sadly. She slowly grabs the picture from me.

"Hey, he was a great man, and will always be as long as we make sure he didn't die in vain. He used to work in this factory when it first opened, and after it closed down, they moved him over to Cryogen seeing as he was about to retire" she says.

"Wait, they moved him over there, do you mean that Cryogen used to own this factory?" I ask.

"Oh yeah, my grandfather used to tell me stories about how they used to do military experiments and stuff on people, but of course, I never believed him, he was old and on edge all the time" she states.

"Well, let's see what's on this USB drive and figure out how we can make this right," I say.

Not even realizing Adrienne was not around I call out her name only for her to walk around the corner in shock, and of course with her nose bleeding.

"Where or should I say when were you?" I ask.

"Uh, just walking around, checking things out making sure everything was cool, and uh well" she pauses.

"What did you see?" I ask.

"Well, I found two metal doors behind all the rubble that looks very sealed, and there appears to be an access box that has weird pictures on it, I am figuring an access code is needed to open them. So, I tried to go back a little bit, to see if I could figure out what happened here, but every time I tried to go back, something kept blocking me. It was very weird, and I can't explain it" she says.

"Hey Amorette, do you know anything about the two doors in the back?" I ask.

"Yeah, my grandpa told me that there were these two sentient beings that they created those two chambers for. That when they were doing their experiments, they opened this void and saw a massive war on the other side with fire and destruction, and seeing this caused a security issue for the government. So, 18 years ago, they opened the void for the final time, and seeing possibly an opportunity the larger being tried to break through, but they used this high energy beam to push him back into the void, causing the factory to start falling apart and closed the void for good. Then, of course, Cryogen was created, and that is about it, or so my crazy grandpa says."

Standing there, I began thinking that this was the beginning, this is what I was looking for the possibility of everything coming in a full circle and giving me the answers, I was looking for.

"Well, anyway I unlocked the coded file, I think it's time," Amorette says. Standing behind her, I begin to realize the truth is there. File after file, project Nemuel gave me the darkest and coldest feeling as if my life were torn into two, and to be honest, that is exactly what happened to us. Our father was not our father, my mother's pictures were on it, watching the videos of her and 7 other women lying on gurneys in this facility brought tears to my eyes.

Watching them strapped down, the audio would cut off and on which made me feel uneasy, but that was a good thing. I could see some of them struggling. Then a final video appears.

"File 459-23-756 Project Nemuel, final study, and last group," a younger Dr. Petersen says. "This is our final chance at developing a serum to help us gain control of this world. One of the beings from the void we opened seems to have been leaving trace amounts of his energy within the facility. Small energy shortages have been happening throughout the city and it's only getting stronger, the last 5 groups we have injected have rejected the serum and are no longer with us. If this fails, then we will be forced to shut the void we created forever and end this project altogether and now we begin" he finishes.

Watching the video my mother and the other women are becoming more and more uncomfortable as the robotic arms are lowered down to inject them with some type of serum I am assuming. Watching the arms begin to inject into their arms, I can see a short energy blast, then another, then a very large one!

"Security breach, security breach, the void has opened we need to charge up the cannon, CHARGE IT NOW!" Dr. Petersen yells.

Watching the women screaming and trying to break from their straps, broken audio is the only thing keeping my sanity in check.

"Oh my God, what is that coming through," Amorette says.

Seeing the screen, I can see a large man, looking human-like but larger. His eyes are glowing white with endless energy, and a crown upon his head which gave him the appearance of a God. His skin was a medium brown color which gave the tattoos that he had on his entire body more definition. He was scary, but then again exquisite at the same time. Watching him come through the void, I noticed the lines of energy that were flowing from him to the arms that were injecting not only my mother, but the other women making them tighten and spasm uncontrollably.

"Fire the cannon now!" Dr. Petersen yells.

"Look, did you see that?" Adrienne exclaims.

Viewing the video before the cannon is fired back and forth, we rewind and play, rewind, and play. There appears to be a short energy blast that comes from his hand and hits a worker there very gently, watching it over and over you can see him take the blast and fall to his knees, then the blast completely engulfs this being and destroys not only him but, the void along with him. The workers run back and forth releasing all the women and helping them to safety. As the video continues you can see Dr. Petersen pointing to the void area and the surrounding facility.

"Get out, we need to go now" he shouts.

Seeing all the workers running out I can see my mother in the distance making her way out the back door and then it hits me. Our powers, our ability to do the things we do, is what happened.

But as I continued to watch the video, things started to get more complicated. The walls were breaking down everywhere, and explosions within the facility would blur out some of the video, and then a pause. As if Adrienne was there making things stop in time. I look at her and get a response.

"Hey that isn't me doing that," she says.

"Doing what?" Amorette asks.

"Nothing" I respond.

Watching the video, the truth comes to light. There appears to be a person standing within the smoke and debris. It's the man that we saw take the blast from that being. He is standing there looking at the monitor, staring, and as the smoke begins to clear, he vanishes and the building finishes falling upon itself, making me worry that something dangerous now is in this world and our government allowed it to happen.

With all of us just staring at the monitor, Amorette glances over at her alarm system as her red-light sensor begins to blink rapidly. Looking at her middle monitor, she sees soldiers coming within the factory, and knows we are caught.

"Oh no guys, you all have to go, I can only hold them off from coming down here for a minute, or" Amorette cannot finish her sentence. An explosion comes from the side of where Adrienne is standing knocking her out cold.

Not even realizing I created a shield around Amorette and me as the blast went off, I feel horrible. Adrienne took the full brunt of that, and I did nothing.

Running over to Adrienne, I slowly lift her off the ground and onto my shoulder, but I can tell my powers are increasing, and turning to Amorette who is just sitting there watching yells to me.

"Go, I will take care of this, you are too important to get caught, I will set off my system it will erase the files, destroy this facility and everything in it, GO! And tell Christian if you see him, I wish things could have been different" she says.

Running towards my car I throw my sister in the back seat and getting in the car I feel like I did at Cryogen. Looking at Amorette one last time she pushes the control, and my car begins to rise out of the factory. Looking out my window, I can see her standing there, and then a shot, she falls to the ground next to her computer as I see General Collins slowly walking in and glaring at me and smiling.

"Finally, the time has come for us to meet, Amorette, is it?" General Collins says.

"We know everything now, you son of a bitch, and we are going to stop you no matter what it takes," she says sadly and breathing very heavily.

"Well, obviously as smart as you are, you probably never figured we would find you, and yet here we are having one final conversation. If I can find you, your little friends will be next. No one is going to stop what has taken me years to develop" he says angrily.

"You're wrong General my friends will stop you and make sure no more pain is brought to this town or the women of Groton. And this, this is for my grandfather Joe" she says slowly.

Clasping onto the remote, Amorette hits a red button that starts erasing all the files, and all the alarms and systems in the factory begin to go off creating a panic in the General's eyes. Looking onto the monitor he can see us begin to race through the factory, but what made his eyes grow larger was a timer on the left-hand side that began a countdown from one minute and decreased very rapidly.

"Get out, get out of here, GO!" he shouted.

As I raced out of the factory the military soldiers that were blocking the exit began firing at my car, I could tell something was wrong because all the red lights and alarms were going off. I began to use my energy to direct the bullets elsewhere, causing them to ricochet off the metal siding in the factory and giving us a chance to escape. As we got closer to the exit, two large trucks were blocking the exit, and feeling the warmth build up inside of me I raise my hand and push them back about 20 feet to allow us to ease through.

Hearing my phone ring, it was Amorette.

"Amorette are you out, did you get out?" I ask frantically.

"Hey everything is ok, don't worry about me just remember what I told you to tell Christian. It's because of him that I have been able to hide here this whole time and never left the town. He always said it would be ok, and to never worry so I never did. Tell him that I...."

Stopping the car and getting out of my vehicle the factory explodes in a large flash of fire and smoke.

At this point, I knew she was gone.

"AMORETTE!!" I scream.

As I stand there crying and realizing that General Collins needed to be stopped, I watch the helicopters and trucks pull away and needed to get to Christian, he would be the only one that can help us at this point, and I think it was time that we all came together again. I needed to tell them the truth and finally put an end to this. Racing through the forest I could hear my sister waking up slowly.

"What happened," she says?

"Amorette's gone, the factory was destroyed, and she never got out," I say sadly.

"Wait what are you talking about, do I need to go back did they see us?"

"No, I don't think so, we just need to get to Christian I am sure he and everyone else can help us put a stop to all of this, plus I don't want to worry mom so after we all talk, we need to get back home before she suspects anything," I say.

"I can't believe it; I can't believe she's gone," Adrienne says.

"We need to be strong, and make sure her and her grandfather didn't die for nothing. Speeding onto the highway our thoughts were somber.

"Sir, they are getting away," a Staff Sergeant says.

"Let them go, I want them to feel free," General Collins says. "Besides, we got that little problem that has bugged me for the last few years out of the way. I want them to enjoy their lives for a while, then when the time is right, I will not only destroy them but make sure everyone remembers me" he says gloating.

Chapter V

"Our First Encounter"

Driving up to Christians' house I could see him sitting on the swing in his backyard slowly swaying back and forth with his head down and watching the trees wither very slowly making me realize that he knew exactly what had happened.

"Christian, are you ok?" I ask.

"I am as fine as anyone who just lost everything could ever be" he responds.

"I saw on the news, what happened, they are saying it was being demolished for environmental purposes, and that there was a gas leak and an explosion occurred and no one was harmed. But I know better than that" he says angrily.

"I am sorry, I am so, so sorry, Amorette wanted to tell you that she is sorry and wished things could have been different between you both. And she tried to tell me something else, but I didn't get the whole message" I say.

"It's ok, I know exactly what she was trying to say, I used to tell her all the time, but she just never could tell me straight out, she would send me riddles and games to play just to always have me end up back at the factory just to tell me to help her. But I knew exactly how much she loved me, I could hear it in her voice, and could see it in her eyes every time I would leave her there. And now all of that is over" he says slowly standing and turning to me with his eyes welled up with anger. "Now he is going to pay, for all of this, for all he has taken away from me."

Looking up at the trees and the surrounding area it becomes gloomy as if the love and joy and been sucked out of everything.

"Christian, please I would don't know how you feel right now, but we have to work together. Anger, frustration, and us falling apart is exactly what he would want" I say. "Amorette wouldn't want you to be like this and neither do I."

"Be like what Alyssa?" he says. "He needs to pay for what he has done; he took my life he took everything that I had planned for us" he yells.

"This isn't you; I understand you are upset, but we need to get everyone together so that we can talk about all of this and what I have come to find out about all of us, who we are, and why all of this happened," I say.

"What, what did you find out that we are all related or something," he says jokingly.

Standing there with my head down I look up at him slowly, he can see in my eyes that there is truth to what he was saying.

"You're kidding me, right?" he asks.

"It's true, that's the reason we need to get everyone back together as we did a few years ago, we also need to get back to school, it's been a few days and I don't want them to start asking questions.

"Fine, but we are not finished talking about this" Christian says walking away.

Watching the plants and trees wither as he walks out into the forest, I knew he was going to be the most challenging to keep under control.

"Let's go, Adrienne, we need to get home so we can be ready for school tomorrow, we have already missed enough, and I have to start preparing for homecoming," I say.

"Seriously, that is what you're worried about, Homecoming?" she asks.

"Amorette was just blown to pieces and all you can worry about is Homecoming?"

"We need to pretend that nothing is different, that everything is still the same. If not, then people will start asking questions and I don't want to have to explain myself to anyone" I state.

"Fine we will go back and pretend nothing ever happened, but I will tell you this if anyone tells me anything, I am going to lose it," Adrienne says.

"Let's get home I am sure mom is worried especially if she saw the news," I say.

Leaving Christians' house, we never even noticed the old white military van sitting at the corner.

"What do you want to do sir?" Private Jackson asks.

"Nothing let them enjoy a few months of school and when the time is right, I will finally get the army that I have always wanted," General Collins says smiling.

Getting home all the lights were on in the house giving me a sense that my mother watched the news.

"Girls are you here, have you seen the news, they said that there was some type of explosion at the old factory that I thought was, uh, well anyway, things are starting to fall apart around town, and I hear they are setting up a curfew for a few months to make sure that everything is ok," she says.

"Well mom, to be honest, remember the girl that was here last night, she was in that factory when it exploded, and I bet they didn't say anything about anyone dying did they?" I ask.

"No, did you go with her to that factory, did you go inside?" she asks.

"We were there, and we saw a lot of things that maybe we need to talk about, what do you think?" I ask her cautiously.

"Like what, what did you see?"

"We needed to get a USB drive decoded and Amorette was the only hope that we had so she unlocked the drive, and we were taken back about 18 years and saw some things that were not only disturbing but is giving us reason to believe that you and our "dad" were holding out on to some things. Plus, this is making me now question Adrienne and our true relationship" I say.

"Ok, look I can guarantee you that you and your sister are blood-related, how I had you was another issue," she says walking away.

"Really mom, an issue?" I ask.

"Not an issue, but more of a complication" she states. "I wanted children so bad and figured I would go through some testing to see if I could have naturally, and they said it would be difficult. So, I tried some testing that facility had, but didn't think everything through and signed all these forms and never wanted any of this to happen" she says sobbing.

Grabbing onto her and hugging her like I never have before she calms down and takes my hand along with my sisters.

"Girls, that evening was the hardest thing I ever had to go through, you wouldn't understand what I went through, but it worked, and I had you, Alyssa, knowing I didn't want for you to be alone, I went to another facility and spent the last penny I had and Adrienne you came into this world. I met your father a few months after you were born Alyssa, and he has always been here for us since day one. But now he is gone, and I feel lost without him" she says sadly.

"Mom, can we ask you a few questions because things are happening, and we are starting to worry about what changes we are going through," I say.

"Honey, you're eighteen, and you and your sister will go through changes, what is it, are you in love, is it a boy, are you having issues at school?" she asks.

"No mom those things we can handle, it's other things," Adrienne says.

"Oh God, I never had the talk with you two, have I?" she asks.

"Ewww gross no mom, it's something else and I think the only way to tell you is to show you," I say.

Standing a few feet back I allow every cell in my body to warm up, I can feel the warmth begin in my chest and flow throughout my body, the red glow filled the room like never before, and slowly rising into the air my mom trips over the living room table but knowing my sister she had a little trick under her sleeve freezing her in midair making sure she did not hurt herself. Adrienne moves the cushioned chair behind her and unfreezes time to make sure she is comfortable.

"You ok mom?" Adrienne asks.

"Uh, sure honey, but how did you, what did you do?" she asks.

"We are starting to develop these, I guess you would call powers and it's not just us, there are others too," Adrienne says.

"There are like seven more besides us that can do all these things, and it's not like we are scared, but after being at that place we feel that there is more to this story than you're telling us" I state.

"Ok, look something did happen that evening when I was at that facility, all of us were lying on these beds with our hands and feet bound to them. The fertilization process had already taken place, so we were kind of out of it when we started hearing these noises and a large explosion that rocked that facility. I couldn't see everything but there was gunfire and yelling and I could hear the soldiers screaming and then a feeling of serenity. My body felt like it was being shocked over and over, but it wasn't painful it was a feeling like I had never felt before. The next thing I know I am waking up at the downtown hospital with no bruising or scratches just a feeling like I had drank all night and had the worst hangover" my mom says.

"We saw the video and we saw you and seven other women being what looked like shocked to death, your bodies were shaking and convulsing, and it was just horrible mom," I say sadly.

"What doesn't make sense is if you had me after Alyssa, but had the treatment done at a regular facility why do I have these powers?" Adrienne asks.

"I don't know love, maybe after all of that happening, I am carrying some type of virus that will affect anyone I come into contact with or maybe in your case who I give birth to," she says looking distraught.

"Mom, you don't have a virus, we are perfectly fine, and we will make sure to find Dad and end all of this and bring our family back together," I say.

"Do not do anything that will put your lives in danger, please" my mother begs.

"We will be ok Mom, don't worry everything is going to work out, we just need to get everyone together, plan out some things and make sure we end all of this once and for all" Adrienne states.

"You are all I have girls and I don't know what I would do if I ever..." watching her reaction I ask Adrienne if she froze her again, but this time looking out the window I can see a dark figure and realize it wasn't her.

"What is that standing outside the window?" Adrienne asks.

"I don't know, but I sure as hell am going to find out right now!"

Slowly raising my arms, I blow a large hole into the kitchen that destroys most of it sending water and debris everywhere. Walking through the hole and into the alleyway I can see him standing there, with glowing yellow eyes and his presence seems overwhelming a bit, but I must stand my ground.

"I got this" Adrienne says running towards him.

"Adrienne STOP!" I yell.

Before I could finish saying anything else, I see his hand glowing yellow swipe across the air knocking her back into the neighbor's garage as if she was nothing. Could this be him I ask myself not even noticing him walking towards me with a glow brighter than the sun? I must stand my ground and feel the warmth within my body hotter than I ever had. The feeling was more intense, but I could not allow him to do to me what he did to my sister, and feeling myself beginning to float off the ground I see him stop, but why? He begins to move again and this time he is brighter than I can handle but seeing him raise his hands towards me a blast is shot in my direction, I return with a blast of my own, yelling in the process. Our two beams meet in the middle causing a catastrophic explosion that knocks not only me but him backward. As he rises, he looks perplexed and stares for a bit, and then he is gone.

"What the hell was that?" Adrienne says.

"I, I don't know, it just felt so natural," I say confused looking at my hands.

"Well, whatever that was we need to use that to our advantage in the future, uh, I mean another time," Adrienne says.

"I don't like this; I think we need to call Christian so he can fix the house and we can talk about all of this with everyone," I say.

In my mind, I do not want to say it, but I think we just saw our real father. Walking into the house all I see is destruction everywhere the kitchen, the side of the house, the dining room table, and the island that my dad built himself, grabbing my cell phone it rings, and oddly enough, it was Christian.

"Hey, I just wanted to apologize for how I acted earlier," he says sadly.

"Christian don't even worry about it, just get over here as fast as you can, we have a lot to talk about" I respond.

Walking past the living room couch I could see my mother lying on the floor with her body shielded by this golden glow, brighter than the sun it seemed, but dim enough to know it was protecting her, and then the flow disappears. Watching her eyes twitching, she slowly opens them and takes in a deep breath. Sitting up she looks around and slowly gets to her feet and slowly walks to her room.

"Good night girls, I will see you in the morning," she says softly.

"Uh, what was that?" Adrienne says confused.

"I don't know, but as long as she didn't notice anything I think we will be ok, but what was that energy that was around mom, it was the same glow and color as that thing had around it, I could feel the same energy that I felt when we were outside," I say.

"What the hell happened here," Christian says.

"Thank God you're here, we need for you to fix this, at least until we can get someone here to fix it, but I can't have my mom see all of this, kind of like you did for."

Before I can continue to say her name, he slowly turns and begins fixing the walls, sink, and furniture with ease.

"You don't have to say her name, I got it," he says sadly.

"Thanks, so much Christian, did you get a hold of anyone," I ask?

"Yeah, everyone, but we need to get back to school and we can meet somewhere afterward," he responds.

"I was thinking that I don't need the school to start asking questions on why we haven't been going and have my mom worry any more than she has been doing. Besides aren't you playing in a couple of days" I ask?

"Yeah, and it's going to be good, I have a few surprises of my own that will make sure those idiots don't mess with us ever again," Christian says.

"Don't do anything dumb, you know that we have to make sure that no one knows about this" I say.

"Do you think the people that killed Amorette care, do you think that if people find out they are going to try and stop us?" he says excitedly.   No one is going to stop us, so quit worrying so much about people finding out ok, and just relax, oh, and your welcome by the way."

The evening grew colder as I could still feel a slight chill coming through the hole that was not there anymore. Going back to school I know is going to be a relief, at least to be able to get things off my mind for a bit. I still have homecoming, prom, and everything else running through my mind and Sam. How am I going to explain this to him, how am I going to tell him everything that is going on without him freaking out and going overboard, or worse than that, him telling everyone else?

"Hey, let's get some rest we have a long day tomorrow and I have a lot of catching up to do tonight so please just chill out and rest," Adrienne says.

"Your right, I have this splitting headache, and not to mention my body feels like it got hit by a huge 18-wheeler" I respond.

"Goodnight sis see you in the morning," she says.

"Good night, Adrienne."

Watching her walk into her room, I hear a slight booming noise, knowing that she just skipped through time somewhere, but where? I just hope she does not do anything that will jeopardize us all.

Chapter VI

"Cassandra and her Issues"

Waking up the next morning I can smell bacon and eggs cooking in the distance and the smell reminds me of the mornings my dad was around. As I slowly walk down the stairs, I glance around the corner to see my mom standing there cooking as she looks out the window.

"Mom, how are you feeling?" I ask.

"I am doing wonderful honey, why do you ask?" she says.

"I just wondered if you remembered last night or anything that happened?" I ask.

"No, I remember this feeling of love last night, like as if I was being held onto and cherished like never before, and then I woke up in my bed and felt sadness and heartache again" she responds.

"Oh, I see well at least you felt something besides pain for a little bit," I say.

"Well, it felt good, but then I remembered your father, I mean Roger and I can't help but miss him so much," she says beginning to cry again.
Holding onto her I can feel her beginning to relax and her body calming down.

"Thanks, honey, I feel much better" she responds.

"Mom, you can say dad I know he has been there for me and Adrienne since the beginning, and he is all I know as a father," I say but remember who I saw yesterday evening.

"Do you feel a draft in here, Jesus it's cold" my mom says.

"No, I don't feel anything" I respond.

"Good morning, and what a glorious morning it is," my sister says.

"Why are you so happy?" I ask.

"Well, I had a wonderful sleep, and we are going back to school, and I am just so excited to be alive," she says.

"Where did you go last night?" I ask.

"UH, nowhere, what do you mean?" she says.

"I know you went somewhere last night, forward, back in time, where did you go?" I ask.

"I did a little recon on what happened last night, and it was the weirdest thing when I went back because you were amazing, but I realized I couldn't stay long because even though I was hiding behind one of the trash containers he turned and looked at me as if he knew I was there," Adrienne says.

"How did he know you were there?" I ask.

"I don't know, but I know he looked right at me, this is something that we are going to need to prepare for, and we are going to need to let everyone know what's going on, this is too big just for the both of us" Adrienne exclaims.

"We will be ok, let's talk about this later I don't want mom hearing us" I respond.

"Girls, do you want breakfast?" she asks.

"Sure mom," I say.

"Ok, so what do you girls have going on for today, Alyssa are you preparing for Homecoming, it seems like it is going to be exciting?" she asks.

"Yes, actually I am, and I have a lot of ideas to make the school better and possibly help the school save money with an energy program" I state.

"Well, that's good love I know how much you have prepared for your final year of school, any ideas on who you are going to ask to the prom?" she asks.

"No, not right now, I just want to get through homecoming which is 3 weeks away and I don't even have a gown to wear" I state.

"Well, I guess this weekend we are going to have to go shopping for something nice, I have some money saved up in an account that your father opened for you and Adrienne and said to only use it when it was necessary," she says.

"That is so great mom, I appreciate it," I respond.

"So how much is in the account," Adrienne says smiling.

"Seriously Adrienne, it doesn't matter how much there is mom if you can help in any way that would be wonderful" I respond.

"Well, I am just saying I saw this new Louis Vuitton belt and I need some new Jordan's, oh and I also need some new pants, the ones I have are all ragged" Adrienne states.

"I will go to the bank later on this afternoon and check into the account to see exactly how much is in there, I am sure it's enough for your prom dress, but an expensive belt and Jordan's I don't know, I will look into it though" she responds.

"Thanks, mom, you're the best" Adrienne gloats.

Kicking her under the table Adrienne smiles selfishly knowing what she is asking for is truly impossible.

"Let's go, I don't want to be late for school," I say.

"Let's try and have a great day girls, I will see you all later this afternoon," my mom says.

Walking up the stairs and getting dressed my mind keeps running in circles about last night, every second, the feeling, the sounds, and the rush of energy that went through my body that I never knew I had. I must be careful and keep this bottled up somehow or I am going to hurt someone.

"Hey, I will be waiting in the car, stop daydreaming and let's go win you the Homecoming Queen award," Adrienne says.

"Are you serious?" I ask.

"Sure, why not, seeing my sister the most powerful being in the universe walking across the football field in your flowing gown getting your crown, and everyone admiring you, why not?" she says.

"I am just saying, you have never wanted to help me with anything and now you want to help me win and I am kind of curious on why the change of heart," I say confused.

"Just want to do what's right and needed," she says smiling. "So, can we go, please?"

Strolling down the steps and watching her swiftly moving out the door I am becoming more and more curious about what her true intentions are. She knows something, but maybe she has seen me win, and knowing that makes me smile, but I still must keep my eye on her.

Driving up to the school I can see everyone staring at me as if something were extremely wrong. Moving from aisle to aisle looking for parking, I finally see it. Up ahead in the distance is a picture of me on the walls of the school with big red exes all over my face, at this time I knew too well who was responsible for this. Getting out of the care the reality sets in.

"Well look who finally graced us with her presence, Mrs. too good to be at school to take in the reality that she will never win Homecoming queen," Cassandra says.

"I am not in the mood for this right now," I say swinging my book bag over my shoulder trying to move past her, but grabbing onto my bag she stops me.

"Hold on just a second, you don't walk off when I am talking to you," she says angrily.

"You don't want to do this Cassandra not right now," I say glaring back at her.

"Do what this?" she says pushing me down onto the floor.
Slowly getting up I see Braelyn, Christian, Sam, and my sister walk over very slowly knowing this is not going to be good for anyone.

"I got this, ok just let me deal with this on my own this time," I say to them.

"It's your war" Christian says walking backward with his arms up.

"Oh look, she needs her backup to take care of her," Cassandra says grinning.

"No, actually I don't Cassandra because what you don't realize is that I am a lot stronger than you think I am, and I think it is time you learned your lesson," I say feeling the warmth growing inside of me.

"Well then make your move and let's settle this," she says.

Slowly moving back and positioning myself to strike, I remember everything I have said the last few days of learning control and making sure we do not do anything foolish that would draw attention to us, slowly standing straight I feel myself calming.

"Cassandra, you can put up pictures of me and talk about me all you want but, in a few months, you will see when the Homecoming queen results come in, right Adrienne?" I ask.

"How am I supposed to know, I am just here for the ride," Adrienne says.

"Think what you want, there is no way in hell you're winning, and I will make sure of that" Cassandra says storming off with her friends.

"Why did you ask me right?" Adrienne asks.

"Well, I thought maybe last night you went into the future and saw me winning," I say.

"Uh no, I told you what I was doing but going ahead to see you win, that wasn't what I was doing, but maybe I should," she says.

"No don't, it's bad enough that I just made myself look like a fool in front of everyone, but almost lost control it's ok," I say.

"Well let me know if you want me to because I need to perfect what I am doing," Adrienne says.

"I will but right now I just want us to concentrate on this afternoon, Christian has all of us meeting up so we can talk about everything, and I wouldn't want to make things worse by getting in trouble," I say.

Walking through the hallway I see at least twenty pictures posted on the walls of me with names drawn across them calling me a pig, a liar, and a freak, but it does not affect me, it is giving me more of a reason to fight harder and beat Cassandra at her own game. Before walking into Mr. Craigs' class, I run into Vincent who nudges my shoulder making sure he got my attention.

"So, you decided to come back huh?" he asks.

"Yeah, what is it to you, I was sick," I say.

"Seems weird how you, Christian, and your sister were gone together were you all sick?" he asks.

"That is none of your business Vincent, maybe a bug is going around," I say.

"Maybe you are the bug because I know exactly what you all were doing and why you were gone for so long" he utters.

"And why was that?" I ask.

"Mr. Collins would you and Alyssa like to join my class today" Mr. Craig states sarcastically.

And then it finally snaps, Vincent is General Collins' son. This is not good, and I know that it is only going to get worse especially if his father is telling him everything that we are involved in, but I must keep my composure so that I can make it appear as if he knows nothing.

"Yes sir, we were both going in right now" I state. Slowly touching Vincent's arm his demeanor changes.

"Uh, yes sir, we were going in right now" he states. "Don't ever touch me again, or you will be sorry," he says angrily.

Looking into his eyes all I see is pain, regret, and anger like I have never seen before, and one day I am sure I will find out why so I will need to keep him closer to me than anyone. Sitting next to Sam was hard but needed to be done.

"Hey there stranger I missed you the last couple of days, is everything alright, I mean with everything going on around town and that explosion, I called your mom, but she didn't answer and thought something had happened to you," he says.

"I am good Sam, and I know I am sorry for not calling you I should have," I respond.

"Just making sure everything is good," he says.

"Hey Alyssa, don't forget about tonight ok, everyone is going to be there

here is the location," Christian says slipping me a piece of paper.

"So, you and Christian huh?" Sam asks.

"No, no way he is just a really good friend, in time you will understand everything, don't worry," I say nicely touching his arm and making him smile.

Coming out of my science class to second period, I can hear someone arguing in the bathroom, and I knew that voice was all too familiar.

"All I did was tell you that I was going to this party tomorrow and there was nothing you can do about it" Adrienne argues.

"Well sweetie, you're not invited and if you think you or your stupid sister can just do as you please, believe me, this party isn't for either one of you" Cassandra gloats.

"What's going on?" I ask.

"Nothing this idiot thinks she runs the entire school and can do what she wants but doesn't realize that her time is up here and there is nothing, she can do about it," Adrienne says.

"Sorry but your wrong, dead wrong," Cassandra says. "If you want to come, go ahead, I am sure this will be good."

"What is your deal Adrienne, why is it that I cannot leave you alone but for a few seconds, and you are already causing issues?" I ask.

"Look, you worry about yourself, and I will deal with my issues, ok? I don't need your help; I can defend myself" she says.

"You know what, you deal with your issues, I won't interfere with you or your problems anymore," I say angrily.

Walking out on her I felt my stomach drop as if I have just given up on my sister who I know needs me more than anything. She is losing control and I feel like I just gave up on the only person that has been there for me from day one. Watching her storm out of the restroom crying, I knew my words hurt more than I wanted, I need to fix it, but I can't right now.

Chapter VII

"A Vision to the Past"

Walking out to my car Sam stops me hoping to get something out of me.

"Hey, would you mind if I came over tonight like we used to do so we can talk a little more about what's going on?" he asks.

"Uh, tonight isn't good Sam I have some really important things to do, but I promise you very soon we will sit down and talk about all of this so that you won't worry so much, is that fine?" I ask.

"Sure, sure whatever you say, you know where to find me, just let me know," he says.

"I promise things will get better, and we can go back to how things used to be" I respond.

"Like how they used to be?" he asks. "And how was that?"

"Us talking, joking, having fun like how things used to be," I say.

"Well, I would rather them go back to 2 years ago when everything was so easy, and we used to hang out and go out together" he responds.

"In time, I promise, I just need this time for me right now," I say. Holding his hand, he smiles back and does so gently with understanding.

"No problem, I am here for you and always will be," he says lovingly.

Walking to my car I could feel his love deep inside but knew right now needed to wait for a bit longer.

Sitting in my car I pull out the note that Christian left me with the directions to our meeting place. I look at it twice to make sure that I am reading it correctly: 1546 Industrial Pkwy, but that is the address to the factory where Amorette died.

"What's up fool, I got with me can she ride with us?" Adrienne says.

"Of course, hey Braelyn how are things?" I ask.

"Good I guess, I got a lashing from Cassandra and the girls because I skipped practice, but I could care less, I am sick and tired of them, but at least cheerleading keeps me out of trouble," Braelyn says.

"So where are we going?" Adrienne asks.

"We apparently, are going to the factory" I state.

"The factory that exploded?" Braelyn asks.

"Yeah, that same one, I am hoping Christian has a plan for all of this, I thought it was closed off by the military, but then again who knows what he is planning," I say.

"Well, we need to be careful, the last time we were there I almost got killed if you forgot," Adrienne says.

"I remember, you don't have to remind me and again I am sorry" I state.

"You almost died, what happened, I don't want to die?" Braelyn asks.

"You're not going to die; well, I mean I don't think you will," Adrienne says laughing.

"You will be fine, don't worry about anything, there are a lot of things we are going to need to talk about and I think with us all there it will make things easier for us to understand and talk about for our future," I say confidently.

"Ok, I am just making sure, I mean I know if anything happens, I can use my power to withstand a blast, but I want to be prepared," Braelyn says.

"Well must be nice to be able to take a blast and walk away as if nothing happened," Adrienne says.

"Well must be nice to be able to jump back and forth in time and change things if need be," Braelyn says.

"No, not change things, I have to be careful with what I do, I cannot just jump back and forth and change things, if I do it can cause a lot of issues not only for myself but for everyone" Adrienne reiterates.

"Ok well, let's get out of here, we have like a twenty-minute drive, and I want us to get something to eat before we get there," I say.

"I want to eat at the drive up what's it called Brenda's Burger's; they have the best hamburgers you will ever have," Adrienne says.

"I love that place too; it is so good, and their service is wonderful," Braelyn says.

"Then Brenda's Burger's it is" I respond.

Driving to the drive-up window, my sister and Braelyn talk about how they hate school because of how people are and how they wished they were homeschooled and never had to worry about dealing with Cassandra and her airhead friends. It makes me think of what this world has come to when it comes to bullying and people just no longer caring about other people's feelings. If things were different, I am sure life would be a lot easier and we could live carefree, but that is not how things have materialized. We live in a world of hate, of bullying that continues in schools and the world, a world that maybe one day we can help and changed, but in time. Arriving at the drive up I can see John and Mike's car sitting there so I knew it was going to be a long evening.

"Hey beautiful, how are things," John says.

"Things are great as long as you leave us alone creep," Adrienne says.

"Well come on, that's not nice, why don't you all come over here so we can talk, you all don't have to be so ugly about things," John says.

"I don't think so, we just want to get some food and go, we don't have time to talk to you," Adrienne says.

As he gets out and slams his door, I can tell John is either drunk or just does not have enough security to be denied.

"Look, I don't know what your deal is, but I am sick and tired of you and your sister thinking you're God's gift to the world and trying to make us look stupid," John says.

"John calm down man," Mike says.

"No, I refuse to sit here and allow these little girls to think they can do as they please. Oh, that's right they weren't invited to the party tomorrow, are you all upset because you can't go?" he asks.

"I don't care if we were invited or not, we are going to that party" Adrienne responds.

"Well, if you do, we got a little surprise for you and your sister," John says grinning. "Later girls."

"Adrienne, we don't need any attention drawn to us, look our food is coming," I say.

"Four double cheeseburgers, five orders of fries, and three cokes, that's $19.50," Keith says.

"I got it guys, my dad gives me an allowance when I do the dishes and stuff," Braelyn says.

"Thanks, Braelyn, really we appreciate it, but why the extra food?" I ask.

"Being in cheerleading takes a toll on my body and being able to do what I do makes my metabolism increase, so I have to keep eating to maintain my figure" she responds smiling.

"Whatever works," Adrienne says.

"Ok, let's get going, we can eat on our way to the factory" I respond.

Driving through the streets the air is beginning to get colder and colder and my only thought is how I am going to explain our situation, and everyone agrees that we need to train and work on ourselves to stop this menacing creature from ever causing more harm. Slowly taking a left on Olympus Drive we arrive at a gated ditch that can easily be accessed through the drainage system.

"Ok, we are here, remember what we talked about, we need to get through the drainage system and into the factory and not be seen, this will be the only way that we can meet up with everyone and finally get prepared for what's coming," I say.

"Fine, fine, let's just go, Braelyn you ready?" Adrienne asks.

"Yes, wait hold on, one more bite," she responds.

"Seriously, let's go!" Adrienne says.

"Geez, ok let's go," Braelyn responds angrily.

Going into the ditch we head our way over to the drainage system that interconnects right to the bottom entryway to the factory, it will be our best bet, but only if I had seen the sensor going off as we passed the entrance things would have been different.

"General Collins, sir?" Private McKenzie says.

"What is it Private?" he asks.

"Our sensor went off at the entrance to the drainage system like you said, we have video of three girls going into the factory sir," he responds.

"It's fine, let them pass, we have small surveillance inside the factory and will be able to see what these little girls are up to, hopefully, if I am right, we will be well on our way to seeing if this serum worked," he says.

"Yes, sir," Private McKenzie responds. "Let them pass," he says over his headset.

Walking into the underground section I can hear people talking and laughing as if a party was being thrown.

"Well, there she is," Christian says. "What took you so long, we were all about to give up on you."

"Sorry, we were hungry and stopped off at Brenda's for some burgers," I respond.

Watching everyone agree in unison, my thought shifted.

"Anyway, so who all is here?" I ask.

"We both are," Dean and David say in unison.

"Megan and I are here too," Cheyenne says.

Flying in from around the corner.

"Hey, everybody, sorry I was being a bit nosey and looking around," Ariel says.

"Ok, looks like everyone is here, so there are a few things that I need to tell you and I want everyone to have an open mind, ok? The powers we have and everything else that comes with it is not exactly as it seems, and to be honest, our fathers who have raised us over the years cannot be considered our fathers" I state.

"What are you talking about?" Christian asks.

"We are all related and our powers were given to us by a being from another dimension," I respond.

"Wait, what you're telling me is that my father is not my father, the only man that has been there my entire life is not even real?" Ariel asks.

"What I am saying is me, Adrienne and Amorette opened the encrypted drive we took from Cryogen and it showed all of our mothers being tortured and tied down to tables as this thing, walked right into our dimension and implanted this energy into them creating us," I respond hesitantly. "Adrienne was born two years later, but that energy was still in my mother."

"Ok, hold on, what you are saying is that not only did something create us, but we are all related because of that?" Cheyenne asks.

"That's unbelievable," Braelyn mutters. "I always wondered why when we met at the park all of us were the same age and born on the same date, I thought it was a coincidence, but that was too perfect of a chance."

"It wasn't a coincidence, and it's not that we are all related it's just that all of us are connected by the anomaly and we need to work together to try and stop it," I say.

"Stop what? What do you know that we don't?" Megan asks.

"The other day I was confronted by this thing, and I kind of used my energy in the alleyway to try and stop it, but it was too powerful and almost knocked me out," I respond.

"You told all of us that we needed to control our powers and keep ourselves secret, why would you do that out in the open?" Ariel asks.

"Look, that wasn't my intention, but I couldn't just let it keep harassing me or us, so I lost control," I say.

"You were wrong for doing that, you were the one that had told us to keep quiet, not to do anything that would expose us," Megan responds.

"I think you need to back off a little," Adrienne says.

"What are you gonna do time traveler, you don't have any other powers besides that, and I can easily knock you on your butt," Cheyenne says.

"Go ahead and try it," Adrienne responds.

Little by little everybody begins to get angry and yell and argue with each other, I can feel the warmth in my body begin to rise and notice a red light filling up the dark parts of the room, as I begin to look around, I can feel myself getting upset and angry, tears begin to fill up in my eyes and my breathing becomes stronger and stronger.

"ENOUGH!" I shout.

I watch as everyone is thrown backward and knocked down to the floor, Dean and David light up the room even brighter as their powers put them in defensive mode, Ariel lifts herself into midair as Braelyn stands rock solid preparing herself for a battle. Christian is standing there in disbelief as everyone is shocked at what I had just done. I can feel a very strong warmth around my body as I look down and notice that I am almost engulfed in a red and orange flame.

"Alyssa, you need to calm down and just breathe, ok?" Christian says.

"I can't, I don't know what to do or stop, what's happening to me?" I ask.

"Sis, you need to chill out, ok? You're scaring us all," my sister responds.

"You all don't get it, none of you all do, we need to train to protect ourselves, we need to learn control and I can't even do that, look at me!" I speak.

"Let me help, you Alyssa, at least let me try," Megan says.

Holding onto my hand she closes her eyes and as she opens them, I can feel the warmth slowly dying out. The flames are lowering, until just a light glow. I think to myself, why do I feel so lightheaded, and then suddenly, I pass out. Laying there I could feel the cold air hitting me and slowly opening my eyes I could see the sun shining down on me like a hot summer's day! Why the sun? Slowly opening my eyes, I can see yellow sand blowing everywhere, but this was not the factory. Where am I? As I raise my head, I can see that I am atop a mountain, but cannot determine where I am. I see this very large figure standing to the right of me he looks so familiar and then it hits me, Cryogen. This was the being that came through the portal that created us, our "father". He slowly raises a diamond staff and points it across the way towards a woman, her blonde hair flowing everywhere, and her eyes, glowing red sitting on a throne made of gold. They both are the size of giants and slowly she rises. Her hand reaches out towards the land and a loud screeching noise comes from her mouth making me cover my ears as it is too much for me to bear. By this time, I open my eyes hundreds of thousands of creatures and men come out from the caverns to race toward the male giant. With his next breath, a siren erupts from his mouth creating crevices in the ground with thousands of men emerging in white racing towards the dark ones. A battle ensues and I can see that the white warriors have powers, as they use them against the dark ones, I can tell that these warriors are experienced as they use multiple attacks against their enemy to drive them back. Out of the corner of my eye though, there are short bursts of energy, and that sound was way too familiar. Adrienne! Watching her use her powers was a sight to see, her skills had developed, and I could see that she was helping this giant. What did he do to her? Why was she helping? As I watched back and forth, she went until at one point she glances up and sees me and within that second, she is gone. Watching the battle unfolding it seems as if the dark enemy was being defeated until the woman raised her hand again and created a deep cavern around the white ones only to have them begin falling deep into the earth. The dark ones began gaining control and I could see her devilish smile as she could see they were winning the battle. I started to get angry again and I could feel my body warming up and beginning to glow. Watching the battle, I wanted to help but, how could I? This was not my war, or so I thought. Trying to control my powers, I did not notice the woman slowly turned to look in my direction as did the male giant. Her expression turned from laughter to anger and fear, looking deep into her eyes, she levitates and begins coming toward me, at this point I never saw that the male had begun his journey to me as well. I began to back up in fear, and I could feel my powers growing stronger and stronger, so I hold my position ready for anything. As she flies towards me even faster the male giant grabs her before she can get to me, and they stumble across the mountain creating a very large indentation on the side of it. I can hear voices in the distance, calling my name, Alyssa, Alyssa, ALYSSA!

"Alyssa are you ok," Christian says.

"Wait, what, what happened?" I ask.

"You were out for a while," he says.

"A while, more like two hours," Adrienne says.

"We were worried about you, so we stayed until you woke up," Christian responds.

"Yeah, we are all here, we wanted to apologize for how we acted and take your word of advice about our training," Megan says. "And I am sorry for knocking you out, it was the only way to get you to calm down."

"It's ok Megan, thank you, but there is one issue that I have," I respond.

"Adrienne, do you have anything to say for yourself?" I ask.

"Uh, what do you mean?" she responds.

"I have a funny feeling that you are holding back on information that we can use" I state.

"What exactly do you mean?" she asks.

"You know, I have been wondering where or when you have been sneaking off to in the middle of the night. You use your powers more than any of us, I am sure, but I know you have information that we can use to stop this thing, don't you?" I ask.

"Ok, ok, look I have been experimenting with my powers and can jump back in time even further than I thought" she responds.

"How much further, the other day you said maybe a week or two maybe a month, but how far?" I ask.

"A millennium?" she responds. "Maybe two or three?"

"A millennium Adrienne? I knew you were up to something" I say.

"Look, it's not a big deal, I can control the time skips and the only issue that I have to deal with is my nose bleeds," she says.

"What do you mean nose bleeds?" Megan asks.

"I have realized that every time I time skip, I leave a part of me, somehow, there, and if anything changes, even the smallest thing I begin to get nosebleeds. So, I follow what I am feeling, and it takes me to the point where something has changed" she says.

"Why didn't you tell me about this?" I ask. "I am your sister and you always said we would never hold anything from each other."

"This, this is the reason I didn't say anything because you are always trying to protect me and I don't need you to protect or help me anymore, I can take care of myself," Adrienne responds angrily.

"So, now you don't need me, right?" I respond. "Well for now on you can defend yourself and deal with your battles because I am done."

"That is how I have always wanted it, you deal with your Homecoming crap, which by the way you win, and I will deal with my life, alone," she says rushing off out of the factory.

I stand there crushed, elated, hurt, happy, all the feelings inside me make me feel like I have lost the only thing that has kept me sane for so many years, but her telling me that I win makes the pain so much harder to bear with. Why did she tell me?

"Hey, congrats Alyssa," Christian says. "Looks like at the homecoming game Friday, you're going to take what you always wanted, and then afterward at the party, you can gloat in front of everybody."

"I didn't want it this way, not like this" I respond sadly. "Ok everyone, it's time to go home, please be safe and let me know if you all need anything."

Slowly, everyone begins to walk out of the factory and walk into the darkness to go home, I feel like my heart was ripped out of my chest, but I had to be strong not only for myself but for everyone, we needed to begin our training but had no clue on where to begin. I start to walk out with Christian not noticing the red light on the camera above our heads going out.

"Sir, what are we going to do sir?" Private McKenzie asks.

"Nothing, we let them do what they need to do, let them train, make them more powerful than what they are now, and when the time is right, we will take advantage of some of their weaknesses, which is each other and then Project Nemuel will be in full effect. No more games I want results, and then I can destroy this so-called God and send him back where he belongs," General Collins says.

Finally arriving home, my mother is sitting on the swing by the side of the house.

"Hey mom, did Adrienne come home?" I ask.

"Yes, she is here honey, and she was crying, what happened?" she responds.

"Just an agree to disagree, situation mom, everything is fine," I say.

"She didn't look happy, but I am sure you got all of this under control. Oh, and don't forget tomorrow we need to look for your homecoming dress for next Friday's game, ok?" she says.

"Sure mom, no problem, after school I will come home, and we can go to the mall" I respond.

"Sounds good, now get rest, you look exhausted," she says.

"Ok mom, I love you very much" I respond.

"I love you too sweetie, goodnight," she says.

Sitting on the swing reminds me of the nights me and my dad used to sit there and talk about my future and what I wanted to do with my life. I wish I knew what was going on and where he was. I will find out soon enough, but I am so tired right now and need to rest, I hope tomorrow is a better day because I know that my mind is continuing to run nonstop. I keep seeing things and having issues sleeping to where not even music or warm baths are soothing me. I am trying to keep my sanity, but it seems like the more I try and relax the more frustrated I become. I need peace and hopefully, all of this will be over soon. Almost walking into the house, I see a golden light coming from the side of the house, as I walk towards it, I can see it instantaneously go out as I go around the corner near the garage. I sometimes wonder if I am going mad.

Chapter VIII

"Could There be Another?"

Waking up the next morning my body is as stiff as a board as if I had been hit by a truck, but I am sure it was that night's events that caused me to feel horrible.... Adrienne! Walking into her room I could see that she had left very early, and I am sure she is stilled upset with me. Walking down the stairs I could smell the bacon and eggs with toast being made, but it was not my mother.

"Hey, how did you sleep?" Adrienne asks.

"Good and you?" I respond.

"I am good, I did a lot of soul searching and skipping last night and just wanted to apologize about last night," she says. "I am having some issues and don't know what to do," she says.

"What's going on?" I say.

"My nose bleeds are becoming overwhelming and a lot stronger and I am beginning to worry that I have done something at some time and don't know what to do because someone or something is changing things and I cannot find the correct time to find out what it is," she responds.

"Are you sure you want my help?" I ask.

"If I didn't, I wouldn't be asking and sure wouldn't be making breakfast for the both of us," she responds.

"Very true, well didn't you say that every time you had a nosebleed you could determine and focus on a specific time and go there and see what has changed?" I ask.

"Yes, the only issue is that the time I keep going to is in the future, and I have seen some things and can't tell anyone what has happened, or it will alter what will happen," she responds.

"Well, what can I do to help?" I ask.

"Just please, whatever you do when the time is right, listen to me," she says.

"Ok, I can do that, are you sure you are ok?" I ask.

"I am fine, just please believe me when I say that all of this, everything that we are doing and going through, you are our only way of making things right in the end," she responds.

"Ok, I promise we will work together to do what we need to do," I say.

"Thank you, so what do you think?" she asks.

Slowly turning the pan around I can tell that the eggs are burnt, and the bacon is very crispy, almost black.

"It looks great, but in the future let's leave our breakfast for mom to do, by the way, where is she?" I ask.

"She is still sleeping, I didn't want to disturb her while she was sleeping, she looked very peaceful," Adrienne says.

"Ok, let me leave her a note so that she doesn't worry" I respond.

"She will be fine, you don't have to take care of all of us, she knows you're getting her after school to look for your Homecoming dress and I am coming with you," she says.

"Oh, you're coming with us, ok sounds like a plan," I respond.

Walking out the door to my car, I sense something is off with my sister, but I am sure I will find out what it is later. Driving into the school parking lot, Cassandra and her airheads are standing near my parking spot for seniors, but I cannot let them get to me, I mean seriously I already know that I win, right?

"Hey creep, looks like her highness decided to grace us with her presence," Cassandra says sarcastically.

"Look, I am not in the mood right now to deal with you or your friends, ok?" I respond.

"I don't care what you think or what you are wanting to deal with, this is my year, my school and you need to disappear along with your sister," she responds.

"Think what you want, but soon there will be a change and you and your friends will soon be a memory at this school," I say.

"Oh really, is that what you think?" she asks.

Before I say anything, I see her hand raise to slap me, and as it is about to happen, I grab her arm stopping the event from occurring.

"No more, Cassandra!" I state. "This ends today, you may be the most popular girl here at this school, but we are tired of you, and this will no longer happen, to any of us."

Staring at her my eyes glow red and I know that she notices because her face fills with fear and she backs off very quickly.

"You're a freak!" she says.

"If only you knew," I respond.

"Let's go girls, I will take care of this situation another time," Cassandra says walking away and into the third hall building.

"Well, guess that escalated quickly, looks like we are going to have to watch our backs until the end of the school year, but I think what you did was worth it," Adrienne gloats. "See you at lunch," she says walking away.

What did I do though? Was trying to outshine Cassandra the best thing to have done, or should I have just let her continue to bully and harass me? I guess in time we will all find out, but for now, I am going to have to be careful.

"Hey Alyssa, so how are you feeling about the Homecoming elections?" Sam asks. "Sorry, I am writing for the school paper and wanted to know your thoughts."

"I feel like things need to change around the school, as you can see, and everyone continues to vote Cassandra in like they have the last 3 years, nothing will ever change," I respond.

"Well, I don't know if I can put that in the article, but I will see what I can come up with," Sam says.

"Take it as you want, and I just wanted to say if we can, after homecoming if you can come over to talk about a few things, I would appreciate it," I ask.

"Sure, you don't know how long I been wanting to talk to you about things as well," he responds.

"Great, I will see you Saturday morning near the hut we built in the woods behind my house?" I ask.

"Sounds like a plan killer, now go win that crown," he says.

Watching him walk away, I think it is time that I explain to him what is going on, things are becoming more serious than I thought and I would hate for him to get hurt or have something worse happen to him. My predicament is how to tell him and explain to him without really showing him, but I will worry about that in a couple of days. Rushing into English class the only seat left is next to Vincent who is glaring at me underneath his black hoodie, but he is the least of my worries.

"So where have you been?" Vincent asks sarcastically.

"None of your business" I respond.

"Seems like someone has been doing things they shouldn't have, like sneaking in and out of places and creating all sorts of trouble for my dad," he says.

"Look I don't know what you're talking about but anything I do is my business and as far as your dad goes, he can rot in hell for all I care," I say angrily.

"You know, you are kind of cute when you get angry" he responds.

"I don't know what your deal is, but you need to leave me alone". Slowly turning my head to him I can feel my eyes burning knowing that they are shining brightly, but before I could do anything his eyes fill black as if his soul was sucked completely out of him.

"Why do you look shocked?" he says. "Did you think you all were the only ones?"

Feeling the sensation go away I slowly get out of my seat and head towards the door and just like that his eyes are back to normal. Running to the girl's bathroom I lock myself in the farthest stall and begin thinking.

"Ok, what was that what the hell just happened, how, why was he able to do that?" I ask myself. "Ok, I have to slow down and think, my mom and seven women make eight and there are nine of us with him that would make ten, this makes no sense" I keep thinking. "Wait, wait, wait, wait, eight women makes eight of us, but David and Dean are twins, so there are nine of us and Adrienne would make 10, she wasn't born until two years later, how could I have missed this, I included her in the total when in reality we were missing one person, Vincent." Slowly gathering my composure, I hear Cassandra and her goons walking into the bathroom.

"Ok, this is how it's going to go down Friday after I win Homecoming Queen, we all need to be on the same page because if Adrienne and her sister show up at this after-party, I want to be sure that they will live to regret it," she says. "First, I want for them to have a great time, nothing too obvious, make them feel at home, and then either Mike or John is going to slip a little something in Alyssa's drink and then the fun will begin, what do you think?"

"Whatever you say C, it sounds good to me," Heather says.

"Yes, anything to teach them a lesson," Michelle, responds.

"Ok, let's get out of here, I don't want anyone to hear" Cassandra states. Accidently pushing down on the toilet paper roll, a squeak is heard loudly coming from my stall, Cassandra and the girls pause.

"Looks like we got an eavesdropper," Cassandra says.

Kicking the door open, I feel my body tighten knowing this was not going to be good.

"Well, well, what do we have here, so I see you like sneaking around just like your mother used to right?" Cassandra asks.

"What are you talking about, you know nothing about my mother, so you need to watch what you say about her," I respond.

"Oh, my mom used to tell me stories about how your poor little mommy couldn't have babies and would cry all the time at the park walking with your dad wishing she could have just one baby," she says.

"Cassandra, you need to stop saying these things, you have no clue what you are talking about or what you are saying!" I respond.

"Oh no, then why did your mom go to that place and get things put inside of her and tested, so you could be born, no wonder you are the way you are and your sister too, you're both freaks," she says coldly.

That warm feeling comes back.

"You need to take it back Cassandra, everything you said is a lie, take it back now or else," I say.

"Or else what, you gonna run and tell your sister to come to help you, or maybe you're gonna go tell your mom and have that whore come down to the school and rat on me," she says.

Grabbing her arm, I can feel that I no longer have control, as I begin to feel the power envelop me, I can see her body begin to steam and heat up, her face begins to bubble slowly, and her clothes begin to smoke. I never even noticed Heather and Michelle running out of the bathroom screaming for help. As her screams begin to snap me back into reality, letting go of her arm was the last thing that I wanted to do, but maybe this will teach her a lesson. Releasing my grip her body begins to heal as if nothing ever happened, but I knew she would never let me forget.

"What is going on here!" Principal Jefferson says running into the girl's bathroom.

"Nothing sir, what do you mean," I respond.

"Look at what she did to me!" Cassandra screams. "Look at me, look at my clothes, my face!"

"What are you talking about Cassandra?" Principal Jefferson asks. "There is nothing wrong with you, are you alright?"

"You did something to me, you did something unnatural, and I am going to make sure you regret it," she says looking at me with horror in her eyes.

"Ok, both of you all get back to class now, and Alyssa, I don't know what's going on with you, but you have been acting different, missing classes, teachers talking about how different you're acting in class, running in and out, are you ok?"

he asks.

"This is my senior year sir, and I guess you could say that I am suffering from senioritis?" I respond.

"Well, either way, you need to get things back in order, and your sister too," he says.

"I understand sir, can I go now?" I ask.

"Yes, and no more issues please, I want to get past this Homecoming and finish up the year in one piece without everyone trying to rip each other apart," he responds.

"Ok sir, have a great rest of your day" I respond walking carefully out of the girl's restroom and into a filled hallway with everyone in the school staring at me and whispering to one another.

"OK, ok, shows over get back to class now!" Principal Jefferson yells to everyone as they slowly disperse back to class. In the corner of the hallway, I could see Vincent glaring at me underneath his black hood and slowly disappearing around the corner to who knows where. Walking to my English class Christian stops me dead in my tracks.

"So, what happened in there?" he asks.

"Nothing, just needed to scare a little sense into Cassandra, she was saying all these things about my mom, and I snapped," I say.

"You need to get a hold of yourself, we cannot risk losing everything we are working for, especially as we begin to train more and more and get a better understanding of who we are," he responds.

"I know, after Homecoming I am sure things will die down, but until then I will make sure that I don't lose it again," I say.

"Sounds good, now good luck I will see you tomorrow after the game Homecoming Queen," he says laughing.

I wish I would have noticed Michelle standing in the opposite hallway and knowing she heard Christians' every word created a path that I was afraid would happen.

"Hey Cassandra, guess what I heard the freak and Christian talking about?" she says.

"What how much they are in love and how she probably wants to have their baby but can't," she responds.

"Nope, they were talking about Homecoming and him congratulating her for winning," she says.

"What are you talking about?" she asks.

"Yep, looks like you might have some competition this time around unless they rigged it already," she responds.

"Look, I don't know why you're gloating like that, who the hell's side are you on anyway? Are you having mental issues like her now?" she asks.

"Uh, no C, I am just saying, you need to do something about this or our reign here is over," she says worriedly.

"My reign here is not over, and that is not going to happen, even if she wins by some miracle, I am going to take care of her," Cassandra says.

"Like you did earlier?" Heather asks.

"Seriously, both of you all are something else, I don't even know why I even bother with you all, you are not even on my level, but I will forgive you this time, but don't ever do it again," Cassandra responds angrily.

"John, Mike, you two want to do me a little favor?" Cassandra asks.

"Well that all depends on what that is and what I get out of it," John says.

"Let's just say we will both get something out of this tomorrow at my party after homecoming, but you need to do every little thing I say," she responds.

"Sounds good, what do you say, brother," John asks Mike with a sinister smile on his face.

"I don't like this, but whatever," he responds.

Slowly hugging John, his glare and smile begin to get bigger and bigger with each word spoken from her evil mouth.

"Well, that sounds like a plan, but how are we?" before he finishes Cassandra puts her finger on his lips.

"Leave that all up to me," she responds.

"Dude, you are way too happy for all of this, we cannot get in trouble again," Mike says.

"Don't even be scared man, let's go so I can fill you in on our little plan, this is going to be our best year yet" John responds.

"Just as long as we don't get in trouble, I am down for anything, but I know you too well, so we got to plan this out the right way, no mistakes," Mike says.

"You're thinking way too far into this, now let's go" John responds.

Walking to my car I begin to think, and it seems like the future has been set into play, and regardless of how things will be, me winning homecoming queen, me losing, me going to this party and something happening will all be a test on me and how I will react to each scenario. I wish I was able to time skip as my sister does, but I think that would hurt me more knowing exactly what would happen and when, if I was able to do so. I will let things be as they are for now, but I must stop worrying about everything that I don't have control over. I need to stay calm and just think about tomorrow and winning the last thing that I feel will make me feel complete. But will it?

Chapter IX

"Homecoming is Just an Event"

Waking up the next morning I felt like I didn't sleep for days but was just a matter of a few hours as I kept tossing and turning worrying about this day and what was going to happen.

"WAKE UP IT'S FRIDAY AND WE GOT A CROWN TO WIN," my sister says running into my room and jumping on me harder than she ever has.

"Come on wake up, mom made breakfast for her queen, and we got to get ready for school so that we can do this thing," she says.

"Adrienne, how do you know that I win, did you go into the future and see something?" I ask.

"What, me, no way, why would I do that?" she responds. "Ok, yes I saw everything, and it was amazing."

"If this is truly what's going to happen, I didn't want to do it like this, not knowing already, I would love to have been surprised instead of me knowing, and now the look on my face will have to be a fake one" I respond.

"Well, then fake it, you have been faking everything else, especially when it comes to your love for Sammy boy," she says laughing.

"What are you talking about, I don't, no you don't know," I say stuttering.

"Look, I know, and I see it every time he is around you, but I get why you're not following through," she says. "I know what it's like to love and be loved and not get it in return, so it's going to be ok," she says holding my hand.

"What do you know about love, I have never seen you with anyone, or even talked to anyone, let alone you talking about a boy you were interested in," I say.

"Well excuse me for trying to talk to you," Adrienne says. "I will let her highness be."

Walking out of my bedroom I can see her body just deflate with sadness, but what is it that she is not telling me? Who is she talking about, well, I guess only time will tell? Making my way downstairs, I can see my mom in her favorite robe and the smell of fresh bacon and eggs, makes my day feel even brighter.

"Well good morning your majesty and how did we sleep last night?" my mom asks.

"Oh yeah, I told her" Adrienne mutters stuffing her face with cereal.

"Adrienne, I told you not to tell anyone," I say.

"Whoa, hold on, when did you tell me not to tell anyone?" she asks. "You did not tell me anything, plus you are not mom, and I don't have to listen to you at all."

"You have caused enough problems for me and everyone else, with your jumping back and forth and your mouth and everything else you do," I respond strongly. Not noticing that her cereal bowl is shaking and begins to crack on the side making her milk spill onto the table.

"Chill Lys, you got issues, and this isn't the time, I have to go, and don't forget to clean up your mess," she says grabbing her bag and walking out the door passing by me and brushing me on the shoulder.

"What is with you two?" My mom asks. "You all were just fine the other day and now this and I know this is a lot more than just your dad being gone. I miss him too, but we need to make sure that we do not fall apart" she says.

"It's hard mom, have you heard anything, I have been thinking about him every day since they took him. Have you heard anything about where they took him or why?" I ask.

"Nothing love, but we will work hard together to find out what happened and get him back, I promise," she responds.

"Mom there are things you don't know, and one day I promise to sit down with you and tell you everything, but for now just know that we will get him back and we will make sure that whoever is doing this is stopped and can never again hurt any of us," I say.

"I trust you honey, and I know you all too well, so don't go getting yourself in any trouble that you cannot get yourself out of" she responds.

"I won't mom," I say holding back tears.

"Oh, by the way, look on the couch and see what I got you," she says.

It was a velvet red dress with a slit up past the knee and a pair of red high heels for tonight's homecoming.

"I hope that it is not too much," my mom asks.

"No mom, it's perfect, I just wish dad could be here," I respond.

"I know me too, now go and if you see your sister walking down the road, please stop and talk to her and give her a ride, she needs you now more than ever," my mom says as she watches me leave the driveway.

"I will," I respond.

Driving down the street I see my sister, walking very slowly but can tell that she is hurt.

"Do you want a ride?" I ask.

"No, I am good, you go do your thing I will be there when I get there," she responds.

"Please just get in the car, it's 3 miles to school and you look tired already, please just get in," I say.

"I don't need your pity or your help, just let me live my life and you go live yours, soon all of this isn't going to matter anyway," she responds.

"Whoa, what do you mean won't matter?" I ask.

"You don't get it yet do you, I know, I see everything and know what is coming and what is going to happen," Adrienne says slowly wiping away her tears. "I just can't say anything because it will change things, and I have done so many things and left parts of my soul in places that I maybe shouldn't have and just can't deal with our future," she says. "Everything, you, me, Christian, Dean, Cheyenne, everyone, I know what will happen to us all and it's killing me inside but have to allow things to be as they are."

Stopping the car, I run to her holding onto her with all my might.

"Adrienne, you don't have to do this alone, and I know I can be overbearing sometimes, but you are my life, you are my sister, and anything that is bothering you we can get through, but you need to talk to me, not just shut me out, do you understand?" I ask.

"Yes, I do, and that's why certain things will have to be done on my own because you won't ever stop caring, and you will continue to shield me from things that I have to get over. You will be gone next year when you graduate, and I will still have two more years of this hell hole and no one to be there for me besides mom who is barely holding on herself," she says.

"Look, I know things will be different next year, but I will always be there for you, no matter what. Yes, we have our disagreements and I sometimes feel like you want to kill me, but I am here for you, through anything and everything," I respond.

"I know you are, but please just let me be me and don't hold me back and allow me sometimes to get in trouble or face things on my own, I know the difference and will always ask for help, if I need it, but until then just allow me to be me and your sister," she says.

"Deal, I promise to allow you to be a spoiled brat, with a big mouth and if you ever need anything, I will wait for you to come and ask me for help, how does that sound?" I ask.

"Sounds perfect," she says.

"Now, please can you get in the car so that we can get to school on time?" I ask.

"Sure, but let's stop off by Braelyn's to pick her up there are a few things that I need to ask her about tonight after Homecoming," she says.

"Sounds good" I respond.

Driving five blocks over I can see Braelyn sitting on her porch in her cheerleader outfit.

"Looking good crazy," Adrienne says.

"Crazy, girl you ain't seen nothing yet, and yes I got the scoop for you, so meet me after school and we can go over what we need to, but it's not going to be good," Braelyn responds.

"Ok, you two, what's going on?" I ask.

"I found out from a little bird at school and Cassandra and the girls are going to put something in your drink to knock you out and they are going to take pictures of you and put them all over the school for everyone to see" she responds.

"I knew it, that big-nosed..." I pause.

"Lys, don't worry, we got this, and I am sure after all of this is said and done, they are going to go down as the laughingstock of Cambridge High School," Adrienne says.

"I do not want either of you doing anything, let things happen as they are supposed to, I am sure that I have enough power to keep my mind straight so just let them try," I respond.

"You have no clue how this is all going to work out, but hey, you don't bother me, and I won't bother you, so we shall see," Adrienne says.

"Seriously, you're just going to let her take pictures of you and embarrass you?" Braelyn asks.

"No, I am going to allow her to think she has total control and then I am going to teach her a lesson she will never forget," I respond.

"Ok, well, if you need anything we will be there. Maybe you should take Sam with you," Braelyn asks.

"That sounds like a good idea, I would like to talk to him about some things and haven't had the time, so that's a great idea," I respond.

"Told you, you like him," Adrienne says smiling.

"Whatever let's get out of here," I state.

Driving towards the school my mind begins to worry about what could happen if I lose control or if whatever they use affects me and I cannot break free from its effects. Well, tonight will be one of the biggest tests of my life, so I need to be sure to concentrate and have Sam by me the whole time if I don't want to get caught up in their games.

As I am driving up to the school, I can see Sam sitting on the bench near the oak tree on the side of the school, I guess this will be my only chance before tonight to ask him to go with me.

"Hey Sam, how are things?" I ask.

"Good, and how are you feeling about tonight?" He continues.

"Well, I am a little nervous, but we will see how things pan out, uh, there was something that I wanted to ask you," I state.

"Yes, I will go with you to the party after homecoming tonight," he says jokingly. "No, I am just kidding what did you want to ask?"

"Well, yes that is exactly what I wanted to know, would be ok going with me to this party, I don't want to be there alone," I say.

"Well, hey, yes, of course, um, do I pick you up, or do you want to get me, or?" He responds.

"Let's take it a little slower, you pick me up at the football field after homecoming and we can go from there, how does that sound?" I ask.

"Sounds great, sweet, ok, well I got to go to school, I mean class at the school, well you know what I mean" he resays laughing nervously.

"Ok Sam, see you in first period."

Watching him walk about fumbling with his books and fidgeting with his backpack I could feel the happiness in him and the small relief that was just lifted off my shoulders. I just need to be sure that everything stays in control, I cannot allow Cassandra to get the upper hand and ruin this evening for me, seeing as I win and all. Walking into the girl's bathroom, the presence of strong perfume and gum chewing lets me know that the airheads are not too far away.

"Look at the competition girls, so sad if you ask me," Cassandra says laughing.

"What do you want Cassandra?" I ask.

"Nothing just standing here wishing you the best of luck and being the better person hope that you make it to my little party after I win," she responds.

"Well, I will be there and hopefully we can put this all behind us, and maybe one day Cassandra, one day, we can be friends and forget any of this happened," I respond.

Shaking her hand, she pulls me closer to her.

"Not even in your wildest dreams will I ever be your friend," she responds.

"Well, I guess that will have to be the way that it is," I say.

"Let's go girls," Cassandra says flicking her dirty blonde hair from one side to the other.

"This evening is going to be the hardest night of my life," I think out loud.

Walking out of the bathroom I see Christian talking with some of the football team.

"Hey Christian, how are you feeling about tonight's game?" I ask.

"I feel, very good, my legs are strong, my body is at one hundred percent, and I feel like we are going to win a state championship this year, what do you all think?" he asks the rest of the team excitedly.

"Not if John or Mike has anything to say about it, but you are good so we will back you up," Chris the varsity center says.

"Well thanks, boys, but I think their time as the hotshots around here has expired and I intend on making sure we make the playoffs this year no matter what," Christian says.

Seeing his happiness makes me feel good, but I am a little concerned with how Christian is playing devil's advocate on what happens with John and Mike, they may not be a threat, but we could lose a lot just by allowing them to get to us.

"Christian, please be careful out there tonight and watch your back, please," I say.

"Don't you worry your pretty little head, everything will be fine once we win the game and you win homecoming, did your mom get you anything to wear tonight?" Christian asks.

"Yes, it is a beautiful dress, and the heels she got me were on point, now go and be careful, please," I say.

"See you tonight, and congrats," he says whispering.
Walking into my science class, I can see Sam sitting there with the biggest smile I have ever seen him have.

"Alright everyone, stand up and move to the front of the class," Mr. Craig says.

"What is all of this?" Mike says.

"We are at a point where we need to pair up for a project that we are going to be doing and will be due at the end of the semester, so be prepared to study and have study nights with your partner if you are intending on passing this class," Mr. Craig says.

"This is BS sir," John says.

"Well, you would know about that wouldn't you John," he responds. "Ok let's start with Sam first, you will be paired up with Brittany," he says. I can see his demeanor change almost immediately.

"Ms. Gonzales, you will be with Mr. Collins, how about that," Mr. Craig suggests.

"Are you serious, an entire year of being matched up with her, there is no way this will ever work," Vincent says.

"I don't like it either, but hey it might be fun," I respond.

"No, it will not be fun, and you have other things to worry about than me," he says.

"I think any issues I have will be handled very soon, so I am free for now," I say smirking.

"Whatever let's just keep this to a school thing please," he says.

"Sounds good to me," I respond.

As he brushes beside me, I can feel a weird emotion coming from him, and it's not anger or pain, it's fear and it's making me wonder what exactly is going on with him and his father. Time will tell.

"Ok, everyone now that you are paired up, let's look at the handouts that I placed in front of your desks, and the topic and project that will be due at the end of the year will be, "Chemistry and Life," Mr. Craig says.

"Chemistry and life what do those two things have to do with each other?" Vincent asks.

"Well, Mr. Collins that's simple, just take a look at your partner, talk amongst each other and figure that part out," Mr. Craig responds.

"No chance, but I will figure it out on my own," Vincent says.

"Ok, now that, that is over with we can move on to the importance of this project," Mr. Craig says slowly turning around and grabbing onto a chemistry flask, it suddenly breaks upon his turn back to us. The whole class begins to laugh as he utters a soft cry as his hand begins to bleed from the glass cutting into him.

Looking to my left I can see Vincent glaring underneath his hood with a very large smile and eyes as black as night, I slowly grab onto his arm.

"Hey, are you ok?" I ask.

"What did I say about you touching me," he responds.

"Look, I know you know already, but this doesn't have to be like this, maybe we can work our way around this?" I ask.

"Work or way around what, you have your mother and so does everyone else, there is no working around anything," he says.

Grabbing onto his backpack he rushes out of the classroom and at that moment, I am starting to realize that he may have lost a lot more than I thought especially with that comment about his mother. Hearing the school bell ring our class is over, and I think it's time for me to talk to Christian and my sister about Vincent, I can no longer keep this to myself anymore.

"Guys, we need to talk, meet me near the football fields during lunch, I think we are going to have an issue with Vincent, and I know maybe I should have said something before, but I just wanted to be sure before I said anything and during class today, I know now we have a problem," I say.

"What are you talking about?" my sister asks.

"Just meet me at the football fields and we will talk about this then," I respond.

"See you then," Christian says.

Walking to my second-period class I can see Vincent standing in between first and second hall looking up into the sky, I can't imagine what he is thinking but I am sure it's nothing good.

"Hey there," Sam says grabbing onto my waist.

"Hey Sam, sorry Mr. Craig didn't put us as partners this semester, you looked kind of bummed, but hey you got Brittany and she is cute and really smart," I respond.

"That's funny, but look I am going to leave early because I have a doctor's appointment, but I will see you after the game so be ready," he responds.

"Of course, see you then," I respond.

Holding onto him I can feel his love and his joy just being able to hold me, I can tell my feelings are growing stronger, but just must give it some time.

Lunchtime rolls around and my journey to the football field is interrupted for a quick second.

"Hey Alyssa, it's me Brittany from chemistry class," she says.

"Hi, Brittany I know who you are," I respond.

"Look I don't want for you to be upset or anything, but I just wanted to know if you knew anything about Sam and if he is dating anyone or anything like that?" she asks me.

"Uh, well, I don't know, why do you ask?" I respond.

"What do you mean you don't know?" she says. "You all have lived on the same block-like forever, and there were always rumors of you all two dating, doesn't he talk to you about anything that happens in his life?" she asks.

"He does, but as far as a girlfriend, I think he is talking to someone that goes to Maple Grove over on the east side of town," I respond, not knowing why.

"Oh, well I got all year to change his mind, so thanks for letting me know," Brittany says.

"No problem good luck," I say.

I am assuming deep inside that I am falling for him, but I got to focus on the meeting we need to have. Walking up to the football bleachers Christian and Adrienne are both talking and joking.

"What's so funny," I ask.

"Nothing, just having a little chit-chat about some things," Christian says.

"Ok, sorry, anyway about Vincent. I have a strong feeling that he is a part of us, a statistic I didn't take into consideration with the video I saw. I saw his eyes, the way he looks at people before things happen and the way he looked at me one day and I can just feel the negative energy within him," I say.

"Whoa, what are you saying that Vincent is connected to all of us?" Adrienne asks.

"More like with us, but not you," I respond.

"What is that supposed to mean?" Adrienne asks concerned.

"I took into consideration the number of women in the video and figured I had all of us accounted for but in reality, I forgot that you were born two years later and not with all of us during that experiment," I say.

"So more of a reason that I have nothing to do with this or any of you all, right?" Adrienne responds.

"Come on Adrienne, she said nothing like that at all," Christian responds.

"I know exactly what she meant, and I can put things together, I am not dumb," Adrienne says angrily. "I get it, all of this, the whole grand picture has everything to do with you all and nothing with me."

"Adrienne, you're not getting it, this has everything to do with you as well, but we just need to know what we are truly up against to cover ourselves; this isn't about just you or me or any individual," I respond.

"I am done with all of this, I will see you tonight, good luck," she says walking away and into the third hall.

"Don't worry about her, she is having issues with this time skipping thing and feels like she needs to get a hold of everything before she loses herself mentally. She says she has seen a lot and needs to regroup. I try to crack jokes with her and sometimes it works, but other times I can see she is just hurting inside," Christian says. "What are we going to do about Vincent?"

"I am going to take it slowly, seeing as he is my partner in science class, I am going to see where we are at as far as what powers he has and what he knows," I say.

"That sounds like a plan, and until then I will see you tonight," Christian responds.

"Yeah, good luck in the game tonight, I am sure you will do great," I say.

"Hopefully" Christian responds.

Walking to my car Adrienne is sitting on the back of it waiting and looking destroyed, I need to talk to her before this gets out of hand.

"Do you want to talk about things, please?" I ask.

"I don't need your kindness, I just want to go home so we can get this evening over with and get this party out of the way, please can we just go," she responds.

"Ok, but before we leave, please understand that this, all of this, has everything to do with you and us, this has nothing to do with Vincent or his evil ways, or Cassandra and her group of morons, or Sam or even mom and dad. This has to deal with all of us, and in the end, we will make the difference, and I know you will be by my side to make a difference, regardless of how we do it," I say.

"Whatever, you say Lys, let's just please go," she responds sadly getting into my car and buckling in.

"Fine, let's go," I say under my breath.

Driving out of the parking lot and towards our house, I can hear her sniffling and hope that she understands that she is a bigger part of this than she realizes. She could be the difference in all of this, and I hope I can get through to her and help her instead of always being a battle between us.

Chapter X

"One Award Down One to Go"

"Alright Alyssa, it's about that time, are you ready to come down?" My mom asks.

"Not really, but I guess," I respond.

As I slowly walk down the stairs in my new high heel shoes, I am careful to not step too fast as my dress continues to linger behind me and catches my back foot every time I walk too fast.

"What do you think?" I ask.

"You look good," Adrienne responds softly.

"Oh, come on Adrienne, your sister looks like a queen," my mom says hugging me ever so tightly.

"Thanks, mom, but I am far from that, and I am running very late, come on Adrienne let's go we still need to pick up Braelyn," I respond.

"Ok, good luck tonight honey, I wish I could be there but I took another shift at the hospital and I am trying to make up for a lost income," my mom says.

"Don't worry mom, I will make sure Adrienne takes videos and pictures of tonight's game, at least so you can see them later," I respond.

"Sounds good honey, good luck I am sure you got this," she says.

Looking at Adrienne I smile very gently and head out the door.

"So after the homecoming game I am going to let you take my car and head out to the house and Sam is going to pick me up from the stadium, do you have your license on you?" I ask.

"Yes, I always have it with me," Adrienne responds.

"I am just making sure, I don't want you getting stopped and having my car towed," I say.

"I have yet to get a ticket unlike your three that you have already," she responds.

"Ok, I get it sorry, I won't be so negative," I say.

"That is the least of your worries," she responds.

Driving into Braelyn's driveway, she comes rushing out in her cheerleader outfit like she is running the 40-yard dash.

"Hey, why are you in such a hurry?" I ask.

"Uh, do you know who Cassandra is, I know I have nothing to fear from her, but she can keep me from performing tonight and we are late," she says.

"Sorry, I will get us there as fast as possible," I respond.

"Thanks, hey Adrienne have you decided on what we talked about yesterday?" she asks.

"Nope, after tonight things will change and I think it's going to change for the better I believe," Adrienne says smiling very sarcastically.

"What are you two talking about?" I ask.

"Nothing, just making sure everything goes smoothly tonight at the party and we have everything planned out to a "T," Braelyn says.

"Ok, well you two please be careful in my car, and let me know if you all leave early from there," I say.

"I wouldn't worry about us leaving early tonight, it's going to be a night to remember," Braelyn responds.

Driving up to the stadium the sound of the band, the screaming of the fans, and the loud announcer let me know that we are winning.

"TOUCHDOWN Cambridge High!!!" The announcer says. "That brings our score after the first quarter Cambridge High School 14, Maple Grove 0."

We are seriously late, especially Braelyn as she should have been there before kick-off.

"I am so dead," Braelyn says. "I should have been here a long time ago and I know that Cassandra is going to sit me out in front of everyone."

"I am so sorry, maybe she won't even notice you were gone, hey Adrienne can't you do something about that?" I ask.

"Ah, yes I can, Braelyn take my hand and close your eyes, you ready?" Adrienne asks.

"Let's do this," she says.

In the instant, they are gone hopefully, Adrienne can fix my mistake and Braelyn doesn't get into trouble. Getting out of the car I walk through the turnstiles into the back walkway where everyone is lined up and ready to go.

"Ok, everyone, Alyssa thank you for joining us this evening, please line up with Keith as he is the last one left without someone," Mr. Craig says.

Nice, Keith, the only one that is six foot five and has no one to stand with making sure that I look very tiny next to him, I know this is a setup.

"Alright now everyone please stay by your partner as we have another quarter left and then it will be showtime," Mr. Craig says excitedly.

"Look who decided to grace us with her presence," I hear from Cassandra as if I had enough to worry about.

"What do you want?" I ask.

"Nothing, just wishing you the best of luck, but I guess you don't need it do you," she says.

"What is that supposed to mean?" I respond.

"Well, it looks like your sister and some other losers, decided they wanted to put multiple votes for you and when this was observed it needed to be corrected, so you see, there was no way you were going to win tonight, and I made sure of that," she says.

Hearing the game continue in the background I walked past everyone knowing that my feelings were hurt but I couldn't let anyone see me cry. Walking to the side of the stands I can see the football game and we were on the verge of scoring.

"Blue 27, blue 27, hut hut," John yells as he quickly moves back into the pocket knowing five defenders are rushing to stop their progress. I can see Christian moving around and going near the back of the endzone and even though

John has the issues he does fires a bullet right to his numbers.

"TOUCHDOWN Cambridge High!!" Says the announcer. "Just like that Cambridge High School has taken a three-touchdown lead and is on their way to winning this game with a blowout."

"Five minutes left," Adrienne says quietly walking up behind me.

"Yeah, I see that, and I also know what you tried to do so I thank you but it didn't work," I respond.

"What are you talking about?" Adrienne asks.

"Your little game of putting duplicate votes for me to win tonight, that's what I am talking about," I say.

"I didn't put multiple votes in anything for you at all," she responds.

"Why would Cassandra say something like that then?" I ask.

"Maybe she is just trying to rile you up to get you upset, who knows," she says.

"You told me, Adrienne, that I win homecoming, you told me that and I believed what you had said," I say feeling the warmth coming up.

"Yes, I did say you win, but that was to get you where you needed to be, at the right time and the right place," she responds. "Ok, maybe I told you a lie, but every scenario has an outcome and if I had told you that you lose, you never would have come and that would certainly mess up a lot of things in the future. I need you here now, to fix a small thing that I changed," she says.

"What did you do Adrienne, what am I correcting?" I ask.

"You will know when the time is right, but until then, good luck," she responds.

Walking away, I just want to dump every ounce of aggression that I have for her right now, but I cannot lose my cool and halftime is here.

"Ok, everyone please line up with the person you were assigned to, and let's please keep this clean ladies and gentlemen, no fighting or bickering whatsoever," Mr. Craig says.

Hearing the marching band perform the march out song, my hopes and dreams have been dashed, especially with me believing my sister and now I am walking out already knowing my fate.

"Ok ladies, chins up and smile," Ms. Setser says as we march out onto the middle of the field with everyone to see.

"I would like to thank everyone for joining us this year for Cambridge High School's Homecoming extravaganza," Principal Jefferson says over the stadium speakers. "This has been a long time coming and would like to congratulate everyone that participated, and worked hard to get the votes needed for this year's homecoming court and to possibly win this year's homecoming king and queen, so let's get to the winners."

And it begins, my downward spiral...

"The two seniors that will be holding the title of duke and duchess are, Mike Montgomery and Heather Johnson" Principal Jefferson calls out enthusiastically but notices that a very small amount of people are clapping. "Ok, thank you for your applause everyone, now the two that will hold the title of prince and princess are Chris Setser and Michelle Green" to where there is a lot more applause but only because Chris is very popular and so is his mom who is almost everyone's math teacher. "Thank you very much, everyone, and now the moment we have all been waiting for. This year's homecoming King is your very own John Montgomery!" Principal Jefferson says very happily. "The football team cheers in excitement along with around 30 other people who have probably known John since he was in pop warner football. "Finally let's take a look at the final votes and let me say this was a very close one, and with the votes coming in at 187 to 185 this year's homecoming queen is, slowing watching Cassandra move closer to the front, my stomach starts to bottom out, "ALYSSA GONZALES!!!" Professor Jefferson says very loudly. There is now a dead silence and I can see Cassandra walk over to Principal Jefferson and rip the card from his hand showing my name on it.

At this point, everyone goes from shock to bewilderment and excitement with the band tooting their horns and beating their drums to the fans in the stands cheering as if we had just won the Super Bowl.

"This is impossible, there is no way that she could have won this," Cassandra says screaming. "We caught her sister cheating and Kenny the secretary opened the boxes and saw that there were multiple votes for her that were not in there before."

"And how would you know how many votes were in there Ms. Blakenship?" Principal Jefferson asks.

"Because I counted them and so did Kenny and he removed a bunch of votes that looked like they were fakes and I know I won this," she continues.

"Well seeing as there seems to be a little dispute over this I will have to talk to Kenny but until then, Alyssa is our winner," he responds.

Walking up very slowly behind and around her I could feel the anger from her as she turned slowly to me and glared at me with disgust.

"This isn't over, but for now I would like to be the bigger person and congratulate you and hope to see you this evening," Cassandra says smirking.

"I will be there and thank you for not being a sore loser, I know how important this was for you," I respond.

"This wasn't important, it was just another game for me and tonight will be my ultimate prize, see you soon," she says.

Walking up to the podium I felt very elated and felt on top of the world.

"Thank you, everyone, thank you for this, it means a lot to me, and want to wish our football team the best of luck the rest of the evening," I say.

"FREAK!" someone shouts in the stands, as everyone begins to chuckle and laugh causing me to feel a sense of anger and hate towards everyone, my feelings get even more crushed when I can hear the opposing team's stands begin to laugh as well. Why? What did I do so wrong to be treated this way and will this ever end. I can feel that I am going to lose it within that second as my eyes begin to fill with bright redness, my arm is touched, it's my sister.

"Come on, let's go, you don't need to stand here and deal with this," she says.

"I am done Adrienne, I cannot deal with this anymore, why are people so mean, who are people like this, I don't get it," I respond.

"In time you will understand and you will no longer be the talk of the town or being made fun of but the reason why we are all still here," she responds.

Holding on to her I could feel drops of rain begin to fall from the sky as everyone begins to take shelter and move from the stands to the walkway and underneath the stadium to stay dry. Looking into the wooded area near the treeline I could see a dark figure with a small hint of gold around him standing there and feared what could happen but as I stopped to pause for s second I could see his hand wave from side to side and the rain suddenly stopped and gave me a sense of comfort watching him back up into the darkness and slowly disappear. It gave me the ability to see it as more than just a threat maybe it was trying to communicate with us or even me, who knows, but at least it gave me time to walk towards the back of the stadium and away from all of these people who slowly regrouped and came back into the stadium to watch the second half. Watching the football team coming out of the field house Christian was leading the way.

"Congrats girl, you deserved it, and hey, see you tonight," he says running past me onto the field.

"Good luck!" I respond.

"Thanks for being there for me," I say to my sister who is still holding onto my arm to comfort my shaking.

"Hey, what am I here for, to fight with you and make your life miserable, well, ok I guess I do sometimes, but I am and will always be your sister, and here for you," she says holding onto my hands. "Now go and let Sam help you get ready for tonight, I got to get Braelyn and figure out what the plan is."

"Please don't go getting yourself into trouble, be there for me please," I respond.

"Ok, don't worry we will be there," she says.

"Thank you," I respond.

Walking away I felt a sense of warmth seeing Sam walking towards me with a blanket in his hands to keep me warm.

"Hey Lys, you ready to head out, or do we need to stop by your house first before we go so you can get dried up and changed?" he asks.

"Let's stop off by my house, I need to get out of this dress and change into something a little more comfortable," I respond.

"Sounds good, oh and congratulations, by the way, you looked beautiful out there, and don't listen to those creeps, you are much more than a freak," he says.

Slowly looking into his eyes I move slowly towards him to give him our first kiss, the only problem, static electricity and the jolt between us was more than amazing.

"Sorry, are you ok?" I ask.

"I am more than ok, let's get you home and onto this party Homecoming queen," he says.

Driving out of the parking area and towards my house, I can feel the love he has for me, and I know now that I love him more than ever, I think after this party it's time for me to talk to him and tell him everything, at least so I know where exactly he is at with all of this and where we will need to be once all of this is over. I just need to keep my mind straight when it comes to us and the fact that we are all still preparing for the worst and preparing for war. Driving up to my house I can see my mom standing outside waiting with a very joyous look on her face.

"I guess I won't even ask how it went with that crown on your head," she says running towards me to greet me with a huge hug.

"No, I won mom, but it wasn't really what I expected," I respond.

"What do you mean honey, what happened?" she asks.

"After trying to talk to everyone, someone in the stands called me a freak," I say. "Do you see me that way?"

"Oh, honey, no matter what you try and do or what you say, there will always be people out there that are haters and just downright ruthless," she says. "But that is their job in life, to hate others because they will never live a happy life and will continue to bully those that they want to be."

"Still, it hurt and thankfully Adrienne was there to get my mind straight and back on track, or I would have lost it," I respond.

"Well, that's your sister for you," she says. "Now get inside and dry off, you got to represent yourself at this party I am hearing so much about around town, you think you are going to be ok with how people were this evening?"

"I will be fine mom, I just need to get this evening over with and move on, this is my final year and I won't allow this to ruin my night," I respond.

"Good thinking Lys," Sam says.

"Oh, Sam, I forgot you were here, well please both of you all go inside and get ready," my mom says.

"Thanks, Mrs. G," Sam responds.

Walking into my house, I am so happy but worried at the same time as I know things can go wrong at any second so I have to prepare Sam for the worst.

"Sam, there is something that I need to tell you and I was going to wait until after the party but I think you need to know now," I say.

"What is it, let me guess you are in love with Christian?" He asks.

"No, of course not and after tonight I would hope you knew the answer to that," I respond.

"Ok, then what is it?" He asks.

"Over the last couple of years there have been some changes that I have gone through, and I don't mean like girl changes, but like weird changes," I say.

"What exactly do you mean changes Lys, I don't get it," he responds.

"I think the only way to explain all of this is to show you," I say. Lifting my hands to my chest, I begin to feel the warmth in my body rise, the room begins to glow a vibrant red and I see him begin to lift himself off of the bed as a red ball of energy begins to develop in front of me. "You see this is what I am talking about."

"That is amazing Alyssa, and how come you haven't told me about this?" He asks.

"I felt like if I said anything this would only make you afraid of me, just like everyone else is, so I kept this to myself, plus there are some things that you just wouldn't understand, things that are happening with some of us and things that we need to work on and through," I respond.

"Afraid?" He asks. "Why would you think I would be afraid of you, I have loved you from the very beginning when we first met in 6th grade, but I was always afraid of saying anything to you because I knew you were always busy and I had the tech club, science club, math club..."

"Ok, I get it," I respond.

"But, never in a million years could I ever be afraid of you, I love you," he says.

"You love me?" I ask. "Do you love me for me?"

"Always, and it has never been any different, why do you think I reacted the way I did when I saw Christian hugging you?" He asks.

"Well, just know that he is a friend a very good friend, but nothing more," I respond.

"That's good to know, and had me worried, I guess I kind of was jealous but didn't know how to tell you how I felt," Sam says.

"It's ok, at least I know now, so would you mind please getting out of my room so I can change?" I ask.

"Oh yes of course, sorry, um, yes see you downstairs," he responds.

Watching him walk out of my room, I can feel the love even more as if we were both connected as one, everything seemed too good to be true, but I have never felt like this before. It was a good feeling. As I finished changing I walked downstairs to see my mom and Sam laughing and joking which made things even easier for me if we were going to do this. My heart was at ease, for now.

"Ok, you ready to go?" I ask.

"Of course he is aren't you Sam," my mom responds.

"Yes, and if I may say so myself, you look wonderful," Sam says.

"Ok, well I will see you later mom, I won't stay out too late, no drinking or partying, and I will be sure to answer my phone if you ever call," I say.

"I trust you honey, and I know you are in good hands" she responds.

"Ok, well I will see you later on tonight, wish me luck," I say.

"You don't need luck honey, you will do great," she says.

Walking out the door and to Sam's car, I can see her standing at the door and waving goodbye as she slowly wipes a tear from her eye. I know right at that moment she knows I am growing up and time is going way too quickly for her.

"So, are you ready to do this?" Sam asks.

"Of course, and please if anything happens tonight, do not say anything about what I showed you," I say.

"Of course not, no need to worry, this will be between you and me," he responds.

"Thanks, that means a lot to me," I say slowly leaning over and kissing him truly for the first time.

"Let's go your highness," he responds.

It seems like we are driving forever, but my stomach is turning with nervousness and it is only a twenty-minute drive. Pulling up to the driveway, it's a huge two-story house, with around fifty cars parked up and down the block and the music is louder than a train.

"Are you sure you're ready for this?" Sam asks one last time.

"I was born ready Sam, let's do this," I respond.

Getting out of the car Adrienne, Braelyn and Cheyenne are standing near the entrance to greet me. The time for my reign has come.

Chapter XI

"No Means No!"

Walking into the house I felt a sense of insecurity but knew that this was something I had to do, regardless of how bad it would get I had to make it known that I was not going to deal with their bitterness or selfishness ever again, but I also had to make sure that I didn't lose my cool nor allow them to get to me to where I would lose control and expose not only myself but all of us here. Adjusting my sash over my chest and raising my head high I walked into the lion's den so to speak.

"Well congratulations Alyssa, look everyone, here is your Homecoming Queen Alyssa Gonzales," Cassandra says as everyone begins to clap loudly making her even more upset than she already is.

"Thank you Cassandra and hopefully we can put all of this behind us and finish out the school year in peace," I say.

"Or in pieces," she responds. "I don't like this any more than you do but let's just let things go and maybe, just maybe we can become friends, who knows, maybe it will be a good thing for us all."

"That could work, let's start by at least shaking hands, what do you think?" I ask.

"Whatever," Cassandra says, grasping my hand tightly and smiling with a grin from ear to ear. "Now let's all have some fun, drinks are in the back, and food is on the dining table if you and your "friends" are hungry."

Watching her walk away I could see Heather and Michelle giving her a thumbs up near the kitchen, now is the time to be on high alert if I don't want something to happen.

"Hey, Sam, can you be sure to watch my surroundings and make sure that if we get something to drink or eat we check it before we consume it," I say.

"Sure, what's going on, you feeling something?" He responds.

"No, I don't have powers like that, but let's just say it's a hunch that something is going to happen and it might not be good," I say.

"No worries, just stay by me and I will take care of you, I mean us, well you know what I mean," he responds.

"Sounds good, and thank you for coming with me," I say slowly kissing him on the lips ever so gently.

"Anything for you Lys, it's always been anything for you," he says.

"Ok, let's go into the kitchen and get us some drinks and something to eat I am starving, and nothing alcoholic please," I say.

"Sounds like a plan," Sam responds.

Walking into the kitchen I can see Mike and John talking to Cassandra near the refrigerator laughing and I am sure it's about me.

"Hey there Alyssa, congratulations on your big win," Mike says. "Looks like you showed Cassandra didn't you."

"It was nothing like that Mike, I did not do this to show up anyone," I say.

"Besides, maybe things can be different after all of this, do you need to continue being a jerk like you've been the last three years. I remember a while back when you use to come running to my house asking for help when Dylan and Jonah used to chase you down the street trying to beat you up every chance they got, do you remember those days?" I ask.

"You need to shut your mouth Alyssa, if you know what's good for you," John says angrily.

"Or what, what are you going to do, bully me like you have this whole time, make me feel small, or are we all going to enjoy our evening?" I ask.

Watching his eyes fill with tears, he approaches me very quickly.

"Whoa, whoa John, that's as far as you go," Sam says slowly moving in front of me.

"Well look who finally got the nerve to say something, but does he have the nerve to do something about it," John says slowly pushing Sam in the chest and back into me.

"I don't want to get into this with you John or your brother but have some respect," Sam says placing his hand on John's chest.

"Seriously, you are going to touch me?" John says grabbing onto Sam's hand and twisting his arm to where Sam lets out a slight grunt of pain.

"Stop it, John, you're going to hurt him, let him go," I say. Not seeing Mike walk up behind me he slowly grabs my waist and moves me away causing me to stumble and fall to the floor. Seeing Sam's face it goes from despair to anger as I see him rise, turn, and hit John across the face almost knocking him out. Mike begins to run towards Sam and I trip him causing him to stumble as well. The crowd begins to cheer and laugh at the two brothers as they slowly jump up and with their embarrassment run out the back door towards the gazebo.

"I never thought you had it in you," I tell Sam.

"Well, I think that time has finally taken its toll on not only you but for me too, I had to defend you even though I knew you could take care of yourself," he responds.

"Well, thank you and I appreciate it," I say reaching out for one of the cups on the counter filled with kool-aid, but never even noticed the pill Michelle dropped into my drink.

"Task completed," Michelle texts Cassandra and Heather letting them know that the game is on.

"Thanks for the help back there," Sam says.

"Who else is going to help you like that," I respond. "Besides, isn't that what girlfriends do, your ride or die."

"Well, I wouldn't want for you to get hurt, but I guess that is something that I will have to get used to which is you taking care of yourself," Sam says smiling.

"We will be fine and I am sure that once the year is over everyone will forget anything that happened this year and we will all go on with our lives and try and forget things and people for that matter," I respond.

Slowly taking a drink I can see my sister rushing over towards me with one hand out and her eyes large with desperation.

"Please don't tell me you drank that?" She asks.

"I was careful and made sure that I watched everyone that was around it, plus wouldn't you already know if something happened or not?" I respond.

"That is why I am worried if you drank whatever was in that cup, then everything from this point is set in motion," Adrienne says. Looking at her I can see her nose slightly begin to bleed. This worries me more than Cassandra or anything else that could happen at this party, at least I have people here that know me.

"Please be careful and don't do anything foolish, things are going to get rough, Sam can I talk to you outside for a minute," Adrienne says.

"Sure, uh, Lys I will be right back," Sam says slowly kissing me on the cheek.

"I will be right here, hurry back," I respond.

Watching them slowly walk out the front door, I feel a hand gently grab my shoulder.

"Hey you, how are you enjoying the party," Cassandra says.

"I am doing good, and I tell you what, these drinks that you made for this party are wonderous," I respond not noticing that I am beginning to see double but my senses are still there.

"Now, now, Alyssa you look like you could use some fresh air, let's go outside to the gazebo so that you can freshen up and we can get to know each other a little better," Cassandra says leading me out the back door to the gazebo where Mike and John are waiting.

"Here you go, sit here Alyssa, it looks like you need to take a load off," Cassandra says sitting me down on the couch as I can feel my mind fading in and out and can see a dark shadow standing in the window but cannot make out who or what it is. "There, there you look like you drank a little too much this evening, John, I think our friend here isn't feeling too well, what do you think?" Cassandra asks.

"She doesn't look well at all, Mike, why don't you sit over there on the couch with our friend so that we can take some pictures and let the whole school know who she is," John says laughing.

"Guys, I don't know about this, I mean we said that we would embarrass her, but I think this is going a little too far don't you think," Mike says slowly moving towards the couch and sitting next to me.

"I don't care how far we go Mike, you are going to do this, and don't worry about the pictures we will be sure to blur out your face when we put them all around the school," John says.

"I don't like this and don't want to do it" Mike responds.

"You're going to do this and do it now or I am going to beat you when we get back home," John says angrily.

"I am going to sit for one picture and nothing else," Mike says.

"Whatever, little girl," Cassandra says laughing as she pulls out her cell phone to begin her little game. "Ok, now just put your arms around her and move her close to you so that it can look like she is kissing you."

I feel Mike's hands slowly move around my waist and I lightly tell him "please stop."

"Guys she is still awake," Mike says.

"Oh yeah, well then maybe she likes being like this, anyone in its right mind would have been out by now, I cannot even take half of a pill and we slipped her two of them," John says.

"Please stop" I mutter very slowly.

"I don't want to do this anymore, I am leaving," Mike says getting up from the couch.

"Please don't leave me here alone with them, help me," I say grabbing onto his arm.

"I cannot help you, Alyssa, I am sorry," Mike says as he quickly runs out the door.

Slowly falling to the floor I can feel the full effects of whatever it is that they gave me but I am still here but dazed.

"Ok, it looks like you are going to have to do it now John," Cassandra says pushing him towards me.

"Ok, but remember what we said, blur out my face and nothing dirty, I am not getting myself caught up in this" John says.

"Oh, you are already caught up and that picture is just in case you decide to turn on me," Cassandra says sarcastically.

"You really can be evil," John says slowly taking off his shirt and laying on the ground next to me.

I can feel the sweat from his body touching me and the smell of his cologne is making me nauseated, but I have to focus and see if I can get past this drug.

"Please stop, get off of me John," I say.

"This will all be over before you know it love, now what about giving me a kiss for the picture?" he asks.

"I don't want to, please stop you're hurting me," I respond. The feeling that I usually get is beginning to come back to me, and I can feel the effects of this drug beginning to fade away.

"What in the hell, this girl is getting hot," John says jumping back off of me.

"I told you she was a freak, now finish what you started," Cassandra says recording every second that is passing by.

Standing up I can see the inside of the gazebo begin to glow red as the lights are off and my body is the only light source in that room.

"I asked you all to stop and leave me alone and now look at what you all have done" I respond with my body slowly lifting off of the ground and my eyes have become black as night as I can see the fear in Cassandra and John's eyes.

"What is this, what the hell is wrong with you freak?" John asks shaking uncontrollably.

"You finally got what you wanted so why not come over here and finish what you started" I respond.

Lifting my hand his body floats through the air to where I am hovering and the fear in his eyes are too satisfying to pass up. Slowly taking my phone out I snap a quick shot of his eyes to remind me of what exactly he looks like. I grab his face with my hands and kiss him ever so gently and begin to see his mouth turn dark and then his face to his whole body as if life was being sucked from him ever so slowly and then there was nothing but a pile of dust.

"OH, MY GOD!!!" Cassandra screams as she reaches for the door not realizing that I had locked it seconds before. "Please, I beg of you, don't hurt me, it was all just a joke, there has to be something that I can do to allow me to make this up to you, I cannot die, I am too pretty and young and popular."

"That is all you think about isn't it, your popularity and who remembers you and your friends? Is that all you care about?" I ask.

"No, I mean there are boys and the people that I hang out with who I care about, I mean I do have a heart," she says.

"A heart, oh yeah that cold thing deep in your chest," I say lifting my hand and seeing her gasp as I change her heart rhythm to an uncontrollable pattern.

"What's wrong Cassandra, are you not feeling well, do you need to take a load off, or do you need to get some fresh air?" I ask.

"I, cannot breathe Alyssa, please, please stop," she says gasping for air.

"It hurts doesn't it, just like you wanted to hurt me, well I took care of John, now I can easily take care of you," I say.

I look outside the window and see my dad standing there telling me to stop, and I can feel my powers starting to fade just as fast as they were brought on. Watching her limp body fall to the floor, I walk outside and slowly see my dad walk around the corner of the gazebo waving me over to follow him.

"Dad, where have you been?" I ask.

"Sorry Alyssa, Adrienne told me this would be the only way to get you to stop so I went along with what she said when she called and told me what was going on," Christian says slowly changing from my dad to himself.

"Alyssa, I am sorry but this was the only way to get you to stop, and believe me I have seen different realities and what you have done to her, so this was our best option, for our future," Adrienne says.

"Ok, I will take your word for it, and Sam I am glad you are still here, I am sorry if you had to see any of that," I say.

"No worries, I got your back and really couldn't do anything if I wanted to seeing as Cheyenne and Braelyn had me pinned up against a wall once Adrienne told me what was going on," Sam says.

"Oh, my God, John, what did I do, what am I supposed to do about what I did to him?" I ask.

"Don't worry about that, I am sure with Cassandra going through what she went through, she is not going to want to say anything, and he was collateral damage" Christian says.

"But, I killed him, I murdered him without even thinking about it, I didn't mean to hurt him, I was just overwhelmed and couldn't stop" I respond.

"This is why we need to work on ourselves if we are intending on doing anything else and trying to figure out our true purpose in this world," Braelyn says.

"I know, but Mike left and he knows that Cassandra, John, and I were the only ones in that room, he is going to come asking questions when he doesn't go home tonight," I say.

Hearing a scream coming from the front of the gazebo it's Heather and Michelle that have found Cassandra lying on the carpeted floor and immediately call for an ambulance as they cannot feel a heartbeat. Chris one of the football trainers begins to perform CPR as Heather turns to look at me and notices my sister smirking.

"You, you did this!" she says excitedly.

"What are you even talking about," Adrienne says. "You are the ones who started this little war of yours, and now we finished it."

"Not you, your sister, and you better hope nothing happens to her because this will all be on you," Heather responds.

"Do you want to go there with me?" I ask.

"Just leave, you and your loser friends need to leave, now!" She yells.

"We were just leaving, let's go everyone," Christian says.

Walking towards the side gate, I can see the ambulance, fire truck, and police cars pulling up to the house quickly and see the paramedics rushing through with a stretcher obviously to get Cassandra to the hospital that Megan volunteers at noticing the name on the side of the ambulance, Maple Grove Memorial.

"I wonder if Megan is volunteering tonight?" I ask.

"I don't know but I can at least tell you Cassandra isn't dead," Cheyenne says. "Believe me if she was I would know, as for John that's a different story."

"I don't need to know anything else, but knowing she is alive helps a little," I respond. "I need to call Megan and find out if she can let me know how she is doing, plus I need to know what exactly is on her phone."

"What do you mean on her phone?" Christian asks.

"I noticed that when all of this was happening she was recording most of what was going on, so I need to know if she has what I did on there or not," I say.

"You need to be careful and start learning how to control yourself, this is getting out of hand and you of all people were the one that told me we needed to be careful," Christian responds.

"I know, and I am working on that but for now please just support me and let's get to the hospital," I say.

"Alright, Adrienne, if you can take Sam home and use your sister's car I will take Alyssa, Cheyenne, and Braelyn to see if Megan is working tonight, she isn't answering any of my calls," Christian says.

"I am going with Alyssa, she and I are together now, so there is no way that I am going to allow her to go anywhere by herself," Sam says.

"Look, Sam, you don't understand anything that is going on right now, and honestly Alyssa can take care of herself" Christian replies.

"Really? That's kind of funny because Alyssa told me everything, there is nothing that I don't know," Sam responds angrily.

"There is still a lot you don't know Sam, please just let Adrienne take you home I will be ok," I say to Sam sadly.

"So, more lies huh, more deceit?" Sam asks.

"This all just came about very quickly and I am not going to get into this right now with you, we are fine, just go home," I say.

"Go home, really after all of this you just want for me to let you," before he can finish he stops as I grab onto his hand.

"Just go home and wait for me, everything will be ok, I promise," I say lightly in his ear.

"Ok, please be careful," he responds.

"I will see you soon," I say giving him a small kiss on the lips.

Watching him walk away hurt me more than it ever has, but we know that this could get dangerous and I don't want to see him get hurt.

"What the hell was that?" Adrienne asks.

"What was what, I told him to go home so he left," I respond.

"No, the whole him changing after you touched his hand, he didn't just go it was as if you made him leave just by touching him," she says. "Oh, it looks like someone has more than one power."

"Nonsense, you just need to talk to people properly, something you will know nothing about," I respond. "Either way, let's get out of here, I can see everyone staring at us as if we were the plague."

"Good idea," Braelyn says.

Getting into the car I feel sick knowing that I have killed someone, destroyed their light, and taken everything away from his family, but what was I to do, he wouldn't get off of me and I felt like I was being physically attacked, no means no, right? Either way, I did what I had to do, and hopefully, we can get

Cassandra's phone and end all of this. As we pulled out I didn't notice Mike standing near the side of the house with tears in his eyes and a look of disgust and a need for revenge. What have I done?

Chapter XII

"Cassandra's Demise"

Pulling up to the hospital we separate to look for Megan and see if she can help us find out where Cassandra is, check her phone, and leave without having to cause any issues for anyone or vice versa.

"We have looked everywhere Alyssa, and I can't find her, are you sure she is working tonight?" Cheyenne asks.

"She has to be, she always answers her phone and the only time she wouldn't especially this late at night is because she is on shift, she is here keep looking," I respond.

"Hey, I checked the doctor's lounge and the ICU wing but I didn't find her either," Christian says.

"I won't even ask how you got in there, but please keep looking, I know she is here," I say.

My phone begins to vibrate and it's Megan.

"Hello, Megan where are you, are you at the hospital?" I ask.

"I am right behind you," Megan says holding the phone against her ear and smiling very sarcastically. Hugging her tight I feel like I want to cry.

"I am so glad I found you, I need your help," I say.

"What's the ask Alyssa?" she responds.

"I need to know where Cassandra is at, what room number, I think she may have recorded me using my powers and I need to know whether it's on her phone or not," I say.

"Ok, let me ask the girls at the desk and see if they can locate her," Megan responds. "Hey, Jenny can you look up a patient and tell me what room she is in."

"She is in the ICU wing fourth floor, she just got out of triage and is sedated for now room 417," Jenny says.

"Great thanks so much," Megan responds.

Turning around Megan looks for me as I have already left and hurried to the elevators to get there as fast as I can.

"You're welcome," Megan says shaking her head and walking off into the emergency room.

Grabbing my phone I message Christian, Cheyenne, and Braelyn and let them know where I am heading, but the pain still lingers in my mind about John and I need to concentrate on Cassandra and her phone, hopefully, she still has it on her and I can check it quickly and leave as if we were never there. Walking near the room, I can see Cassandra sitting up with an IV inserted into her and a heart monitor giving off a silent beeping noise, but who is that sitting in the room with her.

"Well, well, look at what we have here Ms. Blakenship, it looks like someone has been recording things that they shouldn't have been recording," General Collins says. "Now, let's just delete this video and I will be confiscating your phone, per government guidelines I am sure your mother and father have enough money to get you another one, but that more than likely won't be happening as I know now that you know things that are happening in this town and unfortunately you know too much, so we will have to make sure you take a very long nap this evening."

Reaching into his pocket I can see him pulling out a syringe with a red liquid inside of it and moving straight to her IV bag to make sure she is placed in a night of eternal sleep.

"STOP!" I scream grabbing his arm with my hand and slowly moving him away from the bag feeling the energy rise in me.

"If it isn't Ms. Gonzales, looks like you have been working on your powers their little girl," General Collins says. "How are your sister and Amorette, oh that's right she is no longer with us is she."

Feeling my energy rise more than I ever have I send his body flying towards the back wall of the room only for him to stop before he hits the glass door. Looking deeper into the dark I see a shadow come out of the darkness, it's Vincent!

"Nice catch son, now finish her off," General Collins says.

Watching him move slowly towards me I can see a black aura around him, his eyes are black as night and his body is fading in and out so it makes it harder for me to see exactly where he is at. As his hands begin to rise I can see a black light forming in his hands just like my red energy ball that I make whenever I am powering up. The ball is formed and light is beginning to come off of it showing his deadly grin and then it is shot at me with no warning. The only thing I can do is retaliate and create a red force shield around me causing the ball to glance off of me and straight into Cassandra. Her body absorbs the entire ball and she begins to shake violently only to stop and look to the side as her eyes are filled with blackness just like Vincent's.

"You wanted me to do that, didn't you?" I ask.

"It's all in your nature my love, just like all of you are a threat to things that I am doing and creating, poor Cassandra was a threat to you and your kin. Be forewarned though and don't forget that Vincent here is also a part of all of you and his view on things is completely different than how you see them. He wants to be free and show mankind that things can be created not only for defense purposes but to destroy nuisances and threats just like you have done, and what is this your second kill this evening?" General Collins says.

"I am not going to fight in this hospital, but believe me this isn't over and this was not my fault," I respond.

"Oh, according to the video that I have in my possession, it seems like you have a knack for killing things, it's like you were made to do this, isn't that right Vincent?" He asks.

"Yes it is, and when I am done with you, there will no longer be a need for your family either," he responds.

"You need to leave my family out of this, but I won't fight you, Vincent, because in reality, you are my family as well, your father's blood isn't even running through your veins, but if you help me we can find this entity that still roams this earth and destroy it once and for all, and then maybe we can go back to a normal life," I say.

"There is no time for help, no more time for happiness, and no more time for Alyssa Gonzales," Vincent says as he sends a bright flash in my direction knocking me back into the wall and knocking me out cold.

"Alyssa! You're going to pay for that Vincent," Christian yells.

Slowing down his breathing, a dark glow envelops Vincent's body as he directs himself backward along with his father into a black void that allows them to escape as Christian crashes into the shelf cutting his forearm in the process.

"Damn it, what the hell was that," Christian says wrapping his arm with a towel.

"It looked like General Collins," Megan says rushing over to Alyssa to see what damage had been done. "Oh, God Alyssa can you hear me?"

Holding onto my head her hands begin to glow green as her healing abilities begin to take over and wakes me up with a sudden jolt.

"Whoa, whoa, hold on there tiger, you were out you need to sit back and relax, don't try and stand up just yet," Megan says.

"I am alright just get me up please," I respond.

"What the hell was that, was that Vincent?" Megan asks.

"Yes, it seems as if we have another sibling from this experiment that I never took into consideration and had a feeling, but just thought it was all in my mind," I say.

"All in your head, it looks like he was trying to take off your head, how come you never said anything?" Megan asks.

"Because I never would have figured he, of all people, would be special or like us for that matter," I respond.

"We can no longer take anything for granted and we need to get together and regroup and begin training, because it looks like Vincent is a lot stronger or special than you think he is," Christian says. "Can you please help me out here Megan?"

"Of course, I am sorry, let me look at it," Megan responds.

Watching her work is something magical, I mean imagine having the ability to heal things with just a touch, that is something I am very thankful for when it comes to us and this battle we will soon have to fight.

"Thanks, it's a lot better," Christian says. "What about her?"

Megan slowly walks over to her to see if there is anything she can do for her, knowing that her powers can be beneficial even with a small amount of life in a person, but doesn't know if she is too late.

"Don't bother," Cheyenne says. "I saw her walk out of the room a few seconds ago, there is nothing you can do for her."

"Oh, my God, what have I done?" I say beginning to cry and sliding down the wall with my hands covering my face.

"What happened Alyssa?" Megan asks.

"When Vincent attacked me, I went into defensive mode and raised my power higher than I have ever felt it, and deflected his energy blast into Cassandra, I had no way of knowing that this was going to happen," I say.

"Look, this isn't your fault, this is something that General Collins is manipulating and he is trying to get all of us to fight with one another and destroy what we are trying to accomplish, being a family and protecting our family," Christian says.

"Yeah and that, in turn, is another problem we are going to have as Vincent is a part of us as well, his mother was with our mothers during that night when all of us got our "powers" and I don't know if I can fight him, he is our blood," I respond.

"Well, you are going to need to decide and decide quickly because after what he just did he is more of a threat to us than we realize," Megan says.

"I know but you all need to realize that he is a part of us and if we are going to live by our family code then us fighting him throws all of that out the door, what we have promised to one another and even to him," I respond.

"Well, either way, we need to get everyone together and begin our training, this has gone on long enough and we need to not only stop General Collins but find this entity also and salvage what we can of our lives and live a normal life instead of dealing with all of these powers, hiding, and I am just tired Alyssa," Braelyn says walking out the room as Cheyenne follows her to console her.

"She's right Lys, we need to end all of this, don't you want to live a normal life with Sam and have a family and kids later on in life without having to look over your shoulder and worry about who's after you or what could happen?" Christian asks.

"Yes, I am tired just like everyone else is, but I feel like there is more to this than we can imagine and I am afraid of the what-ifs, and what if we are wrong about things and all of this," I say.

"I am scared too, but the stronger we get the less we will have to worry about the what-ifs and move forward instead of backward," Christian responds.

"You're right, I just worry about the future, and I know that Adrienne knows things and that is why she is letting a lot of this happen, but I wish I could just get her to tell me what's going to happen, but I know I would be just pushing things too far and I cannot let this get out of hand, so I am just keeping my distance, but the worse her nosebleeds get it gets me even more and more worried," I say.

"WE will get through this, we just need to begin our training and work together, I think I have a place that we can go to, to train. It's a place that Amorette and I used to go to and wanted to make her new home base but I told her to stay, that I would keep her safe and take care of her, and look at what happened to her," Christian says beginning to sob and slowly produces an orange aura to surround him, something that I have not seen but know that he is upset and hurting.

"Christian, you are going to be fine, we are going to get through this together and I promise you General Collins is going to pay for everything he has done and everyone that he has taken away, including my dad," I respond.

Watching the orange glow fade away, I realize that he is starting to cool off, but I am worried that his power is going to consume him just like it has me, but we will all work on that together and hopefully get through this.

"You all need to go, I am going to have to report this to the head nurse who went on her break and isn't going to like the fact that I turned off the alarm when Cassandra died," Megan says. "Go down the stairway on the left and I will have to turn it back on, thankfully the nurses that were on watch were just knocked out, but I can heal them and wake them up as if nothing ever happened."

"Thanks, Megan, I will call you next weekend, Christian is right we are all going to need to start training and hopefully we can stop all of this death and destruction that they are causing," I say.

"Sounds good, now go before anyone sees you all or worse sees me using my powers that is the last thing we all need," Megan says.

"See you later Megan," Christian responds.

Running through the emergency exit we can hear the monitor alarms being turned back on and hear the sounds of footsteps rushing towards the fourth floor and the echo within the stairwell gets louder and louder as more and more people rush to find out what exactly is going on. The announcement goes off:

"Code blue, code blue all cardiac personnel come to the fourth floor." It makes me sad knowing that they are talking about Cassandra but I have to get that out of my head as we head through the bottom floor and out the back of the hospital near the cafeteria. Running towards the open parking lot, we slow down to not make it so noticeable and see Cheyenne and Braelyn waving at us near the back of the parking lot.

"Oh my God, what happened?" Cheyenne asks.

"Megan had to allow the alarms to go off and all hell broke loose, hopefully, Megan can steer them away from us and give a good explanation of what happened," I say.

"And what if she can't, what are we supposed to do then?" Cheyenne asks.

"There is nothing we can do we will have to work together to make sure that we remain safe and our family is safe, but until then let's go so we can get some rest, we are going to need to get everyone together again and start training, from what I went through a little while ago, I think we are going to need every ounce of power that we have to stop all of this," I respond.

"What exactly happened?" Braelyn asks.

"It is too much to explain, but what I do know is that since Vincent is helping his father, we are going to need to train and train hard, harder than we thought we would need to because he is powerful and I think with all of using our powers together and as a team, we will be able to stop him and his father," I say.

"There is only one thing, and that's with Vincent, in no way are we going to hurt him or fight him, we are going to have to come up with a different way of either distracting him or keeping him at bay as we do what we need to do until it is finished, but in no way are we to hurt him," I say.

"You do understand that after everything and all that we have seen, he is going to try and stop you and kill you, right?" Cheyenne says.

"We have to make a promise all of us that we are not to hurt him in any way if things get out of hand or things get bad I will handle him, but no one is to touch him, defensively you can do anything you need to but he is key in all of this," I respond.

"Ok, that sounds like a plan, but understand that defensively, a lot of us can pack a punch so he better be careful on anything that he tries to do," Braelyn says.

"I am sure when the time comes he will back off," I respond.

Taking Cheyenne's car, Christian and I can sense everyone is on edge.

Chapter XIII

"The Remainned"

Pulling into our driveway I notice that my car is nowhere to be found, and wonder where Sam is, but am also concerned that my sister is not here either. We were gone for a bit but not that long, they should have been back home by now. The sound of racing tires envelops the street as I see my car coming down the road at a high rate of speed, then my brakes are hit hard as she turns quickly into our driveway.

"Seriously, Adrienne where were you and where is Sam?" I ask.

"He is fine, and I went by Ariel's house, she showed me some stuff she has been working on so I had to go to see, why?" Adrienne responded.

"Because I would have figured you would have been home what if we needed you?" I ask.

"All you had to do is call me on my cell phone, it's not like I would never have it on me, don't you think?" Adrienne responds.

"A lot happened, Cassandra is dead and Vincent is very powerful, so we are going to need to get everyone together next weekend and start planning and start training, not only do we have to worry about his being that is roaming around and messing with us, but we also have General Collins and Vincent to worry about and it's about time we end all of this," I say.

"Sounds like a plan, I will get with Ariel, Dean, and David and let them know where are we meeting up," Adrienne says.

"I will send you the pin on your phone for the location, I think you are going to like it, at least Amorette would have and I hope everyone does too," Christian says.

"Well, we are going to have to do something about Monday because you know this is going to be all over the news, and with John's disappearance and Cassandra's death things are going to be spread around and you know how our school is," I say.

"We all know well enough Heather and Michelle are going to be the first to cause us issues, then there is going to be Vincent who I hope doesn't come to school anymore, and with him being my lab partner, this is going to be tough if things get way out of hand," I say.

"Everything is going to work out, I will see you all tomorrow," Christian says walking into the woods towards his house.

"Adrienne, keys, and please let's try and keep things under wraps, you know how the girls at school are and I know that Heather is going to try and accuse me of all of this, so please, for me let's try and act normal," I say.

"Normal? You think that we are normal or any of this is normal Lys?" Adrienne responds.

"I know what this looks like but I just want for you to promise me that you will not cause any issues at school, at least don't start anything with anyone," I say.

"I promise, cross my heart hope to die, I won't start anything, we have been through enough and I know that we all need the rest after what happened last night, I promise you I will not do anything or start anything," Adrienne responds.

"Thank you, sis," Alyssa says.

Holding onto her was the first time in a long time that I was able to feel what she was feeling. Her heart was beating fast and the tightness in her grasp let me know that she did care for me and I knew that I would always be her protector no matter how much she didn't want me to be.

"Awww, how sweet it's about time you too showed how you feel about one another," our mother says.

"Uh, what are you talking about mother, I got cat dander in my eye, that was all," Adrienne says running into the house.

"No worries love, I see all the cats running around here," my mom says.

"Mom, I just wanted to say thanks for everything, and I know dad isn't here but I know how much you all have done for us and I just want to say, I love you,"

I say.

"Well, I love you too honey and so does your father, well you know what I mean," my mom responds.

"I know, and there are some things that you probably are going to hear around town and I don't want for you to get alarmed, but things happened this evening, but we are going to take care of everything," I say.

"What do you mean honey, what happened?" She asks.

"Nothing mom, it's too much to talk about and we have had a horrible night, I know I should have been celebrating tonight, but that was the last thing on my mind, but everything will be ok," I respond.

"Ok, honey if you need anything you know I will always be here for you," my mom says holding onto me tightly.

"I know mom, thanks," I respond.

Walking into the house, I can hear noises coming from my sister's room, but these were sounds that I have never heard before. Walking into her room a bright blue light has encased her being and I can see her eyes are bright like two flashlights in a jet black room. She is floating in the middle of her room but I can see her body trembling, something I have never seen before.

"Adrienne, are you ok?" I ask slowly moving closer to her but didn't know what to do at this point as my fear took over as I began glowing along with her.

"Adrienne, what's wrong with you? I ask again this time a little louder to see if I can knock her out of the trance she is in. Her breathing begins to speed up as I move closer to her. Right before I touch her a bright blue light comes from the corner of her room, it's someone in a grey outfit with a very dark mask on. It seems like they have a voice changer so their voice is distorted and have to concentrate to understand them.

"Whatever you do, do not touch her, she is training her body to withstand some changes that are happening in the future," the person says.

"Who are you and what do you know about my sister?" I ask.

"Don't worry about that you need to come with me there are some things that I need to show you but you have to promise not to share what you are going to see with anyone," it says.

"I promise, but will my sister be ok?" I ask.

"Yes, she is in a cryostasis as long as she is not awoken she will be ok," it responds. "Now please come with me."

Taking their hand I walk into the bright light and lead directly into a room where it seems like hundreds of people are walking back and forth into voids created by who knows what.

"This is the time chamber," it says. "Over the last Epoch, people around the world have been able to move from time to time. Everyone believed that humans started at a specific time period, but here in the time chamber, there is no such thing as time. We have been able to roam around endlessly with no worry as long as there are no major changes in either the past or the future and thank whatever created this realm to help us get back and forth" it says. "We have been noticing that there have been big changes though over the last four months but we are having issues pinpointing where it's coming from but things are leading directly at the future. I am going to do something that we have all been advised not to do and show you a few things before I send you back."

"Wait, who are you?" I ask.

"I am someone that has a viable stake in all of this, but what I am going to show you could help you and your family in the long run, I could lose everything just by showing you this, but right now is the best and only time I can do it," it says.

"Ok, what do we do?" I ask.

"Nothing, just walk over to that room, it will give you a quick glimpse of something you will need to see, it will not give you everything because you can't step through but you will be able to see a few things that may help you in the future," It says.

Walking into the golden light I close my eyes and begin to hear a monitor beeping in the distance. I can see the shadow of a woman laying on a bed sitting up and in pain, I can see the shadow of a man by her side and people running into the room and it looks as if they are trying to help her.

"Look deeper into the situation what do you see?" It asks.

"I don't see anything else, just feel a lot of pain and devastation," I respond.

"I feel cold as if life is being drained away."

"Look closer," it says.

Looking into the fog I can see the woman grabbing onto her stomach and then a bright light appears as she lies back on the table. I can see blasts and explosions that are going off everywhere. There are other people in the room and they are moving closer and closer to her as if there was something they were trying to stop from happening, then I can see the light grow brighter and brighter and then a huge flash, and then nothing.

"Did you feel the energy, did you feel the power?" It asks.

"Yes, it was as if something was coming into this world, something evil, something that shouldn't be here," I respond.

"Take what I have shown you and go back, take what you have learned, and train like you have never trained before. Be the leader they need and the leader they will always look up to when decisions need to be made," it says.

"But what if I fail?" I ask. "What if this future comes to pass and I cannot stop it, what if I lose everyone?" I ask.

"You will have an opportunity to make that decision when the time comes, but until then you will always have everyone there with you, when you need them the most and when the moment seems bleak, just call upon them and they will forever be by your side," it responds.

"Thank you, what should I call you?" I ask.

"We are all called The Remainned, remnants of people we once used to be with bits and pieces spread all-around time, never really knowing whether we are real or one of our doubles we left behind in different time periods," it says.

"We do sometimes feel like we will never get back to our real times but then again being in this time chamber makes time nonexistent, so even thinking about when we left doesn't help us."

"I am sorry, hopefully, my sister doesn't get trapped the way you all have, it must be hard not having family or even knowing how to get back," I say.

"I have been trapped here for an unknown time and I know at a certain point someone will call for me and when they do I will be ready to bring them back to reality, but until then we all wait," it responds.

"Well thank you for all of this, it means a lot to me, I wish Adrienne could have been here to see this, I bet she would have loved it," I say.

"She knows a lot more than you think, but be careful and use this knowledge wisely, cherish the moments because it could end in the snap of a finger," it responds.

Slowly pushing me back into the blue light I can feel my body floating back to my time, but then again what do I even know about time. I know now that it is sacred and can be manipulated so I will have to be careful with everything that I know now. As I turn I can see Adrienne floating in our room as I come through the light her aura begins to dim and then she collapses to the floor.

"Adrienne are you ok?" I ask.

"Hey, what, yes of course I am fine," she responds, slowly collapsing onto her bed and passing out.

"I don't know where or when you were but you missed a lot and the things that I saw were so amazing, but I will leave that as a secret for now and I know we promised each other that we wouldn't keep secrets, but I am sure there is a lot you haven't told me either," I say softly. "Rest well, and will see you in the morning."

The next morning flies by as I feel like I have closed my eyes but only for a second but realize it's ten in the morning and the smell of eggs, bacon, and sausage fill the entire house, as usual. Going down the steps I see my mom standing near the door trembling as if a tiny earthquake was consuming her body.

"Mom are you ok?" I ask as she turns quickly and wipes a tear from her face.

"Oh, yes dear, I am perfectly fine, hey the eggs and bacon are almost ready, are you hungry?" She asks.

"Mom, I can feel what you feel, and I don't want you to worry, ok, we will find dad and we will bring him back home, things are just taking a little longer than usual," I say.

"Honey, please don't do anything foolish, I am sure your dad is perfectly fine and he is just biding his time before they release him from wherever he is at," she says.

"Well if he isn't home by next weekend I am going out to look for him myself," I respond.

"I do not want you getting hurt, do you understand me, I know you are getting older and so is your sister but I would die if anything happened to either one of you!" She says sternly.

"Mom, there are a lot of changes that Adrienne and I are going through, something amazing, and soon we will have dad back home, I promise you," I respond.

"Just watch over your sister, you know how she is," my mom responds as Adrienne creeps around the corner.

"And how is that mom?" She asks.

"You are careless sometimes little one, and your attitude and anger issues make you lose control sometimes, Alyssa has seen it," she responds.

"Look, I am in control of things ok, and no one is going to change my mind on how I am acting and the things that I am doing, understand?" Adrienne says grabbing her jacket and storming out the door.

"Let me go talk to her mom, I will catch up with you later," I say.

"What about your breakfast?" She asks.

"Put it in the fridge I will eat it later, thanks mom," I say running out the door trying to catch her knowing she is faster than lightning.

"Adrienne stop, what is the issue today?" I ask.

"I am sick and tired of everyone saying that there is something wrong with me, everybody makes me feel like I am still a child and that I am out of control," Adrienne says holding back tears.

"Adrienne, mom is just trying to watch out for you and me some of the things she says are true though, don't you think?" I ask.

"The things that she said me being careless, and having anger issues, if she only knew how much you lose control and what you have done" Adrienne responds.

"We said that we would keep things to ourselves, I know what happened at the party, and do you honestly think I enjoy any of this?" I ask.

"It doesn't matter what you think or do, so let me ask you, how was your little trip last night?" Adrienne asks.

"What do you mean, how did you know about that?" I ask.

"Just because I was time skipping last night doesn't mean I lose track of my surroundings and what is happening around me," she responds. "You went somewhere and I want to know where?" She asks.

"That doesn't matter, remember it doesn't matter what I think or what I do, so just mind your own business and remember to keep your mouth shut at school Monday," I respond angrily.

"Don't worry, I will be sure to keep my mouth shut, and you can believe that I will find out where you went, I am the all-knowing," Adrienne says running into the woods passing Christian and bumping into him as she spun around in the weeds.

"What was all that about?"Christian asks.

"Nothing, she is losing it and now is being rude to our mom and I don't know if she is going to keep quiet about everything, so as always I am worried," I respond.

"Look if anything gets out of hand at school I will just wave my little hands, concentrate and create this reality that will mess with them long enough to finish out school until we all get out of here," Christian responds.

"What about Adrienne?" I ask. "She will have another year or two before she even decides what she is going to do with her life, so I cannot risk things changing for a short bit and then them going back and things get worse for her."

"And I fully understand where you're coming from, but you also have to look out for yourself too. I know that Adrienne is going to have issues and it seems like if you ever leave, she will continue to have issues as long as she has the attitude that she has," Christian says. "But none of this is your fault and you have to stop blaming yourself for things that she is causing and can stop from happening."

"I cannot do that, the second that I stop helping her she will fail, and I have been there firsthand when she loses control," I respond.

"Like you do?" Christian asks.

"I know that I have issues, I know I do, but I am trying my hardest to not only take care of her, but everyone else," I say. "I want to be there for everyone and help them as much as I can and be an example, a leader."

"I know what it's like to have to do things for people, believe me when Amorette was here, I knew that I loved her the second that I looked into her eyes, her smile, her warmth, the way she made me feel, just wanted," Christian says.

"But, where did that get me in the end? She is gone and now all I have left is her memory and me trying to control my anger and not cause an issue with reality in this world. I don't want to do something stupid and cause a shift in the earth because I am angry and know she will never come back, but I also have to know when to let go, just like you will have to."

"I understand where you are coming from, and I will do my best to try and learn from all of this and try and let go a little but I cannot guarantee anything," I say.

"And that is fine, just don't give up and you as our leader, that's a good one, I figured I would be the more reasonable choice for that," Christian responds sticking his chest out.

"I don't think so, but hey if you want to challenge me for that spot then be my guest," I say jokingly.

"I just might take you up on that offer, but not right now, right now we need to get everyone together and begin our training," Christian says.

"You're right, after what I saw last night, we are going to need a lot of that, and not just to test things out and see what we can do, but work on ourselves and work as a team," I say.

"What do you mean?" Christian asks.

"Nothing, I had a chance to experience something last night and can't explain what it was, but I experienced a kind of like an out-of-body episode," I say. "I saw something like that time that I passed out at the facility, but this seemed very real this time around and cannot remember a lot but I think we need to prepare ourselves for anything," I say knowing I had to lie a bit to make sure nothing slipped out.

"No worries, I will get a hold of Dean, David, and Cheyenne, I am sure Adrienne is going to Ariel's house which she is doing a lot of recently, and you can get Megan and Braelyn," Christian says.

"Sounds good, so where were you headed off to anyway?" I ask.

"Just to walk into town, I heard that they were having a sale on some football equipment that I was looking at getting," Christian responds.

"You expect me to believe that you were just going into town to look at some "football equipment" that you are possibly going to buy, that is what you're making me believe?" I ask.

"Well, no not that, but ok every Saturday I go to the facility to leave flowers for Amorette, seeing as they are never going to clean out the area because there is supposed "radiation at the facility" and wants everyone to stay away from it, I walk to the very spot where I know she would have been, I take a seat and have a quick chat with her," Christian says.

"And how exactly do you do that?" I ask. "Wait a minute, you're getting a hold of Cheyenne, that's how you are doing it, you're using her to talk to Amorette aren't you?"

"It's something that is helping me right now, to get through all of this," he says. "You seriously think you are the only one that is having issues with all of this? I am trying my hardest not to lose it as well, so anything that I can do or anyone that can help me is well worth my sanity."

"I am sorry, I should never have questioned you, please be safe, and let's set up a game plan for next weekend for all of us to meet up and see what we can come up with as far as training and what we need to work on," I say.

"Thank you for understanding, talk to you soon," Christian says walking down the road and around the block towards town.

Looking into the sky I close my eyes and feel the air against my face, I can smell the fresh air as the sun shines upon me and makes my senses even clearer as I take in a deep breath and slowly let it out. Opening my eyes, I feel the radiation of the sun all over my body but feel a sudden change when my memory comes back of what I saw in the time chamber. I am hoping all of this comes out with us conquering our past, and present and give a change to our futures, but right now that is all I do have, hope.

Chapter XIV

"The Mourning After"

My alarm the next morning reminds me that today is the day that I am going to face my fears, and anxiety to truly find out how the rest of the school year is going to be and possibly the rest of my life. Walking past Adrienne's room I notice that her bed is still made, so either she is already on her way to school or she never came back yesterday. I have to remember to let things go sometimes and let her learn on her own, so that is exactly what I am going to do. Kind of odd though that my mom isn't downstairs cooking breakfast like she has been doing for the last 18 years of my life. Walking by her room I give a gentle knock so as not to wake her if she is still resting.

"Mom, are you ok?" I ask.

Slowly opening the door, I notice her in her robe standing by her window with a vacant stare out into the backyard.

"Mom are you alright?" I ask again grabbing onto her arm this time very gently.

"Oh, my goodness honey you startled me," she responds. "What were you asking me, dear?"

"I asked if you were alright, you were just standing there looking out the window as if you had seen a ghost," I say.

"A ghost, no that is an understatement if you ask me," she responds. "I thought I saw something that I would never want to see again, but I am guessing it's all the stress and everything else that is getting to me," she says.

"What was it that you thought you saw mom?" I ask.

"It was a long time ago honey and there are bits and pieces of things that I still remember, like the when I went into that trance and felt love all around me, that is the same feeling I have been having recently and don't know where it is coming from but it makes me feel so young and alive," my mom says.

"Well, just don't feel too much in love because when dad comes back he is going to need you more than ever" I respond.

"Don't worry about that honey, I will always have a love for your father" my mom reiterates but slowly turns her head and looks back outside with this light glow emanating from her face.

Walking down the stairs I grab my backpack and take a quick breath before opening the door and walking to my car. The fresh air feels good against my skin and the sky is clearer than it has been in a few months. My fears are starting to subside but I still worry about the rest of the year and what is going to happen if I get the scholarship to Kyoto University in Japan, how am I supposed to leave everyone here and just go like nothing. That, I will worry about later, it's time to face the music. Driving up to the school I can sense something is off when I see pictures of Cassandra hung up throughout the school, along the corridors, and even attached to the band hall door, now that says a lot. Some people are wearing black and standing in circles, sobbing, and holding onto each other. This makes me think of how much influence she really had in the school and how many people actually may have admired her or worshipped who she was. Or was it just out of pity that people felt bad or were they genuinely hurting? Only time would tell, but after getting out of my car the fear I had come to fruition. Looking at the back part of second hall, I see Heather and Michelle walking with Braelyn but it looks as if Heather has taken the lead through all of this and completely forgotten about Cassandra. As they walk by I can feel the glare that Heather gives me as she slowly puts on her sunglasses and walks by me as Michelle just looks and turns away, but my concern is with Braelyn as she walks by not even looking at me. That is something we will have to talk about later. Slowly grabbing my bag out of the trunk I feel two arms wrap around me very slowly and feel my heart skip letting me know who it is.

"Good morning Sam, how was your weekend," I ask.

"It was good, didn't hear from you at all, but I figured I would give you your space with everything that happened on Friday," he responds.

"Well thank you very much for being there for me," I say kissing him gently.

Grabbing onto his hand and feeling secure we slowly turn to head towards third hall, but never saw him coming!

"So, you don't think I know what you did Friday at that party do you?" Mike asks.

"What are you talking about?" I respond.

"My brother has been missing since Friday evening, and you and Cassandra were the last two that saw him alive and were with him" Mike responds.

"You need to back off Mike," Sam says slowly moving in between the two of us.

"I don't need to do anything, you need to ask your little girlfriend here, where my brother is at," he says. "Cassandra is dead and my brother has not been seen since that night, so the both of you are going to be responsible for all of this."

"So, I am going to be held responsible for your brother and everything that you, him, and Cassandra tried to do to me that night?" I ask. "All of you are responsible for anything that happened to you all that night, not me. You remember, don't you? You sure looked like you were having fun, going along with everything that Cassandra wanted. Your brother taking the pictures as you moved our body closer to mine."

"Don't even go there, I didn't want to do that and that is why I got up and left" Mike responds.

"Well then maybe you should have stuck around and you would have seen me knock your brother off and run out to the alleyway, I have no clue what happened after that" I respond. "Ask Sam, he picked me up and we left, isn't that right Sam?"

"Yes, it is Alyssa, exactly how she said it happened," Sam says.

"So if I were you, I would go out and help your parents look for him and leave me alone," I say knowing my eyes have begun to glow red with my anger.

"You are a freak just like Cassandra said you were," Mike says walking away.

"But you all will pay for what happened, believe me."

"You ok?" Sam asks.

"Of course I am ok, but I know we are going to have to begin watching our backs because I know exactly how Heather, Michelle, and Mike can be so I know this is going to be a long rest of the year.

"Tell me about it, I don't have any powers like you all but I wish I did so that I can defend myself," Sam says.

"You don't want any of this Sam, I am beginning to think that all of this is more of a curse than it is a gift," I respond.

"You all have something that is special and I am sure that when this is all said and done, you will all be able to use it for good and not for profit or advantage, it's just a matter of having a good leader and everyone following through with what is planned," Sam says.

"I know, I just have to have patience just like you did with me, right?" I ask.

"It was a lot more than patience, it was me knowing how much I loved you but also giving you space and time. I was not going to push you away," Sam responds.

"Well, thank you for what all it is worth, you mean the world to me, let's get to class we are already late," I say.

"Sounds good," Sam responds.

Putting his arm around my shoulders and moving me close to him, reminds me of why I care about him so much and why my love continues to grow. Walking into my science class, I can see Vincent sitting in the corner with his hood over his head as usual, but not once did he ever say anything to me, no comments, nothing. This was very unexpected.

"So I see you made it in today, how was your weekend, did anything exciting happen?" I ask.

"I am not in the mood to talk right now, can we just please get through this class today so that we can go on our way," Vincent says very lightly.

"I am sorry, just didn't know if you remembered what you did Friday night causing a lot of harm to a lot of people," I say but stop as he grabs my hand aggressively. Looking into his eyes I can see them black again but with a huge bruise across his face.

"Right now I don't want to talk, and I don't want to fight, I just want to be left alone, is that too hard for you to understand!" He says shakily.

"Vincent, I know what this is about, you are a part of a bigger plan, something that none of us asked for, but if you let me help you," I say but again pause as his grip gets even tighter.

"I want to be left alone, you don't know what I am going through and you have no clue what my father is putting me through, so please just stop, ok?" Vincent asks.

"Ok, I am sorry we will let this go for now," I respond feeling his grip relax and letting go.

"Thank you, and as far as us being partners, you might as well do the project yourself because there is no way we are going to meet anywhere alone and not create some type of havoc or destruction, it's never going to work," Vincent says.

"We will talk about this later, but all I am asking you is to have an open mind about all of this if I can help you let me at least try please," I say.

"We will talk about this another time, maybe if things were different, but for now just let things go," Vincent responds.

"No problem," I respond.

"Besides you have more important things to worry about than me at this school, and that's beginning with Heather who it seems took over Cassandra's role when she, well you know," Vincent says.

"Yes, I know that, so thank you for creating that," I respond.

"Me?" Vincent asks. "This whole thing could have been avoided if you hadn't put Cassandra in the hospital, to begin with, and she never would have been there that night."

"Well, someone is to blame for this and it sure as hell isn't going to be me for something that you did," I respond.

"We will see about that," Vincent says.

"Let's just start things over today?" I ask. "You look like you have been through enough and I don't have the patience or time right now knowing what I am going to have to go through for the rest of the year."

"I will let things go, but again when the time presents itself, what happened at the hospital will not be the last time that we will need to deal with things together," Vincent says.

"You're right, and the next time we will all be ready," I respond.

"Good luck," Vincent says as he slowly moves his body towards the window and turns away letting me know that our conversation is now over.

The day goes by without a hitch and as the lunch bell rings I know that this will be my biggest test knowing that I am going to have to not only represent the study body but deal with the airheads all at once.

"Hey loser, how was your weekend?" Heather asks as I sit at the corner of the cafeteria trying to mind my own business.

"I am good Heather, Michelle, and Braelyn who I never would have expected seeing with these two," I say.

"Don't worry about me ok, this is exactly where I am supposed to be and need to be," Braelyn says winking her eye.

"Anyway, so I think we need to talk about Friday night and what happened, what do you think?" Heather asks.

"I don't need to talk to anyone about anything, because nothing happened," I respond.

"You expect me to believe that seeing Cassandra laying on the floor unconscious and then finding out that she died at the hospital that night was because of a heart attack?" she says. "You were there and I knew the plan that

Cassandra had created, so you had a lot to do with this."

As I began to speak I had to make sure to keep my composure as students began getting closer and closer to us.

"What plan was that Heather, to put something in my drink, try and knock me unconscious then have Mike and his brother try and take pictures of me doing things to embarrass me?" I ask loudly for everyone to hear.

"No, the plan was to befriend you and place you in the group with us," Heather says. "Look at the text we sent each other that night."

I began to read the text message from Cassandra to Heather and Michelle which said, "Let's just let things go and get her in with us, we need her to help us control the school."

"I don't know what she may have sent you, but that was not your plan and not what you all were trying to do, maybe you should ask John what happened seeing as he and Mike were in that gazebo that night and tried to take pictures of me that I did not consent to," I said. "Why don't we start there?"

"You need to realize that Cassandra was a loving person, and she wanted the best for everyone here, didn't she?" Heather says turning and looking at everyone for validation. People began looking around at each other not giving her what she wanted and began yelling out at her as my words began to resonate in their minds and made them feel uncomfortable with Heather running out of the cafeteria with Michelle in tow.

"You going to?" I ask Braelyn.

"I just wanted to make them feel like they had control and see what it was like to be stared at for the day," Braelyn says. "Plus if they had planned anything I would have been the first to find out about it."

"Well go with them, and keep an ear out, right now with how things are going we will need every advantage we have," I respond.

"Sounds good, see you this weekend," Braelyn says walking out the cafeteria rear entrance.

I saw everyone's faces as they walked back to their corresponding tables, giving me a brief smile and a nod, allowing me to feel wanted and received as their new confidant in the school.

"The days of cliques, bullying, and separation are over," I say sternly. "We all need to work together and be ourselves and not worry about who is going to make fun of us, or bully us or make us feel less than who we are. I hope that everyone can remember Cassandra in a good way, that she is a human being and a person, regardless of what she may have done to you, she was still a part of this school and this community, and she will be extremely missed."

At this point, everyone in the cafeteria began clapping and cheering knowing that there was going to be a change within the school and that brought a smile to my face and honestly made me tear up a bit.

"Whoa, what happened here?" Sam says.

"Nothing just had to set some things straight, and it worked out," I say.

"That's a good thing, at least everyone is on your side and now you can relax a bit," Sam says.

"For now, but we still have a lot to do and this weekend is going to be a turning point because with how Vincent was telling me things today, I don't believe that he and I have had our last conversation" I respond.

"Are you all going to need any help?" Sam asks. "You know how I have access to the chemistry and engineering lab if you all need anything made or looked at," Sam says.

"You know what Sam, I think that might come in handy now that I am thinking about it, what about you and I working together to create suits for us, something that can withstand our powers and you can help me create the algorithms I will need to store the energy and you can come with a way to exert whatever is built up," I say.

"Now that sounds like a plan, let's say you and I meet up before your training session and I will review and take notes of each person's powers and I can work from there, how does that sound?" Sam asks.

"That will work, but for now let's enjoy the last 10 minutes of lunch I am starving and these powers have me completely drained," I respond.

"What did I miss?" Christian says coming up from behind us.

"Looks like everyone is missing out on the excitement," I respond.

"Whoa, sorry I just got off the phone with Dean, David, and Cheyenne and they are in for Saturday, I will send out the location later this afternoon, did you get everyone else?" Christian asks.

"Yes I did, and I will ask Adrienne tonight about Ariel" I respond.

"Alright, well I have to go to practice the football team is short a player so now I am stuck having to learn how to be quarterback" Christian says shaking his head.

"You're going to play quarterback?" I ask. "What about, oh right I forgot, well I am sure you will do fine, just please be careful with Mike after this morning's little meeting I know he is not going to handle this situation very easily."

"I know, I am going to have to come up with something to get his mind back in the game if we intend on winning district and moving on to state" Christian responds.

"Is that your main concern, winning state?" I ask.

"I need to get out of this town, and if I need to take the team to the state championships to do so, I will be scouted and looked at by every Division I school out there needing a quarterback. I got this," Christian responds.

"I am sure you do, but don't take advantage of Mike please, he has been through enough and could use a little pick me up if you know what I mean," I say.

"I got you, no worries, I will make sure he gets his time and will finally get this scholarship that I need and get out of this dump," Christian says.

"Hey, don't talk about our hometown like that, remember if you win a state championship, you are going to put this dump on the map and give us all a reason to celebrate, good luck," I respond.

"Thanks, not like we are going to need it," Christian responds.

"Well don't forget, this weekend, see you Friday at the game," I say.

"See you, Christian," Sam follows.

"Ok now, where were we?" Sam says holding onto my waist as we walk towards the last table knowing we got but a few minutes left.

"Right about here," I respond, kissing him very gently and then biting into my apple as the bell rings loudly letting us know that our lunch is over.

At the end of the day, I feel a little easier but worry about the future and what could happen. Walking to my car I can see Adrienne walking with some girls from our English class towards the woods, I can see Braelyn walking with Heather and Michelle, and I see Christian talking with the football team, in my eyes all is good for now. This weekend will help us all when the time comes to battle General Collins and this entity that is haunting my dreams, it needs to end, and end soon.

Chapter XV

"Training Day"

The rest of the week goes by without any situations or hassles, our football team has now won consecutive games for the first time in a long time. Christian broke six school records in a lot of categories and Braelyn is now co-captain of the cheerleading team with Michelle, as Heather has taken the lead with Cassandra now gone. Ariel and Adrienne have become inseparable and hang out every night, and as for me, it looks like Sam and I have finally become serious.

"Ok, I know that you snuck in and stayed over last night but we need to be careful that my mother doesn't find you here, especially this morning seeing as we always have to eat together as a family like when my dad was around," I say.

"Don't worry, it's not like we did anything, I will just explain that to her," Sam says but pauses in mid-sentence.

Looking at my door Adrienne comes in stumbling, freezes Sam, and drops to the floor and I can tell something is going on because there is blood everywhere.

"What happened to you?" I ask.

"What do you think, something is wrong and it's getting worse, I have never felt like this and it's getting to the point where I am getting sick and tired of these powers and feeling like this," Adrienne says.

"Well, maybe you shouldn't have been jumping back and forth as you have been and maybe this wouldn't have happened," I respond.

"I am literally dying here and you never can just give a second of time to help me out, but would rather put me down as always, Ariel was right about you," Adrienne says harshly.

"What is that supposed to mean, what did she say?" I ask.

"Nothing, don't worry about it, this is why she is the only one that I trust and can confide in anymore," Adrienne says. "You, you're worthless."

"I don't have time for this, we need to be at the location that Christian sent us in an hour and I know your bleeding all over the place, but please unfreeze Sam and get cleaned up," I respond.

"Just like I said, worthless" Adrienne says throwing the towel I gave her on my floor and slamming the door, finally releasing Sam from his bind.

"I came here early and just, got, here" he responds slowly looking at me confused. "Your sister just froze me didn't she?" Sam asks.

"Unfortunately yes," I respond.

"Well, with all of the blood on the floor and on that towel, I am going to assume something bad is happening somewhere at some time, right?" Sam asks.

"Something like that, I think my sister is trying to use her powers to see if she can pinpoint times that the event is happening, that is why I saw her the other night floating and glowing in a trance, but who knows, I can only hope these events don't hurt her too badly," I respond.

"I will take that into consideration when I am designing your suits, something that she can use to harness her powers but also keep her from releasing too much energy so that she isn't leaving any parts of herself in that time," Sam says.

"That would be great, so now if you can see yourself out my window, that would be a good thing for both you and I," I say.

"Very true, ok, I will see you later, don't forget to send me the location," Sam responds.

"Sounds good, I love you," I say.

"I love you too," Sam responds kissing me gently and then going out the window quickly as I can hear my mother coming up the stairs. "Bye!"

The door opens quickly and my mother looks like she hasn't slept in days.

"Sorry honey, I am too exhausted to make anything, can you do it for me and feed your sister, please," My mom says rubbing her dark eyes as it looks like she has been through military training with no sleep.

"Of course, I can, don't worry, I will make some waffles and bacon, I know how to make that at least," I respond.

"Sounds good, I am going to try and sleep, something is off and I have been up trying to find out what it is," My mom responds.

"Get rest mom, I got it," I say moving her towards her room and laying her down in her bed so that she can try and sleep. "Rest," I say as I put my hand over her head and in an instant, she is deep in sleep.

I wonder if this is another power I am developing or how many powers I do have, today I will find out.

"Hey creep, do you want some waffles and bacon," I ask Adrienne as she slowly sits herself down on the couch with toilet paper jammed up her nose.

"Does it look like I want waffles and bacon, yes I want waffles and bacon considering the morning I have had?" Adrienne says.

"Ok, look I am sorry for how I acted, ok, I don't want for us to fight, I need you on my side and with our team mentally and physically," I say. "Have you thought about talking to Megan and seeing if maybe she can help you with this?"

"I have and we are trying to see if any of her powers can stop this from happening or if this will be permanent," Adrienne says.

"Ok well, Sam is going with us this morning and he is going to record all of our biometrics, our energy patterns, movements, fighting patterns, everything and said he will create us suits that can help us if we ever get into a bad situation," I say.

"Well, they better be good because I am done with all of this and maybe just for once get back to a small amount of normalcy," Adrienne says.

"Normalcy?" I say. "There is no such thing as normal for us ever again, it's either we lose these powers and become regular kids or we go on knowing we are going to have to protect the world from any and everything."

"You're right, I guess I am just hoping for better for both you and me, well mainly you," Adrienne says.

"What does that mean?" I ask.

"Nothing, look at the time, we don't have time for breakfast we need to go, do you have the pin on your phone on where we are supposed to meet?" Adrienne asks.

"Yes I do, and this conversation isn't over," I say.

"We will discuss all of this when the time is right," Adrienne responds.

"Sounds good, Mom!" I yell. "We are going, we will be back," forgetting that she went to sleep and probably either didn't hear me or is jolted awake by my screaming, we pause. Nothing, thank goodness.

Driving out to the pin that Christian sent us, the area is beginning to look very familiar. Fairfield Park, if only I thought about it a little bit more, why not? It's where we all came together and found each other one by one, but this time an individual text came through, "Go into the woods near the flagpost" it says. We follow the path and arrive at the flagpost, the wind blowing the United States flag perfectly reminds me of how much I love our country, but a shining light in the woods grabs my attention as I slowly walk towards it and in an instant walk through a forcefield and into something that looks like a stadium with obstacles and makeshift buildings, we have finally arrived.

"So what do you think?" Christian asks.

"I love it, how did you do all of this? I ask.

"Well, a while back Amorette and I kind of figured something like this was going to happen so she created an algorithm to create this stadium with everything we will ever need to practice," Christian says. "There is a little something for everyone, take a look around and welcome to Amorian."

"Amorian?" I ask. "It's very catchy."

"Well, seeing as how we both worked on it we combined our names, I just wished she would have been able to have seen it," Christian says.

"I am sure she is seeing it with all of its glory Christian," I respond.

"I am sure she is, hey here comes everyone else," Christian says as Ariel, Megan, Dean, David, and Braelyn come through the field.

"Whoa, now this is what I am talking about," Ariel says as she takes flight and soars through the arena testing out its parameters and metrics.

"Yeah, go Ariel!!!" Megan yells as Ariel passes by and waves her hand over and lifts Megan and Braelyn off of the ground to join her.

"Yes, now this is what we needed, more room!" Braelyn yells as she attempts to keep her balance.

"How are we supposed to land though," Megan says.

"Well, obviously you won't have to worry about that as you are going to have to sit out of certain things to make sure we are all ok," Ariel says with the wind blowing hard into her face.

"I got this covered, let me go," Braelyn says.

Seeing her turn her body almost into solid rock, Braelyn comes down and slams her fist into the ground with a perfect battle pose.

"That was awesome Braelyn," I say as Ariel and Megan come down and land safely.

"Wait, what did Ariel mean about me not helping if a battle breaks out?" Megan asks.

"Well, unfortunately, you don't have too many fighting powers and your healing capabilities will need to be used, so we are going to have to be sure that you are never seen or hurt," I say.

"Think about it, what if one of us gets hurt or a few of us, we are better as a whole, you are our key to success," Christian says placing his hand on her shoulder.

"You're right, so where do we begin?" Megan asks.

"Well, everyone is here except for Cheyenne but she should be here in about half an hour, so what do you want to work on first?" Christian asks.

"I think we need to focus on concentration and meditation to bring out our true powers," I say.

"But, when I feel like I am bringing out my true powers is when I am upset or mad," Christian responds.

"I know that I remember the hospital, but we need to work on meditating and bringing out our true potential, push come to shove we can use anger as a last resort," I say.

"Whatever works," Christian responds.

"Christian, go ahead and set up the obstacles that Amorette created so we can see what everyone is capable of," I say.

"Sounds good" Christian responds taking out a tablet. "And we are ready for wave one, Dean, David your up. Each creature that is standing before you is AI and a hologram but they can attack you and will learn off of your fighting skills so be quick on your feet and try to change things up a bit."

"Ok, we will try," the twins say in unison.

Watching Dean and David go from their physical form to almost like an astral form is amazing. Dean begins by throwing out a fire orb that distracts the hologram and allows him to generate a beam that cuts straight through it. David begins his power by icing the floor with a sheet of ice causing the hologram to slip allowing him to create a huge block of ice that crushes the hologram making it disappear. Dean and David high-five each other as we are all looking on and within seconds the holograms are regenerated and are now charging at them. David shoots out another blast to create another sheet and the hologram quickly shifts sides to bypass it.

"Remember, they will adapt to your style, you need to change things up," Christian says.

Dean is having issues and seems like he is going in and out of his fire form to where the hologram uses its large wooden club to swipe him about ten feet over our heads.

"What was that?" Dean says grabbing onto his side after falling to the ground.

"These things are holograms, but like I said they will attack you so you have to concentrate and work together," Christian says.

"Fine, no more games," Dean says. "David let's show them what we have been working on."

Standing next to each other I can see a purple glow around them both and can feel an energy I have never felt before, with their hands clenched together I can see them drawing in all of the power they have. Just as the creature is about to hit Dean, both of their eyes open hugely and they morph into this eight-foot purple being with white eyes, and the purple field has now engulfed their giant body, it slowly backs up and a blast comes from his hands causing the creature to disintegrate immediately, the other creature stands no chance as it attempts to come from behind him and it too is vaporized from his eyes this time as it seems to have morphed backward and his face coming from behind his head, its so amazing. Watching them power down their bodies separate into two.

"That was amazing guys, how did you all do that?" I ask.

"Just a little practice and concentration, it helps that we know each other's weaknesses so we molded our fighting style based on that," Dean says.

"If we are ever bound together by anything gold, whether it be a chain or a strap, our powers are lowered almost rendering us unconscious," David says.

"Well, that's a good thing that no one else knows that so please keep that to yourselves," I respond.

"Ok, Ariel you're up," Christian says pushing on buttons causing four flying creatures to appear in mid-air ready to attack.

"Wait, is there any way I can have Braelyn help me on this one?" Ariel asks.

"I don't see why not, Braelyn it looks like your up too," I say.

"Ok, just follow my lead and I will lift you in the air and it will feel as if we are in tandem flying side by side, whenever you want for me to push or throw you, just let me know and I can manipulate our airspeed and make it work," Ariel says.

"Sounds good, I will use rock form first then work onto heavier metals if ok?"Braelyn asks.

"That will work, ok here we go," Ariel says moving her hands from side to side as they lift off of the ground.

Moving very swiftly, Ariel and Braelyn begin to move in patterns first allowing the creatures to get close and then move apart to watch them crash into each other, Braelyn uses her body to shapeshift into rock, concrete, and then onto metals like steel, bronze, and silver. Their patterns are quickly adapted and the creatures begin to pick them off one by one knocking them either further back into the stadium or onto the ground. Ariel dusts herself off and talks to Braelyn for a bit in the far distant corner, and I see Braelyn standing her ground as the creatures begin to swoop towards her. In an instant, Ariel swirls her hands into a swinging motion and Braelyn is hurled towards them at an incredible speed causing them to disintegrate. They quickly reappear but this time behind Ariel causing her to break her concentration and throw Braelyn across the stadium and into the ground causing a huge crevice. The creatures now have Ariel in mid-air and are trying to pull her in a different direction causing her to momentarily close her eyes and then boost herself into a bright bluish color as the beams of light coming off of her cause the creatures to retreat for a bit.

"That's my girl," Adrienne says smiling.

Watching her soar faster and stronger than she ever has, I can see her move by Braelyn and lift her easily as they both are now airborne and ready to fight. They move slowly into the air in unison, turn gently in circles then back down towards the creatures as they are moving quickly towards them as well. Right before impact I can see the bluish light shine brighter and blind the creatures momentarily before Ariel throws Braelyn into supersonic speed and as she does so I can see Braelyn power up into this orange light that makes her rock form look metallic but the color of some unknown metal that any of us have seen. The booming sound of the speed knocks the creatures into a loop as Ariel slaps her hands together and causes them to disintegrate instantaneously. Braelyn slams down hard onto the ground as Ariel slowly glides down showcasing their powers for us to be jealous of.

"So what did you all think?" Ariel asks.

"Beautiful as always," Adrienne responds.

"Uh, yeah that was beautiful and very creative," I say.

"That was something else guys, very nice," Dean and David say in unison.

"Ok, is it my turn yet," Cheyenne says slowly moving her hands in front of her and in circle forms causing the ground to shake a bit Christian quickly pushes a button that creates at least one hundred and fifty ground soldiers with axes and clubs for weapons.

"This is all you are going to test me with," Cheyenne gloats.

"Ok, well let's try five hundred," Christian exclaims as he pushes another red button which quickly changes the ground and rock formations around us lifting us higher into the air as it leaves Cheyenne lower on the ground.

We can see the battle unfolding as she is just standing there as this large amount of creatures begin to run directly at her, at this time I can see Sam move quickly into the stadium.

"Whoa, I did not expect that to happen," Sam says slowly touching his body making sure everything is in its place.

"Hey love, nice of you to join us, we are about to see something magical," I say.

With us moving closer to the edge, we can see Cheyenne standing there and just continuously moving her arms in circular motions with a hazy yellow-green aura beginning to circle her body.

"Watch this guys" Christian responds.

"Watch what, what's going to, ohhhhhhhhhhhhh," Megan says as she begins to see things coming up from the ground beginning to take the form of humanoids.

"What are those?" Braelyn asks.

"Well, Cheyenne can manipulate death and dead tissue, so she and I have been working together and realized that if she concentrates enough she can manipulate dead things, bring them back for a bit to help her fight, and then make them vanish as if they were never there," Christian says smiling.

"Wow, now that is something impressive," I say.

Watching her beginning to run I can see her lift herself off of the ground, but also see Ariel manipulating her a bit to help her move faster with her powers, she spreads her arms even further as more things begin to rise from the earth and begin forming and running towards the creatures, stopping them dead in their tracks, she is lowered down and begins fighting them hand over fist until they are all disintegrated. Her body is surrounded by this yellowish glow and realizes she has fully gained the function of her powers. She brings her hands together like in a prayer and crosses them in front of her with palms facing forward and with a final spreading of her arms, the dead are gone.

"Now that is something we are going to be able to use anytime we are outnumbered," I say.

"Well, I guess I am going to have my work cut out for me, I have some materials and some sensors that I need to get from my car and bring in, to do what I need to do, can you help me go get them?" Sam asks.

"Sure, hey everybody we will be right back, wait for me so I can see what Adrienne has in store for us, and then I would like to go if ok?" I ask.

"Sounds good, but I will go now while you're doing what you need to do because, after today, I need to talk to you all about something me and Ariel learned" Adrienne responds.

"Ok, go ahead we will be right back," I say.

Walking out of the stadium I become increasingly concerned as I know that General Collins is not too far behind trying to catch us and finding this location can destroy us in an instant.

"We need to be careful once we step foot outside of this stadium Sam, you have to promise me that you will be one hundred percent careful and tell me if you see anything or even hear anything from this day forward, do you understand what I am saying?" I ask.

"Of course, I promise Alyssa, I would never do anything to hurt you or harm you in any way" Sam responds.

"I know, I just want for you to be careful but I also need to take everyone else into consideration as well," I say.

"No worries, now let's please go so I can get this stuff back in here and do my job," Sam responds.

"Ok, let's go," I say.

Slowly moving our bodies out of the stadium, it seems very peaceful and quiet but we must remain on high alert for any movement or changes in anything.

"Ok, it looks like the coast is clear let's go towards the football field and make our way around at least to throw anyone off that is nearby," I say.

"Sounds good, but first, let me give you this," Sam says as he slowly comes up to me and kisses me.

"Wow, what was that for?" I ask.

"Just to say I love you very much and can't wait to get to know you," Sam says.

"Well, you have known me for years, but not like this and soon I will show you everything," I respond.

"I can't wait, and maybe later on in the future, we can experience a home and life together like normal people," Sam says.

"I don't see what is going on with all of us as a curse Sam, this is normal to all of us, it's just an added benefit," I say.

"Yeah, but don't you want to have a family and a life where you don't have to look over your shoulders every day like you are now?" Sam asks.

"I am fine with my life now and you in my life, isn't that enough?" I respond.

"It is, for now, but what about the future?" Sam asks.

"Right now, let's worry about the present, and when all of this is over then we can talk about our future because I want that with you," I say.

"And I with you, so knowing that I will make sure that I work on my patience and talk and communicate so that we will always want the same things" Sam responds.

"Thank you, you don't know how much that means to me, now let's go before they send a party to come looking for us," I say.

Running towards the football field, I never noticed the drone overhead watching our every move.

"Well, well, it looks like our little warriors have finally decided to work together as a team and train," General Collins says looking through his monitor with Vincent eagerly pacing back and forth.

"Let me go out there and destroy every single one of them, it's the least I can do for what they did to mom," he says angrily.

"In due time my son, in due time," General Collins says smiling sadistically.

"But all I keep hearing is in time, I want to destroy them now, I have learned enough, you need to allow me to do what I need to do," Vincent says violently.

"I will tell you when and what to do, do you understand?" General collins yells.

"Yeah, of course, dad, no wonder why mom left you," Vincent says throwing out a dark beam from his hands melting the general's coffee cup in seconds.

"Ah, my child if you only knew the truth," General Collins says switching the monitor off and slowly leaving his control center.

Getting to his car was the easy part, now trying to get across from one side to the other with this equipment and not trying to be seen was going to be the tricky part.

"Ok, I know I haven't tried using any of my powers, especially not knowing what my limits are but, I am going to try something, is that ok?" I ask.

"Sure, anything new is a good thing" Sam responds.

Standing there and closing my eyes, I can feel the warmth flow through my body, and I am trying to tell my body to go invisible, telling it to go invisible, telling it to...

"Uh, Alyssa?" Sam says.

"Shhhhh, I am trying to make myself go invisible," I say.

"Yeah, about that, have you seen how you look right now?" Sam asks.

Looking down, I cannot see anything except the grass and the ants that are trying to run up my leg, but I cannot see myself.

"Looks like whatever it is that you are doing is working, can you grab onto the equipment and make it disappear as well?" Sam asks.

"Only one way to find out," I respond.

Grabbing onto the equipment, I can see it slowly begin to disappear as if a cloak was placed over it like in a sci-fi movie.

"Now that is amazing," Sam says.

"Well, if I am going to make equipment disappear, you might as well try and grab onto the equipment and see if it affects you as well," I say.

Seeing him smile and grab onto the equipment, nothing happens, watching him reach out to grab onto my arm, nothing happens.

"Well, I guess it's going to work for you and inanimate objects," Sam says.

"I am sorry, but at least it will look as if you are just out for a walk in the park so please if you are going to talk, talk quietly," I respond.

"Got it, so I had a question and wanted to know what you thought," Sam says.

"And what is that?" I ask.

"You more than likely are going to get that scholarship to do your schooling and internship in Japan next year, how is that going to affect us?" Sam asks.

"Well, I really never thought about that, but what if you come with me, I mean you are good at engineering things, and your mind is so creative when it comes to the things we are going to make for us, why not apply for the scholarship as well?" I respond.

"Well that would be nice but, you know that my mom and dad don't have a lot of money, plus leaving them here to travel that far, with my mom's illness I would be afraid that something would happen and I wouldn't be here to help," he says.

"I understand and believe me I do, I have to leave Adrienne and my mom here by themselves knowing that I will be thousands of miles away and if anything happened I wouldn't be here to help either," I respond.

"So, where does that leave us then?" Sam asks.

"I don't know but hey, we got another half year of school and graduation to plan out, think about what I said, about you applying for that scholarship, at least I won't be in another country with no one to talk to" I state.

"You can always call me or Facetime me," Sam responds.

"True, but it wouldn't be the same, you know that and I know your feelings about leaving your family behind, so just think about it, please?" I ask.

"I will for sure, ok we are here, are you ready?" Sam asks.

"Of course," I respond.

Going into the field, I can see everyone being thrown around by creatures of different sizes, some flying some morphing in and out of the ground, it seems like there is no structure, just explosions, and blasts being sent everywhere. Christian is creating warriors with bows and maces with lion heads on them to attack the creatures, but their patterns are too precise and the creatures adapt to their fighting styles and overpower them instantly. Christian stands with an eagle staff to his side as his powers seem to have increased. Everyone else is attempting their best but seems to be struggling as minion after minion seems to overload their abilities and push them to the brink of exhaustion.

"Set up the markers or whatever you need," I say to Sam as he sets up his system.

"Power up babe, I got all of you all on my mapping system, just be you and try and put out as much power as you can," Sam responds.

Powering up I can feel myself lift off of the ground as Ariel works her wonders behind me, a creature comes in from behind her knocking her to the side but I realize my energy is keeping me airborne, this is different but I have to go with it. Moving from side to side I can see different creatures coming at me from every direction, from the air to the ground I can see them shooting arrows and throwing stones, the creatures in the air are forming patterns to attack me from the side, I know it's a distraction, so I feel my body begin to warm up and see a very bright red glow beginning to encompass the entire arena, the light is so bright I cause the ground forces to halt their advance as it begins to blind them. Seeing this I turn my energy over towards the creatures that have to begin their descent toward me. With one quick arm wave, I disintegrate all of them but feel a blast come up from behind me, which hurtles me towards the mountain landscape causing me to crash into it creating a landslide that covers me up instantaneously. Opening my eyes, I realize its hard for me to breathe and knowing that my life is in jeopardy, I feel the ground and rocks begin to shake, I close my eyes and think of my dad who was forcefully taken from me, and my family, I see Cassandra dying and General Collins laughing, and from within I see an explosion that quickly causes all of the creatures to stop in their tracks. I see my family lying there bruised and beaten, and I slowly begin to rise from the rubble. I feel an intense red aura around my being and all at once, I can see every creature turn and head in my direction. There are roughly five thousand of them all moving at a high rate of speed some magically moving from area to area, some flying at incredible speeds, and some running with all of their might all hoping to get a turn against me. Closing my eyes, I feel the warmth beginning to feel like fire, and with my eyes slowly opening, I see all of them surrounding me as they close in I thrust my hands outwards and with the blink of an eye, they are all gone. There is no explanation for it, but I feel angry and feel out of control.

"Is this all that you have, is there more you can send Christian?" I ask.

"Here goes!" Christian yells.

Watching him push all of the buttons, I can see more and more beings emerging from the ground and the sky, it seemed like legions of these things were coming closer and closer, I can feel my eyes surveying the aerial creatures first, then the ground, but my body seems to have taken over my mind, I cannot control this rage as I am thrusting my hands at every crevice to keep them from reaching me, my aura turns from red to an orange-gold color, I feel a sharp pain in my head and can see that they are gaining ground, my mind is not allowing me to focus and I can see that they are just gaining more and more ground, I cannot feel the hits they are putting on me but feel as if I am losing this battle. Suddenly I feel faint and begin losing consciousness, I can feel my body go limp and see that they are about to attack me from all corners of the arena. I begin to lose complete consciousness and look to my left and see a large golden figure standing there with his arm raised destroying the creatures before hitting me, it seemed so easy, but I finally close my eyes and begin to fall.

"Ariel, you have to catch her?" Adrienne screams.

Moving at what seemed like the speed of light, Ariel swoops in and catches me before hitting the ground.

"That was close, I don't ever want to get that close again," Sam says.

"Please tell me you got everything that you needed," Christian asks.

"Yes, and so much more, you won't believe how much energy all of you all are letting off, it's unbelievable," Sam responds.

"Well, let's hope these suits that you make for us help us keep our powers in check, we are going to need it," Adrienne says.

"I will be sure to take everything into consideration when creating them, don't worry, I got this," Sam says smiling awkwardly.

"Guys, you need to come look at this," Ariel says.

Walking over to where I am laying, my eyes are completely open but filled with gold. All of them look in amazement as I begin to speak a language unknown to all of them.

"What is she saying?" Ariel asks.

"It's Sumerian," Adrienne responds.

"How do you know that," Christian says.

"I wanted to say something before, but it took time for me to go back as far as I needed to," Adrienne says.

"How far back?" Sam says.

"A little over two hundred thousand years," Adrienne says.

"Are you kidding me, Adrienne?" Ariel asks. "You never told me you went that far back, why did you keep that from me?"

"I couldn't say anything, and still can't say anything about the future, but this has to deal with a lot of things that I needed to know exactly what we were up against," Adrienne says. "So here goes."

Adrienne begins telling the story of the Anunnaki a race of deities that came to Earth to harvest life-saving gold from another universe. She also talked about Queen Izanami and King Omo Izanaki who came to earth for the same reasons. At first, they were working as one until Queen Izanami wanted full control over the humans the Anunnaki created from their DNA to work as slaves as well as the gold. They realized that she had to be stopped, but before they could do anything, one by one she began changing the humans by implanting her DNA within them causing them to turn dark and becoming The Lusus Naturae. The Anunnaki knowing that their creations had turned against them pleaded with King Omo, but he knew that his sister was more powerful than all of them combined. He did make a promise to them and told them to give up a piece of their spirit that he would keep in his crown and made sure that when his sister was stopped he would bring them back to peacefully return to their universe. One by one they dispelled a part of themselves that he placed in each diamond of his crown, ten of them to be exact. A war raged on in the corners of what would become Japan as the Anunnaki were destroyed one by one and in the aftermath, King Omo created his army The Enlightened to learn to use kinetic energy to defeat the Queen and her minions. It took two thousand years but she was finally defeated. Holding onto her hand as she died, she vowed to return one day to rule the earth and regain her throne.

"I have seen this war, I have been a part of it and it was not something I would wish even on my worst enemy," Adrienne says. "But all of us, this is why we have the powers we do, not only do we have kinetic abilities but we each have a diety attached to within us. Alyssa has An, I have Haya. Braelyn you have Erra, Christian you have Zababa. Cheyenne, you have Ereskigal, Dean, and David you have Lugalirra and Meslamtaea. Megan, you have Ninisanna and Ariel you have Enlil. We are all now a part of something bigger than just saving the world, we now have the whole universe to worry about."

"So this thing that popped through when King Omo appeared to be destroyed in the video you were watching with Amorette, what is it because it seems to be watching our every move," Christian says.

"I don't know what it is, I have been trying to go back and forward in time but I keep getting shut out in certain parts and don't know why," Adrienne responds.

"Well we need to figure out what it is and how to stop it and General Collins," Ariel says.

"It's here!" I scream waking up from a trance I cannot explain.

"What's here Alyssa?" Sam asks.

"That thing, that thing that is haunting my every move, it helped me when I was losing my energy and consciousness, it was destroying everything around me before I fell," I say.

"Alyssa, that was you doing all of that, and then all of a sudden your aura changed from red to a bright orange-gold color and then you just started lighting up everything, the sky was so bright I could hardly see anything, but that was all you," Christian says.

"No, that wasn't me, but I think we have had enough for today, Sam did you get everything you need?" I ask.

"Yes, I got everything, it will take a little bit of time but I got everything that I needed," Sam responds.

"Ok, everyone let's leave in intervals of ten minutes, I don't want us to be seen," I say.

"Sounds good, let's meet up a week from today, same spot and we can go over some things and work on team attacks," Christian responds.

"Ok, take care everyone, and great job today," I respond.

"Are you sure you are ok?" Ariel asks.

"I am fine just need to rest is all," I respond.

"Ok, be safe," Ariel says.

"You too," I say.

Watching everyone leave gives me a sense of peace but I am still lost on what happened to me. Hopefully, we can put all of this together. As we arrived at my house I could see a van parked outside of the corner lot. As I stood behind Sam's car I see the lights turn on and it speeds away into the night.

"You ok?" Sam asks.

"Yeah just tired, and need some sleep, these next few months before graduation are going to be the longest of my life" I respond.

"Well don't push yourself too hard, after what I saw today, you have enough on your plate and don't want to burn out too soon," Sam says.

"Well, I at least have you to help me keep my head on straight," I say.

"And that is so true, ok well I guess I will see you tomorrow or Monday at school?" Sam asks.

"Monday will be better, I have to rest and get my mind focused, this day took its toll on me," I respond.

"Ok, well I love you," Sam says.

"I love you too, now get home and get rest," I respond kissing him gently.

Watching him drive away I feel butterflies in my stomach for the first time knowing I have someone I can love and trust.

"Ok, I got what you asked for now let my mother go," Sam says on his cell phone.

"Good job Mr. Spencer, now remember the deal was that you would create the suits for them and leave a few blind spots, once that this done, you will see your mother again, is that understood?" General Collins asks.

"Fine, it will take some time but I will get it done, if you hurt her, it will be the last thing you ever do," Sam says.

"Promises, promises, just do what you're told and leave me the USB stick with what I need," General collins says smiling.

"Fine!" Sam says slamming his phone onto his dashboard knowing he has to betray everyone, especially Alyssa.

"Well Mrs. Spencer it looks like your son is going to come through for you," General Collins says. "But, as for you Mr. Gonzales, it looks like your two girls are headed for a world of pain."

"If you hurt any of my family, I will make sure it is the last thing that you ever do," Roger says bloodied and chained to a wall.

"Well, let's just hope they learn to play right and be good girls, and possibly Vincent will allow them to live," General Collins responds.

"Don't bet on that," Vincent says snickering.

"You have no chance against them Vincent, you, them you all are the same everything that happened during that experiment makes all of you connected," Roger says. "You will see once this is all over, you don't stand a chance against any of them."

A purple beam comes from Vincent causing my dad to tense up and begin to convulse.

"No, no, no Vincent, he needs to be alive so that his daughters can see him die and know what your mother went through remember," General Collins says.

"This isn't over Roger, you will pay for what you all did to my mother," Vincent says. "They will all pay."

Chapter XVI

"Introductions are Necessary"

The next few months fly by and our senior prom is at the top of my priority list. Every weekend we have been practicing, harnessing our powers, bringing them to fruition, but this weekend, we will see if Sam put his technology and engineering skills to good use. Our uniforms are done, and it couldn't have come at a better time. All of our eighteenth birthdays are but a mere three weeks away, except for Adrienne, and what better way to celebrate it than having everything in place and ready for General Collins, it worries me that we have gone this long with no contact, no word and Vincent has kept to himself this whole time as well. Something is wrong and it worries me but knowing that we will be complete gives me hope.

"Hey fool, can I talk to you for a bit?" Adrienne says walking into my room.

"Well, I guess I am up now, what's going on? I ask.

"I have a feeling something is happening in the future. Last night I was time skipping and went further than I have ever been able to," Adrienne says. "The only thing is that my nose bleeds have gotten a lot stronger and we need to begin looking into what's happening."

"I agree, something is going on and I am suspecting that General Collins has something to do with this," I respond. "He has been gone for too long and Vincent isn't even making comments or remarks like he usually does."

"Well, hopefully with these new uniforms we are going to be able to harness all of our powers, and then maybe I can test it and see how far in the future I can go," Adrienne responds. "I have not been able to go very far as something has been blocking me but maybe, I will be able to find out what is going to happen with all of us."

"Let's get to school, I have my project to turn in and unfortunately I had to do it myself seeing as Vincent doesn't even want to talk to me," I respond.

"Well, at least you have something to look forward to, how are you and Sam doing?" Adrienne asks.

"We are good, he is just a little stand-offish sometimes and seems like he is on edge, but I am sure it's because of the stress of him making our uniforms and making sure they are right," I respond.

"Yeah, well me and Ariel had a falling out," Adrienne says.

"Uh, what do you mean falling out?" I ask.

"Well, I don't know how to explain it, but I began to have feelings for her when we started hanging out, and one thing led to another, so we have been seeing how things would work with us being in a relationship," Adrienne responds. "Is that ok?"

"Of course it is, and don't listen to anyone else that would say different," I respond. "But, a falling out, what happened?"

"Well, last week we were in the field and we were practicing a throwing maneuver and somehow in between me holding onto her and me getting tossed I skipped into a dark realm," Adrienne responds. "I don't know where I went, but deep in the distance I could see myself holding onto Ariel and she was in my arms, dead."

"That doesn't make sense, aren't you supposed to be able to see things in the future, be able to know what's going to happen, I mean you knew about the homecoming thing and little things here and there?" I ask.

"You don't understand, there are certain things that I can move forward and see, but ever since I started using my powers more and more, I have been stopped at certain points," Adrienne responds. "Going back is the easy part, it's trying to go so far ahead to see what is going to happen to all of us that I cannot do. I freaked out and when I came back she kept asking me what was wrong because I was just lost, and I didn't want to say anything to scare her, so I told her that maybe it just wasn't best for us to continue our relationship. I freaked out, and I know she was hurt, but ever since then she has been ignoring my calls and messages.”

“Well, maybe Sam’s designs will help you harness what you need and allow you to go as far as you need,” I say. “It would be nice to know what lies ahead for everyone.”

“Yeah, that is true, but it scares me sometimes, and even when I move backward in time, I fear I may get lost and not know how to get myself back home,” Adrienne says.

“Believe me, if you ever need to find your way home, I will be there to help guide you,” I respond.

“Ok, well nice talk, maybe one day we can do this again,” Adrienne says.

“Whatever, you go to Ariel’s house and you find a way to make things right, having her mind frustrated and hurt is not going to help us, so you go be the bigger person,” I say.

“Alright, after school I will go to her house, right now I got to come up with something,” Adrienne responds.

Getting out of my bed I begin to get dressed as I can hear Adrienne time skip from her room and who knows where she is going but I hope it’s not somewhere far. What if she becomes lost though, how would I find her?

Smelling the bacon and eggs downstairs snaps me back to reality.

“You on your way out?” My mom says.

“Yeah, the next couple of months are going to be big with prom and me beginning my transition from high school to college, so it’s I am going to be tied up most of the time,” I respond.

“Well don’t forget the little people once you leave for Japan,” she says.

“Mom I am never going to forget about you, and whenever I get the chance I will be sure to call and message you,” I say.

“Honey, you are going to be so busy with your new life that you will more than likely forget about me,” my mom says sadly lowering her head but smiling softly.

"Mom, there is no way, and you never know, maybe one day soon Dad will be back home," I respond.

"Honey, I don't think he is ever going to come back and it pains me to think that, but I have come to terms if that happens," she says. "But I will be strong and hope that he does come home."

"I know he will mom," I say.

"Ok, now you get to school, and don't forget your sister," my mom says.

"She isn't," I stop suddenly.

"Ok, let's go," Adrienne says running down the stairs wiping her nose quickly.

"You alright?" I ask.

"Yes, I am good, now let's go please," She says rushing by everyone and out the door."

"She has seriously lost it," I say kissing my mom and walking out the door.

Driving to school I can see Adrienne continuing to wipe her nose as her nosebleed has become worse.

"Do not get blood all over my car, please," I say handing her a towel that I keep in my gym bag.

"I am sorry, but I had to try something that I have been practicing, but I know something is keeping me from moving forward into the future, I can only get to after senior prom when you get back home and you are not in the best of moods," Adrienne says.

"What is that supposed to mean?" I ask slamming on my brakes.

"Let's just say that something happens at prom, I don't know what it is so don't ask because as soon as I saw you get back home, I returned right away and did not want to know," Adrienne says.

"You need to go forward and tell me what happens," I say.

"I am not doing that, I am going back and forth too much and I think it's starting to take its toll on me," Adrienne responds.

"Ok, well thanks for nothing then, you shouldn't have said anything to me at all piquing my interest, and then nothing," I respond.

"No wonder Ariel isn't talking to you," I say harshly.

"Uncalled for, but I get it," Adrienne says. "Let's just get to school please, I am done."

Putting my car back in drive, we head to the school where I can see Heather, Michelle, and Braelyn handing out flyers to students as they walk into the hallways.

"Oh, here you go love," Heather says handing me a flyer showing she is running for prom queen. "Please don't forget to vote for me for prom queen."

"I can see now that Cassandra is gone you now have a chance at winning something," Adrienne says smirking.

"Well, maybe we can all thank your sister for taking care of both of our issues, isn't that right Alyssa?" Heather says placing her hand on my shoulder.

"I wouldn't do that if I were you," I say.

"Oh, I am so scared, what are you going to show your true nature in front of the whole student body?" Heather asks. "Please go ahead and show everybody who you are."

"Heather, let them pass, they are not worth our time," Braelyn says winking at me.

"Your right, and to think you used to talk to this trash," Heather says. "Let's go girls."

Watching them walk away I see Braelyn turn for a second to look at me and nod giving me a sense of relief that Heather and Michelle will no longer be a problem for any of us. Walking to my science class I almost forgot my project in the car.

"I'll be back I need to get my project," I say to Adrienne knowing she could care less as she walks away waving bye.

Slowly getting to my car I can feel a warmth I hadn't felt in a long time, and slowly turning around I see a large gold being in front of me, and then it goes dark.

Opening my eyes, I am in a dark void, I begin hoping I don't see things like Adrienne saw, but my vision is blurred so I am trying my best to stand, walk, and explore whatever I can. Little by little in the distance, I can see the gold object again approaching me, but as soon as I attempt to use my powers, there is nothing. The being gets closer and closer to me and then I realize it's my dad, his eyes are golden not his usual hazel eyes but I can tell within a second it's not him.

"What do you want?" I ask.

"Just a moment of your time," the being says, but telepathically. "I think it's about time that I finally meet you and let you know a little about what is happening not only within you, but also what's happening to your sister, and I am going to assume my appearance is satisfying?"

"You have some nerve using my father's image for your enjoyment," I say. "And what are you talking about, are you the reason that her nose bleeds keep getting worse and making her go insane?"

"Your sister is amazing and she will be perfect for our collective, but right now she is immersing herself in things she cannot understand and things she should not be playing with," it says.

"What do you know about my sister, all you know is what you did to give us all these powers that we never asked for, and now you run around like a coward showing up whenever you want," I respond noticing a light red spark emit from the darkness.

"You, are just as amazing, but also very dangerous, and there are things that are going to happen in the future, but let me give you a brief history on why we are where we are at," it responds.

It describes how he and his sister had a great battle, and after this battle ended his sister threatened to return. He found the point in time that this will happen but could not give me specifics on when or where. He told me that if she was ever brought back into this world, she would return to Japan where they created the Japanese archipelago, and bring forth her army that has been waiting for her return. He did not want this happening and gave all of us powers to help him, but was worried that how we were using our powers was more for ourselves than for the world. He went on by saying that we were not ready and even with years of training he knew we would fail.

"Soon all of this will be over and I will take back everything that I have given to you all so enjoy what you have for now," it says.

"You can go wherever you want and do whatever you want but we are going to stop you and your sister you freak," I say.

"Freak, no my dear that is you, I am King Omo Izanaki, your creator," he says.

"You are not a King to any of us" I respond. "And my sister will find you and we will stop you because you are cold and have no heart at all," I say watching him get closer and closer to my face.

"No heart, I have given you everything you could desire, the ten of you have powers beyond belief and you use them as parlor tricks, you could be just as I am a God, a savior, but you all have shown me nothing of being a team or helping each other," King Omo says. "When this is over, you all will lose every ounce of power I have given you and you will be human again, isn't that what you all want?"

"Yes, no, I don't know what I want, all I know is that you and from what you have said your sister needs to be stopped," I respond.

"My sister yes, me I am just trying to keep this world safe and not have it destroyed like it almost was many years ago," King Omo states.

"Your threats and candor tell me otherwise," I say. "But in due time we will see who is the coldest of us both."

"You have no room for threats, I can remove your powers now but that will only defeat the purpose," King Omo says. "We will see each other soon, but until then, I will be keeping my eye on you."

Slowly slipping back into unconsciousness I feel myself falling and then something catches me.

"Hey, are you ok?" Sam asks holding onto my body.

"Yes, I am, where is he?" I ask.

"Who?" Sam responds.

"King Omo, he was just here I was talking to him or he was, I don't know but we were talking for like thirty minutes about everything that is happening and everything that is going on," I say.

"Thirty minutes, I saw you walk to your car, you turned around and when I walked up to you, you collapsed it couldn't have been but maybe a second or two," Sam says.

"Well I don't know what happened or where I went but it was a dark void and all of my powers were taken away, I couldn't do anything and he had me there and it felt like an eternity but we have to get everyone together this weekend, did you finish the suits?" I ask.

"Yes I did, and I must say I am very proud of how they came out, it's not only going to help all of you, but me too," he says.

"What do you mean you too?" I ask.

"Nothing, just some research and a paper I am doing on energy, its usage, and how to harness it all, nothing big," Sam says.

"Well harnessing energy is something big, but whatever makes you happy," I respond.

"When all of this is over and we can go back to a normal life and be normal will make me happy," Sam says.

"Crap my science project, can you help me bring it in, I have too many electrical components that need to be put together for it to function," I ask.

"Of course, but what is this?" Sam asks.

"It's a dark matter generator to help us find dark matter easier by increasing the gravitational effect it has on visible matter. This whole void that I was in just now and wherever I went when I met The Remainned has made me think that there is more dark energy than we think there is in the universe. I am wanting to find it all," I say.

"And when you do what are you going to do with it?" Sam asks.

"I am going to put an end to King Omo and his sister and make sure we never have to worry about them again," I say.

"Well let's get past General Collins first then we can worry about this King Omo," Sam responds.

"You are seriously invested in this aren't you babe," I ask.

"Of course I am, why wouldn't I be?" Sam asks. "I want to be able to be there for you and take care of you too."

"Well, hopefully, these suits work, and then we can talk about our future," I say.

"Oh so only if the suits work huh?" Sam asks.

"No, we are going in the right direction, I just don't want for you to get hurt because I don't know what I would do if anything ever happened to you," I respond.

"We will be ok, all of us will," Sam says.

"With the things that I have learned about King Omo and his sister we are going to need everyone to not only work together but be there for each other regardless of what happens," I say.

"And with you as the leader, I put in a special beacon in your suit to radiate a signal and let me know where you are if anything was to happen to you, and that goes for any time as well," Sam says.

"Well, that's a good idea, especially if my sister begins jumping us back and forth and I get lost, now you can find me, your smart," I say.

"Well I just want to be sure I can find you if I need to," Sam says.

"Thank you, and thank you for everything you have done for me and all of us," I say. "I can't wait to try on our suits, now let's get this stuff into class so that I can turn it in for grading and get it back home. Looks like Vincent is going to get a nice grade for doing nothing."

"How has he been?" Sam asks.

"He has not said a word but then again maybe that is a good thing," I respond.

"Well, please be careful with him and that generator, you don't want to go around putting people in voids and never hearing from them again," Sam says.

Carrying in all of the parts and batteries for my generator, his comment piques my interest and gives me an idea if we were ever to run into King Omo again.

Chapter XVII

"Love and Lies"

The school week flies by with no disastrous events or problems, but today is the day we begin our true training as a team and use our suits that will allow us to harness our powers and truly see what we are capable of. The excitement kept me up for most of the night but remembering everything that King Omo told me gives me the passion to train harder and stop him and his sister before they cause any more damage or hurt anyone else.

"Good morning honey, did you sleep well," my mom asks.

"I slept for a bit, just a lot on my mind," I respond. "You usually don't wake me up though what's wrong?"

"I was hearing this pinging noise last night and found a device that has a blinking light on it and I don't know what it is," she says.

"Let me see it," I respond. "It looks like it's a locator, but don't know what it is pointing to."

"Maybe I should just turn it off, I found it near the entranceway of the kitchen behind old books but have never seen it before" she responds.

"I don't know mom, but let me take a look at it, maybe I can solve what it is or where it's coming from," I say.

"Please be careful, you know how my anxiety gets whenever you say you are going to do things," she responds.

"We will be careful," I say.

"What do you mean we, don't get your sister involved in this," she responds.

"Don't worry I am sure she has other issues she is dealing with right now, especially with love," I respond.

"Love?" My mom asks. "When did this happen, who is he?"

"She, you mean, she is in love with a girl mom," I say.

"Oh, well I didn't see that coming, but as long as she is happy, that's what matters most to me," she says.

"Me too, and she is a good person, they are just going through some things, just like us all," I respond.

"Ok, well enjoy your day, I will talk to you this evening," my mom says hugging me tightly.

"See you later mom," I respond.

Slowly getting dressed I begin to think about how King Omo seemed relentless and hell-bent on making sure he stopped his sister's reincarnation no matter what he did to stop it from happening. It scares me mentally not knowing to what lengths he will go to do this, and it also gives me a sense of urgency knowing that there may be a chance we will have to confront him if he has to hurt or kill one of us, so in the meantime, I need to be sure to talk to everyone and make them aware of what is happening. Walking out the door, I see my sister walking towards the house with her hood over her head placed well below her eyes so that I would not see her crying.

"Are you ok?" I ask.

"Yes, I am good, just had an all-night discussion with Ariel about things, and we decided maybe it was best for us to end our relationship with everything that is going on," Adrienne says. "I thought me giving in and talking to her about everything would make our bond stronger, but telling her what I saw and me holding onto her lifeless body, made her think that us being together would cause this."

"None of us know what's going to happen besides you, but you not being able to go further into the future doesn't help us, so maybe Sam's suits will help you do that," I respond.

"I hope so because this is killing me inside and I hurt bad," Adrienne says as I slowly move in to give her a hug not noticing her demeanor change.

"Thanks, I needed that," Adrienne says wiping the tears from her eyes.

"You may want to think about what powers you have."

"Let's go to the park, I don't want to be too late," I say. "Hopefully these suits will help me understand my powers and let me know my true energy peak."

Driving to the park I call Sam and make sure that he will be there on time, which he says he will. Braelyn, Ariel, and everyone else said they will be five to ten minutes late but will be sure to use the backside of the arena to be sure that they are not followed or seen. Parking next to Sam's van I know that I will have to take everything at once to make sure I have everything covered and hidden.

"Hey, Sam," Adrienne says. "Do you have any goodies for us?"

"I wouldn't say goodies, but I got the goods for everyone, here Alyssa," Sam says handing me nine armbands.

"What the heck am I supposed to do with these?" I ask.

"Put that one that is maroon on and then you will know," Sam says as I slowly place it around my left wrist and feel this surge of energy as a black and red suit envelops my body and cushions itself against my skin comfortably.

"What in the world, that is so awesome" Adrienne yells excitedly jumping up and down and clapping her hands. "Where's mine?"

"Take the blue one, Adrienne," Sam says watching my sister snatch it out of my hand and once placed powers up just like mine did, but what was weird was her instantaneously disappearing then reappearing with a shocked look on her face.

"What was that, where or when did you go," I ask.

"I went forward this time and saw a few things that we will have to talk about but only when it is time," Adrienne says.

"Sounds good, but let's go before people see us," I say pushing a button and watching the suit disappear.

"Awww man, I wanted to play with it a little bit, but I get it," Adrienne responds.

"You will have more than enough time to do that today, but inside the arena," I respond.

With the armbands in hand, we proceed to the front of the arena by the trees and I feel a buzzing in my pocket, the locator is going off, and completely forgot about it.

"What is that?" Adrienne asks.

"It's a locator," Sam says.

"How do you know what it is?" I ask.

"I have seen them before online and in books," he says slowly turning to go into the arena.

"What is it trying to locate?" Adrienne asks.

"I don't know, but after our training session today, we are going to find out," I respond.

"We need to, I am worried that this thing is telling someone where we are at," Adrienne responds before I abruptly stop her.

"You're not going with us," I say.

"What do you mean not going with you?" Adrienne asks.

"You're not going with us, me, Sam and Christian are going to find out where this is transmitting from," I respond. "Who knows what this is or where we are going to end up, can't you go forward a bit and tell us what this is?" I ask.

"I have no way of knowing what I did a little bit ago, but I can reassure you that I am going to be very cautious with this new suit and where it takes me," Adrienne responds. "I didn't like what I saw and in time will know more."

"Well, if by chance you can see where this leads us, please let us know," I say.

"I will be sure to," Adrienne responds walking into the arena with the bands. "We all are going to need to know."

"Ok well, my job is done here, I need to get back home and take care of some other projects that I have been working on," Sam says.

"So you are not going to stay?" I ask.

"No, I need to finish this stuff up and can't waste any time," Sam says walking off towards his car.

"Hey can I come by tomorrow, I need to ask your mom about prom and wondered if," I say before being stopped mid-sentence.

"NO! Sam says turning around quickly. "I mean not right now, my mom and dad are going through some things, so right now isn't the right time."

"Ok, I am sorry, do you need anything, you haven't said anything about this," I ask.

"No, I will be fine, just need to finish these projects, I love you, call me when you all are done," Sam says walking away but seeing him slowly wipe his eyes. Something is wrong I think walking into the arena.

"Everything is in place, they have the suits, now let my mother go," Sam says to General Collins from his cell.

"In due time young man, I need to make sure that these suits work first, then I can think about letting your precious mother go," General Collins responds.

"They work, and if you don't let my mother go by next weekend I will make sure that you regret ever messing with my family," Sam says.

"You cannot make threats to me Mr. Spencer, with one quick snap my son will make sure that your mother is never found," General Collins says as Sam's mother screams in the background.

"I gave you the USB drive, and now the suits have trackers on them, what more do you want from me?" Sam asks.

"I want all of them dead," General Collins responds. "Beginning with your girlfriend."

"Please I am begging you, don't hurt her or my mother," Sam says.

"I will do as I please, now just a little longer and you will see your mother in due time," General Collins says.

"Fine, don't ever call me again," Sam responds.

I wish my sister had gone forward enough to see all of this but right now none of us were aware of anything.

"Alright Alyssa, you ready?" Christian asks.

"Is everyone here?" I ask.

"Yes, everyone is here," Christian responds. "These suits are something else, I can only imagine what they can do for us."

"Is everyone ready, on the count of three, two, one, now?" Christian says as I can hear the clicking of each band set off this slight humming sound, then a sudden flash from each of us as the suits envelop our bodies and create a rainbow effect all over the arena as our powers are glowing brightly.

"Oh my God, look at this pink Aura I have," Ariel says.

"Why is mine green?" Braelyn asks.

"Probably because you're like the Hulk," Christian says knowing Braelyn has issues about her weight but destroys things just like the Hulk does.

"Adrienne, are you not going to turn yours on?" Ariel asks.

"Uh, no not right now, I did outside the arena and it works so I am good for now, all I can do is jump back and forth in time and shoot blasts from my gauntlets that my sister made for me, I can't do much," Adrienne says slowly covering her band with her hoodie sleeve.

"You are much more than that Adrienne," Ariel says.

"Seems like you don't see it that way," Adrienne responds slowly walking away into the corner of the arena.

"What was all that about?" Braelyn asks.

"Nothing, Adrienne is just having some issues with her body is all," I say.

"Tell me about it, I think I gained five pounds yesterday and ate like five times, I need to cut back but these powers make me so hungry," Braelyn says.

"She will be ok, right Ariel?" I ask.

"Uh, sure she will be fine," she responds before flying away toward Adrienne.

"Hey, are you ok?" Ariel asks.

"I am fine," Adrienne responds wiping the tears from her eyes.

"You don't look fine, look maybe we can talk for a second?" Ariel asks.

"What can we possibly talk about, I am hurt and I know what I said and saw but you have no clue that this is going to happen, none of us do, there has to be ways to change the future and I will be sure with what I saw earlier, I will do what I must, even if that means me dying," Adrienne says.

"What did you see Adrienne?" Ariel asks.

"What I am going to tell you, do not tell anyone, please this will have to remain between us, promise me?" Adrienne asks.

"I promise you, and only you," Ariel says.

"I saw the birth of a baby, but this King Omo had it in his hands and he was trying to kill it with his energy as they were both glowing, so I know this King Omo supposedly knows when his sister is being reborn and I am thinking this is the time frame, but it was so blurry I couldn't make out anything else, who was giving birth, anything," Adrienne says. "I am worried that we won't be able to stop him, but we will have to try, so at any moment if I ever tell you anything and we are not able to, you are going to need to stop him somehow."

"I will do anything for you, just let me know," Ariel responds hugging my sister, and then slowly kissing her on the lips. "You are my everything and I am sorry for hurting you and us arguing, I love you."

"I love you too and we are going to stop the future from happening, there is no way you are dying," Adrienne says. "Now let's go kick some ass."

Helping her fly back to where we are positioned, Adrienne turns on her band and her suit shines brightly along with ours.

"You ready to do this sis?" I ask.

"Let's do this," Adrienne responds.

With the push of a button, Christian sends out the entire legion of creatures against us with no stopping the onslaught, it was either we worked together to stop them from advancing on us or we would all suffer.

"Adrienne, use your powers to push yourself atop the mountain to distract them from us," I say. "Christian, you Braelyn, and the twins take the lower path on the left, Ariel you take Cheyenne and distract the aerial creatures until I can muster enough energy to take them out on the backside."

"Got it!" everyone yells.

In an instant, everyone is exactly where they need to be and we begin our battle, hammering out hit after hit, blast after blast, and keeping them at bay. They cannot penetrate our defenses and are falling one by one. My leadership has improved and I can tell that we are one, we have finally used all of our powers as a collective and destroyed the last of the creatures.

"Now that was amazing," Adrienne says. "We are going to be unstoppable."

"You think, that was beyond amazing, I could feel my powers flowing through me as if we were all using each other's powers," Ariel says.

"It did feel great," David says.

"Yeah, great," Dean follows.

"So now what Alyssa, what else do we need to do to be ready?" Christian asks.

"I think we are ready, now it's time for us to take down General Collins and Vincent, then work our way back to this King Omo," I say.

"Are you sure we are ready?" Braelyn asks.

"I believe as long as we trust each other and we work together as a family, there is no way we will lose, I promise everyone, on my life," I respond.

"We will follow you, no matter what happens, we will win as a family or lose as a family, no questions asked," Christian says.

"Thank you, everyone, now let's get out of here and get some rest, don't forget prom is a few weeks away, and I want to finish out the year with a bang," I say.

"Our school is having fireworks after the prom," Megan says as Cheyenne pounds her fist in a yes movement.

"Yes, we are," Cheyenne responds.

"Dean and David, what are you all two going to do?" I ask.

"Our mom has a pizza party that they are going to throw for me and my brother, it's our favorite so we are going to hang out at home," Dean says.

"Yeah, our home, it's safer there," David responds.

"Well, we cannot have our family eating alone, let's say everyone meets around eight-thirty at Dean and David's and have some pizza then we can sneak them into our prom disguised by the magical Christian, which I am sure you can make them look completely different?" I ask.

"In all seriousness that sounds like a wonderful plan, what do you say, Dean, David?" Christian asks.

"That would be great everyone, thanks so much," Dean and David say in unison.

"No problem, just be ready to party and dance all night long," I respond. Christian, do you mind sticking around for a bit?"

"Sure what's up?" He asks.

"I have a locator that keeps going off and I need for you to go with me and Sam to find out what it is or where it's transmitting from, can you go with us?" I ask.

"Of course, call Sam and have him meet us at the field so we can go from there, if you look at the locator it seems like it's near the old zoo and I know a back way into the place," Christian responds.

"Sounds good, and thanks," I say.

"Anything for family," he responds walking out of Amorian.

Calling Sam to let him know we are done, I get a busy signal then it rings, I am thinking maybe it's the interference of the arena, or maybe it could be something else.

"Good job my dear, you and your family keep training, keep growing, keep developing your powers so that when the time is right, I can finally send this being back to where it came from," General Collins says, shutting off a monitor that has every one of our vitals and power levels on it. "You will become what I need and what is rightfully mine."

"You won't get away with this Collins, you and Dr. Peterson will get exactly what you asked for but in a bad way," Roger says chained to the wall. "My daughters will be sure to stop you no matter what it takes."

"Your daughters will no longer be my problem once I take all of their powers away and my Vincent ends their life just like we are going to end King Omo's," General Collins says. "You are our bait, and Sam made sure to allow them to find you, so for now I say goodbye, and I won't be seeing you soon."

"Sam, it's Alyssa, where are you?" I ask.

"Sorry, I lost track of time, I am pulling up in ten minutes," Sam says.

"Is everything ok, you seem off today?" I ask.

"I am good, just a lot on my mind, and with school almost over, I am barely applying for scholarships and worried I won't get in anywhere," he says.

"Do you want me to talk to the dean at my school?" I ask. "I am sure I can get you an interview if you need one."

"No, that's ok, I will just need to push a little harder than I usually do, but I will be fine, so how did it go?" Sam asks.

"It went wonderful, oh and as far as this locator, we will need to meet up with Christian tonight in the field, he says it is pointing him to the old zoo, so we may have a clue on what it is," I say.

"Well, that's good news, I wonder how it got in your house," he says. "I am sure we will find out who exactly it is leading to."

"What do you mean who Sam? Why would you say who, instead of what?" I ask.

"I don't know I am just saying locators like that usually lead to a person or to something that has a beacon on it for calls of help," Sam says driving up to the park. "Can we go please?" he asks as I slowly disconnect and walk to the car now having this fuzzy feeling in my stomach. I am worried and I am starting to have issues with my trust. I love him and trust him, maybe a little too much, but I feel like he is hiding something. I call Adrienne as I am walking, but I get her voicemail.

"Adrienne, I need you to go back in time over the last 3 days, and see what has been going on in our house, near the kitchen entrance, see if you can notice anything off or someone that should not be there, I need to know right away," I say.

Disconnecting and getting in Sam's car, I never realize that he has a device that begins to jam the frequency in my phone.

"Pick up your phone Alyssa, come on!" Adrienne says angrily.

"What's wrong honey," our mom says.

"I am trying to get a hold of Alyssa, that tracker you found, it was planted by Sam, he left it here and I am worried about what could happen to her because I can't see or move around for some reason, I mean, nevermind mom, I can't explain what is happening and it's frustrating," Adrienne says rushing out the door and down the street to Ariel's house.

I never knew she cared this much but, why couldn't she go forward to see where we were or where we were going? Something again was blocking her ability to move forward and this time we would need her more than ever. I never realized that we drove past my sister as we went towards the field to meet Christian. Driving up I can see him in the woods near the dead oak tree with his hands in his pockets and shaking his head.

"Something doesn't feel right, you find this device going off in your house, and have no way of knowing how it got there," Christian says. "You now want us to go into the old zoo that has been abandoned for ten years because this thing is giving off a signal of some sort and we are going in alone without everyone?"

"I know how this may feel, but I don't want my sister involved and for some reason, something is stopping her from going back and forth again so it's frustrating that she cannot help us," I say. "Damn I forgot my phone."

"I will get it, you both stay here," Sam says going towards the car.

"You getting bad juju vibes from him?" Christian asks.

"You too?" I respond. "I thought it was just me, but we will see how things go, I don't want to believe things just off of intuition, but it's usually right."

"Here he comes," Christian says.

"Here you go," Christian says handing me my phone and didn't even realize that the battery was removed. Walking towards the abandoned zoo my stomach has that funny tickle again, I keep thinking to myself, it will be fine.

Chapter XVIII

"My Father's Return Home"

Reaching the outer fence of the abandoned zoo, graffiti, beer bottles, old food containers, and trash is littered beyond belief. I remember when my dad and mom used to bring me and my sister here for a family weekend, but right now it's just a shell of what it used to be.

"Wow, I remember when my parents used to bring me here," Christian says.

"Yeah I was thinking the same thing, but hopefully we can find whatever this locator is leading us to quick or risk us needing a tetanus shot," I respond.

"Tell me about it," Sam says.

Walking through the rusted fence I can hear a faint noise coming from the left corner of the old bear facility.

"Do you hear that, it sounds like a generator?" I say.

"Yeah I do hear that, but where is Sam?" Christian asks.

"I have no clue, he was right next to me," but before I could say another word I can see a missile coming right at us, lifting my hands I destroy the missile and engulf its blast in a cocoon.

"Christian, you need to power up," I yell as I see him push the armband and his suit allows him to create energy blasts with his hands.

Soldiers are surrounding us little by little and I know that we have found something that we should not have. Pushing my armband my suit surrounds me quickly and allows me to grab numerous soldiers without hurting them and knocking them unconscious into the wall. Christian subdued the other remaining soldiers as he used his form-changing abilities and made them think General Collins ordered them to stop.

"Well, that seemed kind of easy, what do you think?" I ask.

"Yeah a little too easy, but back there in the back there is a light, let's go look and see what is back there," Christian responds.

Going through the bottom of the bear cages I can see that there is another locked cage that has a new padlock on it. Using my powers the lock breaks like a toy. Going through the door, I stand there in shock as a known figure stands before me chained to the wall.

"Dad?" I ask.

"Baby girl, you shouldn't have come," my dad says.

"Dad, oh my God, I can't believe I found you, why are you here, what did they do to you?"I ask.

"I am fine, but you need to leave this is a trap and Sam led you here for a reason," he says.

"What are you talking about?" I ask.

"General Collins had his mother and he made him place a locator at the house to lead you here, but you need to leave," my dad says.

"So this whole time he has been lying to us?" I ask.

"He had no choice, you would have done the same thing if the situation was reversed," he says.

"No, I would have found a way to save you, but he just lied to me and made me believe that he loved me," I say.

"But I do love you," Sam says as Vincent and his father walk him into the room by his neck. "I am sorry Alyssa, they had my mother, and now that I am here I have realized that she is gone."

"Well, I did say in time you both would be together again, so I think it's time that you both are rejoined, what do you think Vincent?" General Collins asks.

"Alyssa, they had me put," but before he could say anything, I see Vincent open up a void and throw Sam into it, and slowly see his body disappear into empty darkness.

Not holding back I gather all of my energy and shoot a dark red beam that transitions to gold and I can feel all of my love, hate, and powers focused just on them, but before it destroys them, Vincent creates a portal allowing for him and his father to escape. I can feel Christian and my father pulling on me but having issues as I am standing my ground and my powers are keeping me from moving. I can feel the pain, the screaming is not only in my head but is coming directly from me as I know that Sam is gone. Even though he lied to me, he did what anyone would have done, what I would have done, and knowing this I feel my eyes close as my body goes unconscious. Waking up violently I notice that I am back home.

"Where is he, where is General Collins?" I ask aggressively.

"He is gone honey, and you need to relax, the whole time you were laying here you were wrapped in a gold cocoon-like energy and it was scaring your mother," my father says.

"I need to find him, Dad, he took everything away from me, we had just started talking about our life, our future," I respond.

"Believe me, I know what you are feeling, when they took me I lost all sense of reality, I felt like I was going to die not knowing whether I would ever see you all again," my dad says. "I can only empathize with you on what happened but I am here with you, we are all here for you."

"My heart hurts bad, I feel like my heart was ripped out of my chest, what am I supposed to do now?" I ask.

"You fight, honey, you fight like never before and you make sure that his death is not in vain," my dad responds. "You make sure that if you are going to end this, you end it and end it for good because General Collins is not going to stop until he has you or he kills you."

"It's not only him, but it's Vincent too," I say.

"Honey, you have to understand that Vincent is a part of you all and he is only acting this way because his father has made him believe that you killed his mother," my dad says.

"How could he do that?" I ask.

"Because he believes that his son is the key to stopping King Omo and the more he uses his powers, the stronger he is getting and thinks that if he can get him to full strength he can banish him into a void and keep him from destroying the earth along with his sister," my dad responds.

"That is not what is going on though dad, King Omo is trying to stop his sister from being reborn and he knows when but we don't," I say. "Adrienne has tried numerous times to go into the future to see when or what's happening but something is blocking her from going far."

"That's not entirely true," Adrienne says. "When I first put on the suit, it sent me forward and I saw the birth of a child. I think King Omo was trying to kill this baby because they were both glowing and just when I was about to see what else was happening it went dark and I came back."

"Why didn't you tell me this back then?" I ask.

"Because you had enough going on and I needed to see if this was just a vision or a time I went to," Adrienne responds.

"Well to be honest a while back when you were in your room meditating, I went to a time chamber and met something that showed me a vision similar to it and it was a woman in a hospital holding onto her stomach and then it seemed like there was an explosion and people all around her, so this has to be the time," I say.

"At least we know that much, but my issue is when and where," Adrienne responds.

"You both have to focus and get prom over with and then focus and try and time skip to see if you can get more details on when and where," my dad says.

Watching my door slowly open I can hear my mother's keys and purse drop to the floor.

"Roger?" my mother says as she slowly moves forward to my dad for the first time in months and grabs onto him like never before. "Oh, my God love your home."

"Yes, I am ok, a little worse for wear but Alyssa helped me and got me back home, to you" my dad responds as my mother squeezes him tightly.

"Well I am so glad you are back, but what's going on?" she asks.

"We are trying to decide what we are going to do for prom as far as chaperoning and stuff like that, right Lys?" My dad asks as he turns and winks.

"Chaperoning, you just got back, you have bruises and cuts all over your face, and look like you could rest for a year," my mom responds.

"No way, I am good and feel more alive than ever," my dad says.

"Well girls, I think me and your dad need to have a little alone time, so we are going to sleep and you all can finish this conversation without us," my mom says as she walks out of the room grasping onto my father's hand. "Plus I will need to bandage him up and make sure that he is fine."

"Ewww gross, you too are going to make out, nasty," Adrienne says.

"We are going to do none of that, I just need to make sure that your father heals properly," my mom says. "I need to nurse him back to health."

"Still mom, let him breathe, he just got back," I say.

"Honey, when you and Sam finally realize your love for one another and allow it to blossom, you too will feel what I feel when I am with your father," she said not knowing the events that have transpired.

"Mom, Sam is gone," I respond slowly placing my hands over my face.

"What do you mean gone, did he leave town?" she asks.

"No, mom he is dead, he died this evening and dad didn't want to say anything," I respond.

"Dead, there is no way, you have to be mistaken, Roger is this true?" My mom asks quietly.

"I am afraid it is, when Alyssa and Christian came to save me, Sam was with them and General Collins ended his life, along with his mothers," my dad says.

"I am so sorry my love, I know his father is out of town, he said he was leaving for some work," my mom responds. "Who is going to tell him?"

"When he gets back I will let him know," my dad responds.

"Alyssa, we will get through this, our family is strong and we will be there to help you through all of this, I promise," my mom says hugging me softly.

"Thanks, mom, you go help dad and we will talk about this soon," I respond.

"Good night everyone, Roger let's let them be," my mom says walking out of my room.

"So what are we going to do now?" Adrienne asks.

"I am guessing we go about our business, but sooner or later we are going to need to try and find out when this event you both saw is going to happen," Christian says.

"We will do that right after prom, right now I just want to be alone, I need to think about what our next move is, this is going to be tough trying to manage prom and me losing Sam, I lost my love and need to figure things out," I respond.

"You take your time we will regroup after prom, we all have our powers down and know what we need to know when the time comes," Christian says. "You all get some rest, a few more weeks than we can end all of this."

"Thanks, see you Monday," I respond.

"Bye Christian," Adrienne says sitting down on the bed next to me.

"So what are we going to do?" Adrienne asks.

"The only thing we can do is find a way to get you to move forward and see everything that you can when this event happens, maybe get a name or anything that will give us a direction," I respond.

"I have tried over and over, I am beginning to think that King Omo is blocking my every move and that is why I cannot see anything solid during this timeframe," Adrienne responds. "Everything is blurry, but I know it's him."

"Let's try again after prom, hopefully, nothing happens and we get past these next couple of weeks. I heard Jennifer saying that Vincent was checking out early from school and his father had him homeschooled the last few weeks," I say.

"Must be nice, but then again, him not being at school helps us as well," Adrienne responds.

"Ok, get rest we will talk about this more later," I say.

"Good night sis," Adrienne says with a small smile.

"Good night, and get rest, no time skipping," I respond.

"You know me," she says walking out of the room and making that familiar sound I am so used to.

"Good luck," I say laying down and resting my mind.

Far away near General Collin's home on the Fort Reagan Military Installation, Vincent and his father are deep below the base attempting to open voids that are guaranteed to keep King Omo from escaping.

"See that metal structure in the corner, now concentrate to create the void right below it," General Collins says. "The ones you are creating are at least 3 feet away and you have to push or throw someone into it so that will no longer work if you are wanting to get rid of this being and your old schoolmates."

"I am trying dad, it's not as easy as you think," Vincent says.

"Concentrate Vincent, use your mind and create it right below the structure," General Collins pesters.

"I am doing everything I can, it's only coming up beside it or above it, I can't," Vincent stops as his father slaps him across the face.

"You are so pitiful, just like your friends at least they have suits that harness their energy and help them use their powers to the fullest," General Collins says. "Sorry Sam couldn't create one for you, maybe then you could have done something right."

"Don't touch me again," Vincent says underneath his breath.

"Excuse me, what did you say?" General Collins asks.

"I said don't touch me again, just because I have these powers doesn't give you the right to control me like a dog," Vincent says. "I am your son and wished you would see me like that, not your project or your destroyer."

"Do not forget what your friends did to your mother when that explosion happened. She was trapped inside because they told her that you were inside. There was nothing I could do once she went inside," General Collins says knowing that his mother died as a result of him trying to use another liquid that slowly killed her. Cremation was the only way of getting rid of her body, but lying to Vincent allowed General Collins to expose his rage.

"Don't talk about my mother, she was everything to me and she kept me sane, now that she is gone I have nothing, no one, and you aren't helping me!" Vincent yells as he powers up and creates the void right below the structure causing it to get sucked in and disappear.

"Yes, my boy that is it, that is the way you need to perform when the time comes," General Collins says.

"You have no idea what I am capable of, but everyone will always remember the name Vincent Collins," Vincent says as he smirks at his accomplishment.

"Dr. Peterson, how are we coming along with the plasma cannon that I have been asking for, for the last six months?" General Collins asks. "I need to be sure it is up and capable of capturing their powers."

"It is ready and fully functional," Dr. Peterson says handing him the cannon. "All you need to do is when they show their true forms, point the cannon and fire," Dr. Peterson stops as General Collins lifts the cannon towards Vincent.

"What are you doing?" Vincent asks.

"Nothing son, just making sure this thing works," General Collins says slowly pulling the trigger as a beam of light emits from the cannon engulfing Vincent.

"Dad, please it hurts!" Vincent yells as he is dropped to his knees.

"Try and use your powers son, try," General Collins yells hoping that the cannon works.

"I can't, I can't do anything, my body feels like it's on fire," Vincent says.

"Try harder you sniveling child," General Collins says watching as his son drops lower to the ground and then goes unconscious. "Very well."

General Collins turns off the cannon knowing that it is a success and walks over to where Vincent's body is lying motionless.

"Now I have the power," General Collins says smiling looking at a vial attached to the cannon filled with a black substance.

"You are going to have to be sure to use it when you need it the most, you will only have ten shots before you have to charge it up again and that will take at least three minutes," Dr. Peterson says. "It's going to hit them hard and knock them down but only for a couple of minutes, you won't have enough time for that charge though."

"When it is used, there will be no need for a second charge," General Collins says. "I will end all of this once and for all, and take everything that I have worked for over the last 18 years and become a God!"

"Do you think playing with these kinds of things won't have any repercussions?" Dr. Peterson asks.

"Repercussions?" General Collins asks. "When this ends, I will be the most powerful being in all of the world, and there will be no one in the universe that can stop me."

"And the children?" Dr. Peterson asks.

"They will be but a memory, I will make sure of that," General Collins says smiling.

"God help us," Dr. Peterson says walking away.

Chapter XIX

"My Prom Dress is Better Than Yours"

The next few weeks fly by with prom meetings, decorations, the setup in the gym, as well as getting the band and deciding on a house band that plays at the Majestic all the time, they were Sam's favorite. Between the food and the drinks that we were needing in bulk, I walked around the halls with no excitement or flair. Sam's funeral was this past weekend and I was not happy my heart was still torn in two, and knowing that I would never see Sam again made it even worse. There was nothing to say goodbye to, nobody, nothing, and I still see him in my dreams and thoughts being thrown into the void by Vincent, and the terror on his face is played over and over again. It hurts but I need to be strong for my family as well.

"Hey, Alyssa," Brittany says walking over to me. "I am very sorry about Sam, he was a good person."

"Thank you, that means a lot to me," I respond.

"I have this USB drive that he gave to me to give to you if anything ever happened to him, I found it kind of odd, but here you go," she says handing me the silver USB drive that has "for you" written on it.

Taking my laptop out of my bag I walk out to the bleachers near the football field to see what is on it.

"Hey love, I guess if you are watching this something bad happened," Sam says on the video. "I know that you are going to hate me when you find out what I have done, but I just wanted to say that I am sorry and apologize for deceiving you, but I had no other choice. I want you to know that I do love you very much, and my heart will always be with you. Second, General Collins had me put in tracking devices within the suits so he would know exactly where you all were at all times. If you look at your armband, there is a red button on the far left-hand side of it, push it. As you can see there was a small homing beacon that popped out, you are good to go and he will never be able to track you again. Please do the same for everyone else's. Finally, the only thing that he never knew about was that I knew he and Dr. Peterson were creating a pulse cannon of some sort that would hinder anyone from using their powers if it were ever directed at them. He is hoping to use this weapon on all of you including King Omo and render you all powerless. Once this happens your powers will be gone for a short time but you will be you again, normal. I have, however, put in a safety protocol in your suits so that if the beam is ever used on you or anyone else, the effects will only enhance your powers not remove them but only for a short time so you will feel the effects of the blast, but as soon as the effects wear off, you all will be stronger than ever, who knows maybe you all can use this time to defeat King Omo or stop whatever it is he is doing. Man, General Collins is going to be in for a surprise when he uses that cannon he will not realize what hit him. Oh, one last thing, I have a surprise for you but you will get that at the end of all of this, just know that I love you Alyssa and even though I am not there, I miss you so much."

Slowly closing my laptop and placing it in my backpack the emotion is so overwhelming and I feel like I am about to explode as it begins to rain, feeling my energy take hold, I click my armband and as my suit surrounds me I rise quickly into the sky past the dark clouds and rain that has surrounded me into the morning light, above the clouds, and into the suns beams. The feeling is so warm and gives me a sense of hope that now we will have an advantage over General Collins. Flying around I feel free, hopeful, and know that soon our time will come to end all of this so we can live a somewhat normal life. My faith is restored and my heart is content, for now.

Invisibly moving across the city I can see everyone enjoying the day and living what appears to be happy lives. I intend on keeping this city safe and making sure that nothing happens to anyone, anymore. Slowing getting back to school, I pick up my backpack as the rain has disappeared and I deactivate my suit to continue my day at school.

"Hey, where have you been?" Christian asks.

"Just clearing my head, this weekend's prom has taken its toll along with Sam's death and General Collins this has been the longest year of my life," I say.

"I feel you, but at least we can get this event over with and truly start concentrating on how we stop General Collins, Vincent, and King Omo from causing any more harm," Christian says.

"You are right about that, hey, let me see your armband," I ask pushing on the red button and watching the tracker pop out of the band. "There now you are good to go."

"What was that?" he asks.

"Sam put in trackers that General Collins had him put in our suits so call everyone and let them know what to do, but I am going to leave just one active on my sister's suit," I say.

"So you aren't going to tell her?" Christian asks.

"I am going to act like I took it out because I am sure Ariel will say something but it will still be active," I say.

"You're truly playing with fire, but I like the idea," Christian responds.

"Ok, well I will see you tomorrow evening, I have to go with my mom and sister to go get my dress for prom, it was already ordered and should be ready tonight," I respond.

"Sounds good, see you tomorrow and be sure to save me a dance," he says walking off.

There is only one person that I would have loved to dance the first and last dance with, but I know everything happens for a reason.

The final bell rings as I am walking outside to my car when Heather stops me abruptly.

"I just want you to know that even though Cassandra is no longer here, God rest her soul, I am going to make sure that you do not win prom queen this year," Heather says.

"You know what, I don't have time for this and have enough to worry about," I respond.

"Oh, that's right, eye for an eye and I guess since we lost our Cassandra it was only right for you to lose your love, right?" she asks.

"You do not want to start something you can't finish Heather, let this be your only warning," I say.

"Big woman, trying to keep her feelings in check but we all know that you are a loser, just like your sister, and just like your mother," she says.

"Well, I guess we are all just losers, but I would rather be a loser than be a second-best to Cassandra and even though she is gone, you're still her shadow, a never was," I respond getting into my car before flipping her off driving towards the exit home.

"She will pay for what she has done, she will never forget tomorrow for as long as she lives," Heather says.

Driving up to the house, I can see my mom, sister, and dad sitting outside on the porch swing talking and laughing, I can see their smiles and laughter which reminds me that I have to remain strong as there will always be happiness and joy as long as I have faith.

"Hey honey, are you ready to go?" My mom asks.

"Of course, I have been waiting for this day my entire life," I respond.

"It's going to be just one night Lys, and when it's over then what?" Adrienne responds.

"Well, then I prepare to leave for Japan two weeks later or did you forget," I respond.

"Oh, yeah I forgot," she says walking into the house.

"Adrienne I didn't mean anything by that," I say as my mother holds my arm.

"Let her go honey," my mom says.

"I can't, she means the world to me and I do not want to hurt her," I respond running into the house and up the stairs to her locked door.

"Adrienne, I am sorry I didn't mean to comment, I know how hard it's going to be for you when I leave, but right now I need you more than ever and need you by my side, I am sorry," I say as the door unlocks and she runs out hugging me tightly.

"I am sorry too, I love you and hope you have a wonderful prom, so let's go get your dress and get you ready for tomorrow," Adrienne responds.

"Sounds like a plan," I say walking out of the house with my arms around her shoulder.

"Aww, now that is a sight to see, I am happy you all can put things aside and be there for one another," my mom says.

"Is it me or do you look like your getting older Adrienne?" My dad says.

"Uh, no I am good, I am still sixteen, why would you say that?" Adrienne responds.

"You have small bags under your eyes, I guess you're just tired," my dad says.

"Your probably right, I haven't been sleeping right for the last few days," she responds.

Removing my arm from her shoulder I look into her eyes and notice that she is a bit older, a bit different, and suddenly I see my mom and dad standing there, frozen.

"I know that you are not my sister, but when are you from?" I ask.

"I am from five years from now and you have to make a decision soon and I am here to help you," she says.

"Where is my sister from now?" I ask.

"She is in the time chamber, and she will be here soon so what I have to say I must say quickly," she says. "You are the key to stopping all of this and soon you will have to decide on how it ends."

"How does it end?" I ask.

"Not good, but know that King Omo is here to help us not to be the enemy, he could have taken everything from all of us and made us normal again but he didn't, but that is all I can tell you, if I change anything it can be catastrophic to your future, to my future," she says.

"I need to know more," I respond.

"There is nothing more that I can tell you besides you keeping your head on straight and making sure you make the right choice in the end," she responds. "Now I have to go, but please know that I will always be here for you no matter what happens, be careful."

As quickly as she walks in the door, my sister walks out and everything unfreezes leaving me with a shocked look on my face.

"You look like you saw a ghost, are you ok?" Adrienne asks.

"I am fine, let's just go, please mom," I say.

"Sure honey, geez my head is all fuzzy right now, we will be back honey," my mom says kissing my dad.

"You all have fun, and don't spend too much on my credit card," he says.

"I need some new shoes, please, can I get something?" Adrienne asks.

"Yes, you can get shoes, honey please get her some new shoes so I don't have to hear it later," my dad says.

"Ok, we will be back later," my mom responds.

Driving towards the city mall everything the older Adrienne told me had me on edge and scenario after scenario keeps running through my mind. What did she mean by the right choice in the end? My mind is going in a million different directions and I know now that all of this will end with my decision, and I am worried.

"Ok girls here we are," my mother says driving up to Maple Grove Mall. "We need to make this quick because you have a manicure and pedicure appointment in an hour, so let's go in and out," my mom says.

"I will run to the Van's store and pick out the shoes while you both go get her dress," Adrienne responds.

"Perfect dear, here is the card, and don't get crazy with it," my mom says.

Walking into the store, I see my dress hanging in a beige cover as the bright red shines from the front, and feel excited about tomorrow's prom.

"There she is," Ms. Valdez says as she grabs the dress from the front rack. "Are you ready to try it on my dear?"

"Of course," I say grabbing it from her hands and moving quickly to the first dressing room I see. The dress fits perfectly and I begin to sob as my sister comes in holding onto a box. "Did you get the shoes you wanted?"

"Yes I did, here," she says as she hands me the box and finds a pair of red high heels that are my size.

"Are these for me?" I ask.

"No, they are for me because I am making a fashion statement and want to start dressing like a girl," Adrienne responds sarcastically.

"Well thank you, this means a lot to me," I say.

"Of course it does, and I will be there with you to make sure you make the right choices, until the end," she responds as I slowly look up at her and hug her tightly.

"Ok, I can't breathe weirdo," she says.

"Ok, so what do you think, how does it look," I say as I slowly walk out and show my mom.

"Well isn't that a nice dress and man those legs," Mike says as he walks into the store from the outside of the mall.

"Excuse me but you need to mind your manners young man," my mom says.

"You need to shut your mouth," he says as he walks over towards me and my sister who I have grabbed onto to keep her from doing anything dumb.

"Looks like someone is going to have fun at the prom tomorrow, I guess it's too bad that my brother, Cassandra, and hell Sam can't make it, how convenient for you," he says.

"You need to apologize to my mother and then leave us alone," I say.

"Honey, I am just getting started, you owe me your life for what you did to my brother," he says clenching his fist.

"I have no clue what happened to your brother, he was there one minute then gone the next," I respond.

"Well, let's just say that regardless of what happened you will be held accountable for his death and we all will make sure that happens," he says.

"Do what you want, but today is not the day," I say as I see Sherriff Polk walking into the store removing his hat.

"Lily, how are you ma'am, and what do we have here, Mike Montgomery now what brings you to these parts of my town," Sherriff Polk says.

"Nothing Sherriff, just trying to tie up some loose ends before prom is all," Mike says.

"Well, you can do that in your town, but in my town, you have no right to be tying up anything," Sherriff Polk responds. "You and your brother caused enough problems over the last three years and now that he is gone it seems like things are a lot quieter and better around here."

Mike looks directly into his eyes and I can see his eyes begin to tear up.

"This isn't over freak, I will catch you another time," he says.

Watching them walk out of the shop was not only a stress reliever but allowed me to breathe for a minute.

"Sorry about that ladies, you all have a fun time at prom, and good to see you again Lily," Sherriff Polk says smiling at my mom.

"Uh, what was all that about?" I ask.

"Nothing dear, let's go before those boys come back," she says.

"Why are you acting funny?" I ask.

"No reason, I just remember when me and Sherriff Polk went to school together and he and my boyfriend at that time had it out and almost came to blows for me," my mom says.

"Well, just as long as nothing was going on when dad was missing," Adrienne responds.

"There is no way honey, Sherriff Polk is a good man, and his wife is an amazing woman," my mom says.

"Alright, it's time to go, I can see Mike across the street and I don't feel like dealing with him," I respond.

Walking to our car, I can feel Mike staring at me and know that prom will more than likely be when he strikes, I have to be careful, we all do.

Chapter XX

"Prom Night Part I"

The morning is brisk as I wake up and take a deep breath standing in my room with my bedroom window open. I know that tonight will be the last chance for me to shine before leaving for Japan and changing my life forever. I wished things would have been different and Sam was here to pick me up and give me the night of my life, but I guess I am going to have to create an evening for the both of us. It's weird like I can still feel him, next to me trying to get out of a void that he is trapped in and he can only see us, but we cannot see him. Sam if you are out there, know that I love you and I will never forget you. Then a small tap on my shoulder and I turn, but what was that another one of King Omo's tricks, I had to watch myself because he could attack at any time and my trust is not how it used to be so my spidey senses are on extra high alert.

"Alyssa dear, are you getting ready?" My mom asks.

"Mom, it's not for another twelve hours, why would I be getting ready right now?" I ask.

"Believe me, dear, whenever you get married, you will understand that you will never have enough time and you are going to feel rushed, I am just trying to get you prepared," she says.

"Married mom, I am not even thinking about that right now, not for at least another seven or eight years," I respond.

"Well, whatever you want dear, have you seen your sister?" She asks.

"No, is she not in her room?" I ask.

Walking into her room, I can tell something bad happened, her furniture, bed, sheets, and clothing are thrown everywhere like a tornado hit her room and stayed there for hours.

"Oh my God Roger!" my mother screams running into the room as she searches desperately for her.

My father runs by me and I can tell he is worried as my mother is throwing things left and right looking for a sign of life. He grabs her closely and falls to his knees with her as she crumples to the ground in pain. Listening to the pain in my mother's voice I see my dad motion me over to them.

"Hold her, please it's going to help," he says.

"What do you mean?" I ask.

"Just hold her," he says again.

Holding onto her I can feel the tension in her body as she grasps me tightly crying and screaming and then a sense of her body easing itself into asleep.

"What happened?" I ask my dad.

"One thing I learned very early on was that you not only had a strong power within yourself, but you also had multiple powers combined, and having the ability to ease people's minds and control their feelings was one of them," he says.

"I guess that is why I caused Vincent to calm his anger and get others to see things my way when I just touched them," I respond.

"Yes, you did it to us several times but took me a little bit to catch on, it's a good power to have when the situation gets rough or if you run into a scenario when the other person is out of line or not thinking straight," he responds.

"Well, I have to get ready and I don't know where Adrienne is at but I will try and find her after prom if I can," I say to my dad as he lifts my mom to take her to their room.

"You have a good time tonight honey, I will talk to your mom and try to reason with her," he says.

"I understand, there are a lot of things I have wanted to say to her, but have refrained from doing so as I felt she would just be put in more danger if she knew too much, I mean we have shown her a little but not much," I say.

"Now that is speaking like a true leader," my dad says. "Now don't worry about us, I will go out and look for Adrienne when I know your mom is good, I just wish there was a way for me to track her."

"Uh, actually there is, when Sam told me about the trackers he put on the suits, I never told Adrienne about it so hers is still active" I respond. "Use this tracker that I made the other day as it is set on her frequency so it will be able to tell you where she is at, but be careful because General Collins can track her as well."

"I will be careful, now go get them tonight," my dad responds slowly shutting their bedroom door.

Slowly closing my bedroom door, I began to worry even more knowing what Vincent is capable of, but I must keep my head in check just in case anything happens at prom. I began messaging everyone, especially Ariel, to see if anyone has seen my sister or if she told anyone that she would be time-skipping for long periods, but the responses were nothing that I had hoped for as my emotions began to rise, and noticed quickly as my darkroom began to fill with a reddish light that was all too familiar. Closing my eyes and taking deep breaths helps me as I can see the light fade to a light pink hue, the color is pleasant and keeps me in check. My phone begins to ring and my hopes are dashed when I see Christian's name on my screen.

"Hey, um I don't know where you are at mentally, but just checking in to make sure you are ready for tonight," he says. "I have the limo picking us all up around seven, if that is ok with you?"

"That is perfect," I respond. "And I will be ok for tonight."

"Just making sure, and we would all understand if you didn't go," he says. "I also know we need to be prepared just in case anything happens, especially with Adrienne gone, for now."

"I agree and thank you for your concern, we all will need to be on our toes tonight," I respond.

"I got something for you, so please don't let me forget," Christian says.

"I don't like surprises Christian, and you know that," I respond.

"I am sure you will love this one," he says.

"Ok, I will see you all then," I respond.

Slowly pulling back my hair, I begin to put on my foundation and have to remind myself not to cry. Images of Sam keep running through my head but now that I am putting on my make-up I can't allow it to smear, that's the last thing that I need. I can hear my bedroom door open slowly.

"Hey love, do you need my help?" My mom asks.

"No, mom you need to rest, I got everything under control," I respond.

"There is no way that I am going to miss out on helping you get ready, I remember when my prom came around and my date came in his sixty-eight cherry-red Camaro to pick me up, but your grandmother had to work late so she was unable to help me," my mom says. "Your grandfather was there, but he was already asleep by the time I had to go after he worked his long night shift."

"Well, if you want to help me, mom, then you can help me with my make-up and hair if you can," I ask.

"Of course, now I don't know too much about contouring like all of these DIY girls perform, but I am going to show you a thing or two," my mom says.

As the day continued to speed by we talked for hours about her life and what I want to accomplish when I finally leave for Japan. We laugh, smile, and cry but she gives me comfort and a sense of security that I had lost along the way.

"Your father is going to drop you all off, right?" She asks.

"No, mom I had told you all that Christian and the others got us a limo to take us to prom then to dinner," I say.

"Oh, well, ok that's fine, you be safe," she responds.

"Of course, I will mom, as long as we all stick together nothing will happen," I say.

"With your sister missing and your dad being gone for so long, I just worry now more than usual, I am sorry," my mom responds.

"We will be good mom, let me go put this on and see if I can pass for decent," I say walking into the bathroom.

As I slide on my prom dress I zip it up, fix my hair, look directly into the mirror and realize that I look wonderful. Walking out of the bathroom, my father sees me and comes into my room.

"You are beautiful honey," my dad says. "You look just like your mother in her prom pictures many moons ago."

"Thanks, dad that means a lot," I respond.

"Just be sure to take care of yourself," he says.

"I know dad, we will be fine for the hundredth time," I respond laughing at the notion.

Hearing the doorbell ring, I know that it's time. I feel a rush of excitement through my body, but then a sudden jolt of fear reminds me to stay humble, moving quickly down the stairs I can hear people on the other side of the door.

"Is the prom queen ready!" Christian yells as I walk outside.

"I am not going to win, and if I do it's going to be a long shot knowing Heather will do anything to finalize her senior year with that title, and if I don't it's ok," I respond.

"Well, I said I had a surprise for you and here it is," Christian says revealing a corsage from behind his back.

"Oh my God Christian, that is a beautiful flower, where did you get it?" I ask.

"Well, Sam told me that if anything ever happened to him I would need to pick it up from the flower shop and give it to you, I never thought I would have to but I guess things didn't go as he planned, I am sorry," Christian says.

"Please don't be, this means a lot to me, so thank you," I respond.

"So are we ready to go?" Dean says from the back of the car.

"Oh I forgot that Dean and David were coming with us, are you going to be able to hide them?" I ask Christian.

"Of course, it's not as hard as you think," he says.

"Well, I wouldn't know but let's get going I want to get this over with," I respond.

"Sounds good, but we need to stop off and pick up Ariel first," Christian responds.

"I thought she wasn't going to come with Adrienne missing and everything?" I ask.

"I know how all of this was affecting her and I need for her to focus on something else than your sister, so I asked her to come with us," Christian says.

"I understand and maybe that will help her, let's go everyone," I say.

Driving away I turn around and see my mother and father standing at the doorway waving goodbye, it makes me happy knowing that they are together again. Driving up to Ariel's house she is waiting on the curb for us.

"Hey girl, you ready to party?" Christian asks.

"I am going to try and get my mind off of Adrienne being gone, I seriously doubt I am going to have an ounce of fun," she says.

"Well, get in, we are running a little bit late and need to make our grand entrance," Dean says.

"Yeah, a very grand entrance," David says behind him.

"I forgot you two were going with us, ok, I don't want to feel all mushy right now and have a lot on my mind, so let's get out of here please," Ariel responds.

Getting in the limo she brushes by me and I can feel the pain that she is hiding, I can feel the love and pain flowing through her.

"Hey we are going to find her," I say to her.

"I hope so because if Vincent did anything to her or if anything happened to her, there is going to be a lot of payback," she responds.

"I understand and we will do everything to find her and we will deal with what happened to her in the right way," I say. "Guys we are here, let's do this."

Getting out of the car there is nothing but eyes all around staring at us as if we are diseased and making me feel like my make-up is completely messed up but I have to think positive, just tonight and I am done with this school.

"Look at her dress, I guess mommy didn't have enough money to put you in something nice for a change, could she?" Heather says laughing and flipping her hair as she walks into the building.

"Don't mind her," Christian says. "It's just a show she is putting on because she knows without Cassandra, she is nothing."

"I know, I am just sick and tired of her antics, but now that all of this will be over soon and I am going to have to hear it from my sister on how Michelle is going to act when they are seniors in two years," I respond.

"Let's just get inside, walk around a bit and then shake some, how about that?" Christian asks.

"That sounds like a plan, let's go," I say.

Walking into the front entrance I can see pictures throughout the hall, from team photos to my win during homecoming, pictures of me and Christian and some with my sister, but also near the doorway is a picture of me and Sam. I have never seen this picture and don't ever remember taking it near the football field in the bleachers. I begin to tear up when I feel a hand on my shoulder.

"So what do you think," Ariel says. "I took this picture of you and him hugging on the bleachers, I didn't know what you all were talking about, but I thought this was a good one," she says.

"I love it, thank you so much," I respond.

"I thought about displaying it as soon as we walk in but figured it being in the actual prom area was even better," she says.

"The beginning, the end, either way, I love it," I say hugging her.

"Ok, now that we got all of the mushiness out of the way, let's party," Christian says grabbing onto our arms and leading us into the hall.

The music was wonderful from dance to techno, and the atmosphere was on fire. I could see everyone smiling and never knew how good Christian and Ariel could dance. I could feel the rhythm through my body and allowed it to flow as if this was my last day on earth. Everyone was having the time of their lives and gave me a sense of euphoria, but also knew that this was my final night as a senior and in this town. I had to make this night a memorable night.

"Let's go get a drink!" Christian yells.

"What?" I respond.

"Let's get a drink, my throat is dry!" he yells again.

Walking towards the refreshment stand I can see Braelyn has found her way from the airheads.

"Hey, what's going on?" I ask.

"We have a problem and it's going to be a big one," she responds.

"What is it?" I ask.

"Supposedly the results are in for homecoming queen," she responds.

"Ok, so Heather wins, why is that a problem?" Christian asks watching Braelyn shaking her head no. "You're kidding me, Alyssa wins?"

"Yes, and Heather already knows, so that is our problem, I cannot find Mike, so I am figuring that he will be involved too," Braelyn responds.

"You're kidding me right?" I ask.

"Knowing how well you want tonight to go, you got the crown but just be careful and watch your back, I can only do so much but we need everyone to watch her moves," Braelyn responds.

"Thanks, I don't even have a speech written, with Sam gone I didn't even think about me winning this thing," I respond.

"Well, whatever you say, just say it from the heart, you've always been good at that," Christian says. "Let's go dance, we got a lot to celebrate tonight."

Walking onto the dance floor, I never noticed Heather and Michelle standing in the far corner watching my every move.

"So what did you tell her?" Heather asks.

"Nothing at all, she asked how I was doing and I said ok, and that was about it, I didn't tell her anything else," Braelyn responds.

"You better not have, I could care less if I go to jail, this ends tonight and I will be sure that everyone in this town always remembers the Gonzales name," Heather says slowly walking to the back of the hall for an unknown reason.

"Heather, please don't do anything that's going to hurt her," Braelyn says as they walk into the darkness of the hall.

The night could not be going any better as we are dancing the night away and all of my issues and problems seem to be placed on the back burner for now, but I can't stop thinking about Sam and I slowly stop dancing and begin to walk off of the dance floor.

"Alright guys, this will be the first slow dance of the evening, so grab the one you love and listen to the rhythm of the music," the DJ says as I am near the seats and feel a hand near my elbow.

"Do you mind if I get this dance," Christian says.

"I don't feel like dancing right now," I say.

"Look, close your eyes," he says.

Closing my eyes I can tell there is something different.

"Now open them," he says as I slowly do and notice that he looks just like Sam and know that I am the only one that can see this.

"Thank you, but you didn't have to do this," I say.

"I know I didn't but I just wanted for you to have a great time, you deserve it more than anyone else does in this school," Christian responds.

"There are a lot of things that we all deserve, but I am seeing that happiness is not one of them," I respond.

"Don't say that you are smart, have a full scholarship, the strongest out of all of us even when we are combined more than likely," he says. "I know that Sam is gone, but you need to move on with your life, if not you will regret things that you never took the chance on," he says.

"You're wrong Christian, I don't regret anything and every choice that I make from this point forward will always be how Sam and I wanted our lives to be," I say. "There is no changing that, ever."

"I am sorry," Christian says changing himself back to his form.

"No worries, just know that he will always be a part of me and no one will ever change that," I say.

"I am sorry, I just thought this would make you happy," Christian says.

"It did and thank you so much, it made my night," I respond.

Walking towards the back of the hall, I decide to sit by the ice sculpture and not partake in the school song. It has been a ritual every year for all seniors to hold hands and sing the school song as we celebrate our last year in high school, but feel that doing this without Sam would be a mistake.

"Ok, everyone, I can see one senior that is trying to sit this one out, so let's give a big hand and round of applause to see if we can get the homecoming queen to come out and join us for her last chance at singing our school song," Principal Jefferson says clapping and yelling my name. "Let's go, Alyssa!"

The screaming gets louder and louder and I can feel the energy as they continue to yell my name and begin to scream and cheer as I slowly rise from my seat. Slowly walking towards the crowd I can see Christian running towards me with a shock on his face. Look at everyone I can see some of them pointing up with their hands over their mouths. As I raise my head, I can see a liquid substance falling from the rafters. Feeling the texture it's like a clear jelly and thinking about Braelyn's warning, I feel as if the whole school was behind this travesty, and watching the feathers coming down from the ceiling, I know exactly who did this, Heather! The fear is gone within me, and I feel as if payback, is necessary and warranted, the glow begins to light up the inside of the hall. I know that every time I feel this way I have promised myself that no matter what I was going to keep control of my powers, but this was the last straw. There was a time when I felt like things were going to get better if I won Homecoming, then had the feeling that if I won Prom Queen that I would have a clearer path on what I wanted, but I was wrong. It was time.

"Alyssa, what are you doing?" Christian asks.

"Something I should have done a long time ago, and don't try and stop me please, I am done being the good one, it's time for a change," I say as I slowly feel the red glow envelop my body and everyone around me begins to run towards the exit doors.

Chapter XXI

"Prom Night Part II"

Looking around I can see Principal Jefferson and everyone else running down the hallway and realize that all of the doors are locked and there was no escape.

"Alyssa, please, you don't want to do this, we have been good all year on keeping all of this a secret, you are going to destroy everything we have worked for, and we will do what we need to, to stop you," Christian says.

Looking at the group I can see them powering up and their suits moving across their bodies very slowly as they stand in fighting positions. Funny, I completely forgot the twins were here the whole time, but even with them being there, it wasn't going to be enough to stop me.

"Dean and David, we need to make her realize that what she is doing is wrong, we need to work together and make sure she doesn't hurt anyone," Christian says.

"How are we supposed to do that, she is more powerful than any of us are," Ariel responds.

"I think I know of a way, but you are going to have to distract her long enough to allow me to do what I need to," Christian says.

"Go do what you need we will try and see if we can do anything to slow her down, but with the way she is looking I hope we have time," Dean says.

"Yeah, plenty of time," David responds.

I can see things that I haven't been able to before, I can see the aura that people are letting off, some are black and some are white, but the black ones are the ones that I am more concerned about as they are a sign of negativity and those types of people need to be stopped, they can no longer keep bullying people and need to be erased from existence. I know exactly who needs to be erased first and looking up I send a beam brighter than the sun towards Heather and Michelle but notice that it is blocked by Braelyn.

"Alyssa, I know what they have done to you, but you cannot do this, this isn't you," she says.

"How do you know who I am or what I even am, I have been given these powers from King Omo, and he has given me the greatest power of them all," I say. "The power of creation as I was the creator of our universe and father to the Gods, but now the mother to them all."

Seeing that Braelyn isn't back down I send another shot directly at her in hopes that it will ricochet into the girls behind her, but her powers have fully developed and she uses both hands to block my energy and force it directly back to me causing me to jump to my safety.

"Please Alyssa, don't do this," Braelyn says.

"It's too late for me to stop, and I feel like I do not want to," I respond.

Standing there I feel my energy growing stronger and see that my aura has changed from red to a bright orange color.

"Alyssa, we don't want to do this, but you need to stop you are going too far," Ariel says floating next to Braelyn with Dean and David by their side.

"Do you believe that all of you can stop me?" I ask.

"We may not be able to stop you, but we are going to do everything to help everyone here," Dean says.

Looking to my left and right, I notice that David has melted the locks and everyone is beginning to exit the hall. I can tell their distraction has worked, for now.

"I will allow them to leave, but you all will not be given the same courtesy," I say as I notice that my body has grown an extra two feet since the transformation.

"Alyssa look at yourself please, look at what you have done," Ariel says as I slowly look and notice destruction and chaos surrounding me.

"You need to look at how we have been treated, like losers and unknowns, as if we didn't even exist," I say. "I will no longer allow any of us to be harmed or be talked about behind our backs, I am the creator and the beginning and no one will take that away from me or us."

"Alyssa, you have lost your mind, none of us are Gods, we are just teenagers who are scared, but we have a leader, you, to help us on our way and help us understand that we are a family," Ariel shouts. "Don't you remember how far we have come as a family?"

I begin to see flashbacks of our training sessions and us talking and laughing and joking around as we went about our lives, but the anger continues to overshadow the happiness and I fall back into place.

"There is no family, only us making sure that King Omo is stopped before he destroys this world or our universe, and I will not allow this to happen, and none of you all will stop me," I say.

"We are not trying to stop you but we are here to help you, you are not thinking straight," Braelyn says.

"What do you know about how I am thinking, if you knew then you would be able to stop this," I say as I slowly rear back and send multiple blasts from my eyes and hands knocking everyone to the ground and back away from me.

"Oh God that hurt, I was not prepared for that," Dean says.

"Yeah me either," David responds slowly.

"Don't let her get ahead of us, we need to somehow get behind her and get Braelyn to hold her from behind so that we can try and knock her out, it's our only chance," Ariel says.

"I will try and distract her from the air, Braelyn you are going to need to go through the back of the hall and around the corridor to get behind her, Dean and David see if you can conjure up your Gods and fight her with her own medicine," Ariel says.

"We will try but we can only hold it for so long, you all will need to try and hurry," they say in unison.

"Braelyn, do you even know what your God can do?" Ariel asks.

"No, but I am going to try and do my best, and hopefully it's enough," Braelyn says.

Running through the back of the hall, Braelyn notices two girls cowardly behind the tables, it's Heather and Michelle.

"Braelyn, we are so sorry this happened," Heather says. "We didn't mean for it to go this far."

"Yes, you did, you both did and I can only imagine how much worse it would have been if Cassandra was here, so remember what you did and if we can stop her, try and live a good life, try and do something for someone besides yourselves," Braelyn says as she runs off into the back corridor behind a blue curtain.

"Ok, seriously just the three of you against me?" I say.

"Well, not just the three of us, let me introduce you to two others who have been dying to join us," Dean and David said.

Standing in identical poses they slowly close their eyes and a red and blue aura begins to encompass their bodies. As their energy soars the Gods Lugalirra and Meslamtaea emerge, the divine twins but also guardians of death and the underworld. Their bodies begin to merge and begin an onslaught on me that I quickly have to dodge to not get hit. I look up in the air and see the emergence of Enlil, the lord of the air. His presence is just as commanding as mine, but I must keep ahead of them to keep them from stopping me.

"You look wonderful my brothers and sisters, we have arisen again to claim our rightful place on this planet," I say.

"No, An, this is not how we wanted things to be, we cared for the humans we created, and we need to help them instead of destroying them," Enlil says. "We did not come here to rule over them, but to work with them and help them harvest gold so we could survive and allow them to benefit from its value."

"Yes, but Queen Izanami took all of that from us and I will not allow that to happen again, no matter what I have to do," An says.

"Sister, if you want to fight us, then we are all lost," Lugalirra and Meslamtaea say in unison.

"You will have to destroy me to stop this purge, this cleanse, that the Earth must go through so that King Omo and his sister may never return and we can continue our rule over these humans," An says.

Slowing feeling another surge of power I can see the entire hall light up into a golden color, my power is its climax and the others feel and fear it.

"Move now," Enlil says as she descends towards me and emits rays from her eyes that I can block with my hand.

The twins move their hands together and a purple beam emits from their bodies as I stop it with my other hand.

"After all of the millenias that we have been gone, this is all the power that you have, all the fight you have?" I ask.

"No, not to fight you, but to distract you," Enlil says.

Slowly closing my eyes I realize that I have been tricked. Knowing Braelyn is behind me I can feel the energy of my sister Erra emerging. The God of War and plagues, I brace myself for death, but hope for the best. I can feel the blow to the back of my head and I am out cold.

"She is down, her energy has rescinded and she is back to her normal form," Erra says powering down.

Dean, David, and Ariel also power down and stand beside my body.

"What are we supposed to do when she wakes up?" Ariel says.

"I don't know but whatever you all did was unbelievable," Christian says walking into the hall from the front entrance.

"And where the hell were you through all of this?" Dean asks.

"Yeah, where were you?" David responds.

"I was trying to save all of us from being exposed," Christian responds.

"Let's get her out of here and I will explain it at her house, we have people coming to enjoy their prom.”

Slowly lifting me over his shoulder and walking towards the back everyone turns to see the entire class walking into the event as if nothing ever happened. This was a story that needed to be explained but we all had to get out of there.

Driving up to my house, I could hear everything that was happening but could not wake up for the life of me. I could hear my mom scream and then my dad telling Ariel to get his medical bag from the back of his car.

“Here you go sir,” Ariel says.

“Ok, what exactly happened?” My dad asks. “I can inject her with adrenaline but need to know if she was using her powers, if so I will have to use a lesser dose.”

“Yes, she was using it all, it took four of us just to stop her,” Christian says.

Taking the cap off of the needle he injects me right into my heart, causing me to jump straight up, and in defense mode, my powers were still effective.

“What happened to me, what’s going on?” I ask.

“You were in full power mode tonight, we kind of knocked you out but you are good now, your dad helped you,” Christian says.

“Ok, thanks dad, but what about the prom Christian, what did I do?” I ask sadly.

“I took care of it, I used my powers and created a live band outside and had everyone believe that it was the beginning of prom and then everyone came into the hall like nothing ever happened, I was pretty impressed with myself, and I believe it worked,” Christian says.

“I just need to rest, we all need to regroup tomorrow at Amorian, I need to make things right and make sure that we are all on the same page,” I respond.

“That sounds like a plan, ok I will message everyone else, you get some rest and hopefully your sister will show up, has anyone seen her?” Christian asks.

“No, none of us have and as time is passing by, we are becoming more and more worried that she may be lost somewhere or sometime,” my dad says.

"Well, if you see her sir, please message me and let me know, I am worried about her and miss her very much," Ariel says.

"I will for sure, now everyone go get rest, you all are going to need it," my dad says.

With his arm around my shoulders, he leads me up the stairs to my room knowing that my powers are getting harder to control.

"Do you want to talk about it?" My dad asks.

"Does it look like I want to talk about it, dad?" I respond.

"Sometimes things happen, look at me, I was gone for so long that coming home was more of a shock than being chained up, but I had to get over my fears," my dad says. "You are afraid and I can see it in your eyes, but you need to try and control your anger and your fears."

"I am trying dad, it's hard, but I understand where you're coming from, you went through a lot and if you can do it, so can I," I respond.

"That's my girl, now you get some rest, and be fully charged in the morning to help your friends and get rid of General Collins and this King Omo if need be," he says. "I love you, Alyssa."

"I love you too dad, goodnight," I say.

Closing my eyes, I keep having flashbacks of the prom and how I tried to hurt my family, I really need to gain control of these powers and hopefully, we can all come together to help me. Tomorrow has to be better.

"Rest well little one, you will all be in for a surprise tomorrow," General Collins says sitting in the van across the block. "You all are going to wish you were never born."

Chapter XXII

"A King is Born"

Waking up the next morning, I slowly walk towards my sister's room and slowly open the door. I can see that everything has been fixed and everything has been put back in its place, only my mom would do such a thing and it reminds me that my sister has not come back. Walking out I notice an envelope on her workstation. Opening it I know it's from her:

"I know it's hard with me not being there right now, but understand that all of this is for a reason. I have left parts of me strewn across time and if you are reading this, then I am trapped somehow and working my way to get back," Adrienne writes. "Know that I love you very much and everything will work out in the end, time is on our side, Love Adrienne."

Slowly wiping the tears from my eyes, the letter lets me know that she will be ok, I just wish I knew when she would be back. Walking to my room, I put my armband on knowing that this all can come to an end very soon, and General Collins is getting closer and closer to us. I wish Sam was here, I am sure he would be able to tell me what I needed to feel, but for now, I have to depend and rely on my brothers and sisters and try and control my anger, this has gone on long enough. Getting in my car I see all of the family's outside enjoying their weekend, some having a barbeque, some just riding their bikes, and it reminds me of how I used to love being normal or at least feeling normal before all of this happened to me, to us. I never felt so hopeless driving to Amorian but also had a small sense of hope knowing that we will all be together if anything happens. Driving up to the park, I can see families walking around, holding hands and enjoying their day, slowly getting out of the car I begin to walk towards the back end of the park and see Christian near the trees waving at me. The feelings I am having are that of anger and happiness, please God give me the strength to control them.

"Hey Alyssa, are you ready?" Christian asks.

"I really just need to talk to everybody about what happened and see what I can do to make things right again," I say.

"Just speak from the heart, everything else will follow along," Christian says.

"Let's go in before anyone sees us," I respond.

"General Collins, what are we going to do?" Dr. Peterson asks as he, General Collins, and Vincent sit in the parking area in their white military van.

"I am going to make sure that today goes down in history as the day King Collins is born, and the world becomes mine, now Dr. Peterson besides myself, you are the only one that knows how the cannon works and what the cannon is for, correct?" General Collins asks.

"Of course, now if for some reason the," Dr. Peterson stops as he hears the cannon charging up and being pointed at him. "What are you doing, you activated the killswitch, please don't do this."

"Dad don't!" Vincent screams as General Collins pulls the trigger hitting Dr. Peterson in the chest disintegrating him in a second. "Why, you know that no one is going to try and stop you, let alone Dr. Peterson."

"I need to tie up all loose ends son, do you want to be the next?" He asks.

"I just want all of this over, just like Alyssa and Adrienne does," Vincent responds.

"So are you taking a liking to your siblings?" General Collins asks.

"I just feel like there is more to this that I am not being told, mom's death, these powers, everything," Vincent responds.

"Well, maybe there are some things that need to be kept hidden, and those things that need to be altered just a bit, but you need to stay on the path and complete our plan," General Collins says. "You need to keep your mind focused on the goal and not listen to anything any of them say, is that clear?"

"Why are you so worried about what they say?" Vincent asks.

"Please don't make me use this weapon on you as well, just know that they are out to trick you and I know how gullible you are so tricking you is easy," General Collins says. "Once I drain them of all of their powers, I am going to use those powers to wipe them off the face of the earth."

"I thought you were just going to wipe them of their powers, you said nothing about killing all of them, why the sudden change?" Vincent asks.

"It seems to me that you have taken a stronger interest in them than what you are leading me to believe," General Collins says. "You know what they did, you know what happened to your mother, you want them gone too."

"Yes, but I wanted to be the one to complete this task, not you," Vincent responds. "Let me be the one that does it."

"You will have your time son, now let's go in so that we can get our revenge," General Collins says as they both get out of the vehicle and walk into a black void that Vincent created.

"Alright, now that we are all here, I just wanted to apologize for last night," I say.

"We really need to come up with a plan on how we can keep ourselves from losing control," Ariel says. "That night could have gotten out of hand and thankfully we were able to keep you from going over the edge."

"Well I thank you all very much, you don't know how lost I was when I changed, it felt exciting, but felt like I had no control, there are parts that I don't' even remember," I say.

"Well, maybe we can do something about that today, what if we harness our energy and see how we can work together?" Christian asks.

"That sounds like a plan but what are we supposed to do with Adrienne not here?" Braelyn asks.

"She will be ok, I am sure she has everything planned out, but I am sure Ariel you will be able to help her, right?" I ask.

"That isn't a problem, but we need to make sure last night never happens again, so where do we begin?" Ariel asks.

"I think we need to power up and see what true powers we have and focus on our energy as a unit," I say.

"That sounds good, alright everyone, let's do this," Christian says pushing on his armband and lighting up the arena like never before.

Each one of us takes turns powering up to full force and looking around the arena it is lit like a rainbow, our kinetic energy combined can almost power the sun, it seems.

"Well, isn't this a pleasant treat, thank you for all being here on this special occasion," General Collins says walking out of a void and blasting me in the chest with his cannon and knocking me over the boulders.

"Alyssa!" Christian screams as he races towards General Collins only to be blasted back into the rocks as well.

One by one, my family races towards him to stop him only to be blasted by his cannon and fall to the floor not knowing what we had just done. Walking from around the rocks I can see everyone laying on the floor struggling to get up. What have we done?

"You see Vincent, now you can have your fun," General Collins says. "And now that I have what I want, you can finish off Ms. Gonzales and her family, or should I just destroy them?"

"No, I have this," Vincent says as he grabs my arms and pushes me through a black void only to end up at the other end of the arena. "You need to tell me the truth about my mother."

"What are you talking about?" I ask. "I know that your mother died, but what does that have to do with me or any of us?"

"My father told me you all forced her to go to the facility that was destroyed and she died in that explosion, telling her that I was there," he says.

"Vincent, we would never have done anything like that," I say. "I don't know who lied to you but we didn't do anything to her."

"You're lying, I can see it in your eyes, and I am going to finish this once and for all," Vincent says as he raises his hands and his eyes go black.

"Vincent, don't do this," Adrienne says as she comes from a blue void and touches his shoulder. "Here let me show you."

Vincent's eyes begin to glow blue and his body is stiff as a board but you can tell Adrienne is showing him everything as she closes her eyes and begins to breathe deeply.

"You see, it was your father that did this, not us," Adrienne says.

"I am so sorry, for everything, I knew that Sam wasn't lying but I had to make it seem like he was gone," Vincent says.

"What do you mean to make it seem?" I ask.

"You'll see, let's go," Vincent says as he holds my should and we are transported back to the entrance.

"Now, that I have all of your powers I am going to use them to make this world a better place," General Collins says as he disconnects the vial from the cannon and injects himself causing him to begin to convulse uncontrollably.

His body begins to contort violently and then a shimmer of light begins to emit from his eyes and then his mouth from there his entire body is engulfed in a pure white light as his body rises in the air he begins to double and quadruple in size, the armor begins to show on his shoulders then arms and the crown on his head is covered in diamonds.

"Finally I can begin my reign over the earth and then the universe," General Collins says as he looks at his hands and then at us.

"I knew this was going to happen," Vincent says. "I should have listened to Sam earlier, but at least this time around I can make things right."

"What are you talking about Vincent?" I ask before seeing everyone stand and power up to begin their battle with King Collins.

"No time right now, go help them, I need to really concentrate on our next move, please keep him distracted," Vincent says.

"You better have a good plan, we are going to need everything and everyone if we are going to stop him," I respond.

"I agree," Vincent responds as he sits behind the rocks and a black aura begins to surround him, but I don't have any more time to waste.

Powering up I can see everyone already in their God form, standing in a battle position, the feeling of all of us together is extreme and comforting at the same time, my sister appears next to me as I reveal my true form.

"Let's do this sis," Adrienne says.

"General Collins, you have desecrated our powers and have become something unnatural," I say. "You will allow us to take our powers back or face the consequences.

"Child, none of you are a match for me, so skip the pleasantries and let's finish this," King Collins says.

"Don't mind if we do, everyone, move now!" I yell.

"Our attacks begin from the ground and then move to the sky, his military background is putting us at a disadvantage but hopefully one of us can get a clean hit to see where we are at. Ariel has taken to the sky with Braelyn as the twins are working their powers to keep him from moving around quickly. I have created a beam that he is holding at bay and everyone else, is holding their own. I can see him begin to struggle but it seems as if our powers are no match for his considering he has all of our powers combined into one. Ariel falls from the sky as one of her energy beams is directed back towards her and Braelyn seems to lose control of her body as she crumbles to the floor and then back solid again. The twins are struggling to keep together as their powers are thrust back to them as it begins separating them slowly. I can feel my energy as if I am sitting in the hot sun and it feels as if I am about to catch on fire.

"Do you honestly think you are going to win?" King Collins asks.

"It's not about winning, it's about stopping you once and for all," I respond as my beam begins to take a gold appearance.

"Ah yes, there you go, bring me everything you all have," he responds as we begin to attack harder and from every corner. "Bring me your all!"

I can feel the ground beginning to shake as he stops my beam and his armor begins to turn into diamonds just like his crown rebounding my beam back into me, but also into everyone else as it seems as if he absorbed my power. Everyone drops to the ground in an instant and it seems like there is no way of stopping him. Being knocked back into the side of the rocks, I can see Vincent stand and he is much bigger than I remember.

"I told you I had a surprise," Vincent says as he moves his hands in a circular motion and a void opens up near King Collins.

"What are you doing son, what is this?" He asks.

"My gift to you dad, for killing my mother," Vincent responds as a figure comes from within the void, it's Sam!

"Surprised to see me aren't you, well, here is a little gift from my mother to you," Sam says as he raises a huge cannon and fires it directly into King Collins.

"What is this, what have you done?" he asks.

"Just giving my friends back what you stole from them," Sam responds.

I can see him fall to his knees and all of our powers are being stripped from him, one by one, and returning to us. As he falls we rise, standing over him, begging is his only option.

"Vincent please, I am your father, why have you done this?" General Collins asks.

"I listened, for the first time I listened, and seeing Sam's reaction to losing his mother because of me, I owed it to him for her death," Vincent responds. "I hid him, knowing something was off and Adrienne showing me the truth, you killed my mother, so bringing him back to stop you was the only way. Yes, I worked with him and helped Dr. Peterson create a cannon that would reverse what you have done. I bet you never saw that coming did you?"

"Well, I must say, I am very proud of you, but I did make sure that there was a contingency plan if things did not go my way," General Collins says. "While all of you were battling me, I used the last of my powers to bring you a gift of sorts."

Looking near the entrance there was a black egg-shaped bomb that had numbers counting down seconds, showing we only had an hour left before it detonated.

"Why didn't I see this?" Adrienne asks out loud as she runs towards the bomb to see what she can do.

Looking around I see smoke and chaos, but more importantly, I can feel love, happiness, and contentment.

"Hey, Alyssa, sorry I had to stay hidden for a while," Sam says as he slowly hugs me from behind.

Holding onto him I felt every emotion possible, and only knew that my love for him would continue to grow.

"I cannot believe you are alive, I was so lost without you," I respond.

"Hey, don't worry, I am ok, and you can thank Vincent for all of this, it was his idea," Sam says.

"But after everything he did?" I respond.

"I know, but he was lost and brainwashed, it took me and your sister forever just to convince him," he responds.

"My sister?" I ask.

"Yes, your sister was with us most of the time, trying to get him to listen to what she had to say, but getting through to him took a long time, technically," Sam says. "The good thing is Adrienne took him to some type of time chamber to talk to him so what seemed like months for him was only like ten seconds for me."

"Uh, guys, I think we can do the catch-up thing later, we have a bigger problem," Adrienne says.

"Why didn't you see this Adrienne?" Christian asks.

"I think his power could have blocked me from seeing this event from ever happening, but knowing what and when we need to go, I think we can use this to our advantage," Adrienne responds. "Alyssa, what are we looking at here?"

"This is a hydrogen bomb, and it will destroy the entire city if it goes off here" I respond.

"What are we going to do Alyssa," Ariel asks.

"I can try and diffuse it, but I would need all of my engineering tools which are back at school," I respond.

"No, we are going to take this thing with us, I think I have found the time that King Omo is talking about and we are going to need to stop him from taking any innocent lives," Adrienne responds.

"Ok, so what do we need to do?" Braelyn asks.

"Everyone needs to gather around the bomb, I am going to meditate for a brief second and should be able to transport all of us to this time," Adrienne says.

"Hold on for a second, what about me?" General Collins asks. "You cannot leave me here, I have no way out and."

"Oh, don't worry General Collins, this deals with you too, and you're going with us," Adrienne responds handcuffing him to the bomb.

"What are you doing, take these cuffs off of me, are you crazy?" General Collins asks.

"You wanted to play God remember, now I think it's time you met a real one," Adrienne says.

Holding onto the bomb and closing her eyes, my sister's aura begins to glow brightly and then I feel very lightheaded. Looking around I see us traveling very fast and then stopping inside a hospital that is in utter chaos.

"Are we all here?" Adrienne asks. "Hey, what year is it?"

"What, what year, 2031," and nurse states running out of the labor and delivery wing.

"Everyone stay behind me and follow me, this is it, this is the time, and we need to stop King Omo at any cost," Adrienne says.

Looking at everyone we power up to our God levels and run into the darkness of the wing, this is our biggest test ever, and this may be our only chance to stop him. I worry that we are not prepared for this but we all have agreed that no matter what happens we were going to stop him at any cost. I pray that all of us are enough.

<h1 style="text-align:center">Chapter XXIII</h1>

<h2 style="text-align:center">"Reincarnation is a Child's Game"</h2>

Running into the wing the darkness comes and goes as the lights from the hospital are flickering on and off. You can smell the chaos and death that has already occurred, the smoke and fire begin to get stronger, and realize that there is a bright golden light at the end of the wing. We slowly move towards one of the rooms that are open and to our shock, we see the bodies of infants lying in their beds, lifeless. King Omo is behind this and we must stop him from hurting anyone else.

"I cannot believe he did this," Braelyn says. "Look at this, how could anyone do this?"

"We need to split up and look for him, he has to be somewhere in this wing," Adrienne responds.

"I don't think we should split up, we need every ounce of power that we have and use it all at the same time," I say.

"I am with Alyssa on this one," Vincent utters. "One thing my dad did teach me and that was the power of working together and unifying our abilities as one."

"Let's move through that corridor and out the side, but we must move together, Christian, you watch our back, and Vincent, watch our sides as good as you can," I say.

"On it," Christian responds.

Moving through the corridor I notice a bright light coming from the end of the wing, as we get closer I can hear a woman screaming. The sounds are eerily familiar as my mind flashes back to the vision I was shown in the time chamber. Could this be the same point in time that I say? Only one way to find out. Hiding near the entrance we see two tall white figures standing guard.

"Adrienne, this is what I heard and saw when I was taken to the time chamber, do you know anything about it?" I ask.

"No," she says looking away telling me she knows more than she is saying.

"We need to get into that room, but I don't know what to do about those two things standing near the doorway," I say as the screams get louder and louder.

"We will distract them and you can sneak in from that side area, guys we need to create a distraction," Christian says.

"You all create the distraction and I will create a void for Alyssa to get through once they move, they will see her if she goes through that area," Vincent says.

"Thanks, Vincent," I respond.

"Ok on the count of three, one, two, three," Christian says as they run and blast a few times into the wall by the two guards.

Watching Vincent move his arms from side to side, he creates a void that I easily access and end up right in front of the doors to the delivery wing. Walking in slowly, I can hear a woman screaming as I move towards a room lit up only by the flickering lights that are still functioning after the destruction. In the corner, I can see King Omo sitting in a meditative state floating a foot above the ground. I can see a doctor sitting in a delivery position as a woman is crying and in pain. The sheet is covering her from the waist up so I cannot see her face, but see a man sitting with his back to me consoling her and nurses running around frantically.

"Come on honey, one more push and this will be all over," the doctor says.

Watching her beardown I can see King Omo's eyes slowly open with a white light emitting from them.

"There you go, almost there, and there she is," the doctor says as King Omo moves swiftly and takes the baby from her hands knocking her to the ground. Watching her get up she runs past me and out of the delivery room.

"There you are my dear," King Omo says looking deeply into her eyes as a beam comes from his locking them together.

"Don't hurt my daughter," the father yells as he runs toward King Omo only to be thrown back into the wall and killed instantly. The mother is moving but with barely enough energy to do just that.

"King Omo, this needs to end, do you even know if that is your sister?" I ask.

"What does it matter child, even if it isn't I will make sure that no child is left unchecked," he responds. "I cannot take that chance and neither can you all. I have been searching and through time and space and know this is the right time."

"What about all of the innocent lives you took, the chaos and destruction that you created, is this the life that you wanted for us?" I ask.

"You have no clue what you are talking about little one," he responds. "By keeping my sister from realizing who she is, I will have saved the lives of millions of souls. Now let me finish what I started."

"We cannot let you do that," Christian says dragging in the bodyguards that were keeping the wing protected. "You have caused enough chaos and it's time for you to go back where you came from. Adrienne, we don't have a lot of time and that bomb is about to go off, we need to do everything possible to not only stop him but get that bomb off the planet."

"Let me worry about getting them off of the planet, you all just get him in that corner of the room and I will do the rest," Vincent says. "I owe you all at least that much, regardless of what happens you do as I say."

"Let's do this everyone," Christian says.

Backing up to be with my family, I see King Omo placing the baby in a small incubator and she is motionless. Looking to my left I can see Adrienne taking the mother out of the room and to safety.

"I know that you all feel what you are doing is best, but you need to let me complete what I have set out to do," King Omo says. "You have no clue what my sister is capable of."

"From what we have seen, you are out of control and we are all going to stop you no matter what we have to do," I respond. "It's time everyone, please trust me and let's finish this once and for all."

Watching everyone powering up even higher, the room begins to fill again with every color of the spectrum, and looking at King Omo he begins to smile.

"Yes, finally you have come together as one, as a family, and your powers are beyond how they were so many years ago," King Omo says. "I told you to trust me and I would make sure that you would be born-again, but now you have to trust me one more time and let me finish what I started. I want to protect you and this world, but I cannot do that if you try and stop me."

"You have done enough damage and now we must protect the Earth on our own, protect our people, and our loved ones," I respond. "Now!"

Each one of us closes our eyes and our bodies begin to unite, one by one our powers and each other are absorbed into one being, a pure God. Opening our eyes, we see the world as it truly is, made of pure energy, and as we stand there looking at King Omo, he doesn't seem as intimidating as he once did. Our minds are one, and we can think faster than we act, the time has come to end all of this and get ourselves back home and leave these wonderful beings at peace.

"You all have impressed me," King Omo says. "And now it is my turn."

Looking into his eyes, they begin to glow brightly, and then his size doubles but is also covered in gold armor with a long golden sword and shield.

"Are you sure you want to do this?" He asks.

"It is our duty to protect all of those that are here on earth or born of this earth regardless of who they are, they are our creation," I respond.

"And you are mine," he says as he moves quickly towards us for the first attack.

We begin to fight, throwing everything that we have at him, our powers, our energy, our love, and all of it was holding him at bay, we just hope that Vincent plans out what he needs to.

"Can you all hear me?" Vincent asks.

"Yes, we can hear you, what do you want for us to do?" We ask.

"I need for you to continue your onslaught, I have developed and created a portal so that once it envelops him, it will take the bomb with him as well and place him in a suspended animation chamber," Vincent responds. "But we have to do everything at the same time, Sam I need for you to help me push in the bomb."

"You let us know. we are having an issue keeping ourselves combined, I don't know if it's the battle or if we are losing our strength and powering down," we respond.

"Give me five minutes, the bomb has five minutes and ten seconds remaining, we need to do this quickly," Vincent responds.

Looking back at King Omo, we can see that he is tiring as well, his armor has taken a beating and it is no longer shining as it did, and his sword is developing cracks. We move in closer to see if we can bind him and move him towards the corner of the room.

"It looks like you are tiring King Omo, I thought that you were strong enough to defeat us?" We ask.

"Child, I told you that when the time was right, you would regret it if you ever interfered with my plans, it is time to take things back," he responds lifting his hand and touching our chest knocking us back causing us to separate and feel our powers begin to leave us.

"What did you do?" I ask.

"I took back what I gave you, now I can finish what I need to without any worry," King Omo says.

Looking at each other we are human again, we have failed and we have no clue what to do now.

"You see, I told you that when the time would come I would take everything back from you and all of this would be over," King Omo says.

"Nothing is ever over, and do you honestly think that we didn't have a plan B?" I say. "Adrienne?"

King Omo never realized that Adrienne, even though was there, never combined with us, so she and Vincent still had their powers. Waving her hands across her chest, a portal opened and it was us, from five minutes ago and we looked on as they used their powers to bind King Omo and push him back as Vincent began the opening of his portal.

"How did you do this?" King Omo asks.

"Easy, while you were busy taking their powers, I had Vincent send me through one of his portals that you could not see or feel, plus being in the time chamber stops anything from seeing true time," Adrienne says.

"You need to push him all the way back, the portal is open, you need to use everything you have and push!" Vincent yells holding the portal open.

"You cannot do this to me, I gave you your powers back, you owe me your lives," King Omo says looking to his right.

Standing there is a golden figure, the figure of a woman with a long golden staff, beautiful blonde hair, and eyes like diamonds, but who was she?

"No, no, you all have to stop," King Omo says.

Using every ounce of power they have, they push him deep into the portal as Sam pushes in the bomb along with him. As the portal closes the timer on the bomb stops with a second left and all we see is his outstretched arm searching for help. Standing in the room, we see ourselves begin to separate one by one and we feel at peace.

"Uh, hi, I don't know what to say or ask," I say.

"What is there to say, but your welcome, and we are sorry that you lost your powers but we have an idea on how to fix that," my double says to me.

Holding out her hand I take hers and she moves into me, like a ghost moving into a body and taking over. I feel the power again, as does everyone else as their double moves into them, and without using my armband I power up showing everyone that we no longer need the bands to become who we were meant to be.

"Well, I guess you don't need me anymore," Sam says laughing.

"I do have an issue though, who was that woman that was in the corner with him?" I ask.

"What woman?" Adrienne responds.

"Are you talking about me?" Queen Izanami says. "Sorry young ones but I must be on my way, here, here is a gift from me to you," she says moving her staff towards me blasting me in the process. I am out. Falling to the floor everybody runs to me and sees that I am out cold.

"Megan, please, what's wrong with her?" Adrienne asks.

"I am checking her and it seems like she is in a deep coma, she is still in there but I can feel as if she is trapped in her mind," Megan says.

"Can you fix her?" Adrienne asks.

"There is nothing I can do, she will need to find her own way out, this is up to her now to find her way back," Megan responds.

Queen Izanami walks gingerly twirling her staff out the rear entrance of the hospital seeing General Collins cowering on the floor.

"Please, please don't kill me," General Collins says.

"Kill you, why you are going to be my new pet, General Collins is it?" She asks.

"Yes, and thank you, my queen, I am at your service," he responds as they both disappear into thin air.